WHERE THE ROAD TAKES ME

Also by Jay McLean

Combative

WHERE THE ROAD TAKES ME

JAY McLEAN

SKYSCAPE

SKYSCAPE

This is a work of fiction. Names, characters, organizations, places, events, and incidents are either products of the author's imagination or are used fictitiously.

Text copyright © 2015 Jay McLean
All rights reserved.

No part of this book may be reproduced, or stored in a retrieval system, or transmitted in any form or by any means, electronic, mechanical, photocopying, recording, or otherwise, without express written permission of the publisher.

Published by Skyscape, New York

www.apub.com

Amazon, the Amazon logo, and Skyscape are trademarks of Amazon.com, Inc., or its affiliates.

ISBN-13: 9781477849408
ISBN-10: 1477849408

Cover design by Shasti O'Leary-Soudant

Library of Congress Control Number: 2014916998

Printed in the United States of America

To anyone who has been lost, and those who find them

PROLOGUE

You know how sometimes you can tell that something is about to happen, even though there are no physical signs? Like when the hair on the back of your neck stands up, or your palms begin to sweat, or butterflies form in your stomach? Like, the beating of your heart thumps faster, harder—and even though you're staring down at the floors of the familiar hallways of high school—you know that when you lift your gaze, something's going to *change*? And then you look up—and the beating of your heart stops for a split second. The boy with the messy dark hair and the piercing blue eyes is watching you—a hint of a smile on his beautiful face that's enough to kick your heart back into gear. But then he turns around and walks away—not for him—but for you. Because he knows that is what you want, and you know that he only wants you to be happy.

Blake Hunter—he was my *change*.

CHAPTER ONE

There was that familiar ache that I loved so much—a burn in my chest that spread to the rest of my body. There was just one other feeling I loved more. Well—two, if you included the high of sex.

Numbness.

A constant state of numbness was my euphoria.

You couldn't tell. No one could.

My feet thudded against the pavement. Sweat dripped from my hairline, down my neck, and onto my bare back. I shut my eyes, urging the numbness to kick in. I wanted to feel it everywhere. Not just in my body but everywhere. *Maybe I should quit basketball and take up smoking weed as a hobby.* I laughed to myself—Dad would love that. Another reason to kick my ass.

I rounded the corner with my eyes still shut. I knew that path in the park better than I knew my own home. Which is why I was running at two in the morning on a Saturday night. Sunday morning? Whatever.

I was five steps past the corner—the numbness had just started to seep in—when I bumped into something. My eyes sprang open, and I found myself staring at someone on the ground.

"Fuck, I'm sorry," I huffed, trying to level my breathing. I rested my hands on my knees, waiting for the thumping in my heart to calm itself. My skin stung and my muscles throbbed from the impact of our bodies. I was six foot three, and my frame matched the constant training and rigorous workouts it endured. Her—I couldn't tell what she looked like—but I knew this much: if the collision had hurt me, it must've almost killed her.

She slowly came to a sitting position, resting her ass on her heels. Her head was bent, and her loose blonde hair formed a curtain around her face. She lifted her hands, palms up, and examined them. *Blood.*

"Shit! I'm so sorry." A wave of panic whooshed through me. Squatting in front of her, I took her hands to study the damage. She yanked them away and sniffed, straightening her legs out in front of her. Her short-ass skirt left nothing to the imagination.

"Dammit," she whispered, her head still down.

My gaze moved from the hem of her skirt to her knees. *Blood.*

"Fuck, I'm so sorry," I said for the third time.

It was dark, the only light coming from the moon and a lamp-post fifteen yards away. I wanted to see her face, but I sure as hell wasn't going to ask her to look at me. "Are you okay?"

Before she could answer, a rustling from the bushes interrupted us.

A guy stepped out, close to my age. He looked rough, rougher than the kids I hung out with—and I use that term loosely. He wiped the back of his hand across his mouth, then eyed it. *Blood.* His eyes narrowed. Looking down at the girl in front of me, he seethed, "You fucking whore!"

Slowly, she stood up.

I swear I could actually hear the clicking of the pieces as it all fell into place in my mind.

Him—with his fat lip, torn shirt, and undone fly.

Her—now fully standing. The top of her tank was ripped, exposing one bra-covered breast.

I watched as her lips pursed and her eyes narrowed to slits, but then fire flamed in them as she yelled, "Fuck you!"

He took a step toward her with his hand raised.

Before I knew it, I was between them, gripping his forearm, my other arm behind me, wrapped around her waist. I could feel her shallow breaths against my back.

"Who the fuck are you?" he demanded, trying to pull away from my hold.

"Blake. Who the fuck are *you*?"

He laughed once, a snarl on his lips and a challenge in his eyes. "What are you, her bodyguard?"

I lifted my chin and squared my shoulders. I towered over him, eying him down. I knew I could take him. Easily. "I don't know, dickface. Does she need one?"

He tried again to withdraw his arm. I grasped it tighter. Then a cynical laugh escaped him. "Good luck. She's a fucking tease—dresses like a whore but won't even suck dick." He looked around my shoulder at her. "You cock-teasing slut!"

Something in me snapped.

Blood rushed to my ears, and the numbness I'd hoped for was well and truly gone. My arm—the one previously wrapped around her—moved fast. My fingers had formed a fist and would have made contact with his face—

Would have—if not for the tiny blonde girl standing in front of me. Between my intended target and me. With her entire body weight, she pulled my arm downwards, her eyes widening. "Don't," she said. "It's not worth it." Her voice was quiet, but her expression screamed for me to let it go. I was so surprised by her actions that I dropped Dickface's raised arm.

Glaring at the guy behind her, I tried for an even tone as I warned, "You got three seconds to get out of here before I beat your ass."

Her warm hands were now pressed against my chest, their pressure causing me to inhale sharply. My eyes fell to hers. They were pleading.

I heard "fuck this" and then heavy footsteps thumping against the pavement, the sound growing gradually more distant. My eyes, though, they never left hers.

After what felt like forever, she looked away.

I blinked for what seemed like the first time.

She suddenly noticed that her hands were still on my chest. "Shit. I'm sorry," she said, pulling them away and hiding them behind her back.

I swallowed. It was thick and embarrassingly loud, louder than the beating of my heart in my eardrums. "Are you okay?" I asked her. Bending slightly, I finally relaxed enough to catch my breath.

"Yeah, are you?"

Straightening, I studied her warily. She was a mess. Scraped knees. Disheveled hair. Shoe missing. I looked away when I caught sight of her purple bra, openly exposed from her torn top.

She cleared her throat.

I returned my gaze to her once she'd crossed her arms over her chest, hiding herself. She bit the corner of her lip, but everything else was still. There was no movement, not until she slowly raised her hand and wiped her cheek. "Thank you," she whispered.

My eyebrows bunched. It'd been a while since I'd heard such genuine sincerity. "It's no problem. Really."

She tried to smile and then adjusted her top while taking off her remaining shoe. Then she just stood there, barefoot and shivering. One arm at her side, holding her one and only heel, the other covering her breast. "Well, thanks for saving me." She laughed softly, jerking her head toward the path behind us. "I better get going."

I nodded, chewing on my thumb. Then some sense kicked in, and I stepped in front of her, blocking her from walking away. "You shouldn't be walking anywhere alone, especially—" I cut myself off. "Dressed like that" was definitely the wrong thing to say. Instead, I opted for "especially this late at night."

Her smile was tight. "I'll be fine," she assured me, looking around at the darkness surrounding us.

She shivered again.

I pulled out my shirt, which I'd tucked into my shorts' waistband, and handed it to her. "It's probably wet—from my sweat—and it might smell a little funky, but you'll be warmer."

Her face relaxed, and her lips curled up. "Thank you, Blake."

"You're welcome, umm . . . ?"

She paused, searching my face. "Abby."

"Abby." I nodded in confirmation. "At least let me walk you wherever you need to go."

She seemed to hesitate before nodding slowly. "I need to find my purse and my phone." She studied me for a moment. "I don't suppose you're hiding a phone anywhere on you I can use for light?"

I looked down at my running shorts and sneakers. "No. But it's in my car . . ." I pointed in the direction of the parking lot. "We can grab it and come back."

She cursed under her breath. "It's okay. I don't think we'll be able to find our way back here. Not when it's this dark. I'll come back in the morning or something."

I smiled. Knowing that park as well as I did had its perks. "I know where we are. It's fine."

Grimacing, she asked, "Are you sure? You're not . . . on your way somewhere?"

My laughter echoed through the still air. "Yes, Abby, I'm sure. Where would I be going dressed like this?"

She smiled then. Amusement danced in her eyes. "I don't know." She shrugged. "To kill someone?"

"What?" I asked, surprised at her sharp wit. I turned and began moving toward the lot.

When she caught up to me, she continued. "Think about it. How many times do you hear on the news about dead bodies being found in parks? You know who always finds them? Joggers."

I turned to her, tilting my head slightly, trying to work out whether she was serious or not. She tried to hide her smile before adding, "It seems a little suspicious to me—you joggers always being first on the scene and all. My theory is that you're all a bunch of murderers, and you get away with it, using the jogger clause. Makes me wonder if you have some underground club where you compare notes and brag about pulling off these murders."

I threw back my head and laughed. "That's one amazing theory."

"Well," she said, nudging my side with her elbow, "at least when you murder me, you'll know that I was onto you, buddy."

"Yet, here you are—walking with me in pitch-black darkness, at two in the morning, to a more-than-likely abandoned parking lot, under the impression I'm going to get you back to your necessities. You're not even slightly afraid of what might happen to you?" All joking aside, she had to be a little worried. Surely.

The air around us turned thick. "No, Blake. I know I'm safe with you."

She said my name as if it had a different meaning.

We walked the rest of the way to my car in silence.

CHAPTER TWO

I opened the car door, pulled out a bottle of water, and handed it to her. She thanked me before gulping half of it down in one swig. Searching through my gym bag in the backseat, I found a sweatshirt for me, then handed her my letterman jacket. I watched as she shrugged it on. It looked huge on her, bigger than it did on Hannah. With her fingers curled around the edge of the sleeves, she slowly worked each of the buttons from the bottom up. It hung lower than the skirt she wore, almost down to her knees. "What?" Her voice pulled me from my thoughts.

I shook my head, trying to clear it. "Shoes," I mumbled.

"What?" she asked again.

I turned and sifted through the shit on the floor of the back-seat. I knew I'd seen a pair of Hannah's flip-flops there somewhere. She'd refused to take them back when I'd told her I'd found them. Maybe it was her way of claiming her territory. Better than her panties or bra, I guessed. Once I'd found them, I dropped them on the ground in front of Abby's feet.

She smirked. "Girlfriend's?"

"Sister's," I lied. *Why the fuck did I just lie?*

It was obvious she didn't believe me, but she didn't question me, just slipped them on and waited with her hands in the jacket pockets.

We set off, back to where I'd run into her, phone and flashlight in tow. It was awkward. I figured she had to know I'd lied about having a girlfriend. I broke the silence. "So, you go to school around here? I mean, what? How old are you anyway? I figure you're around my age. I'm a senior." Then quickly, I added, "I'm eighteen, though." *Yeah, because that was important.* I shook my head at myself.

"Here's the thing, *Blake*." She used that same tone with my name again. Before I could ask her what that was about, she continued, "Let's not do the whole, awkward, get-to-know-you thing. In reality, we'll probably never see each other again after tonight. Okay?"

"Um . . . okay."

"Good." After a pause, she added, "I don't normally dress—or look—like this."

Facing her, I wondered why she'd say something like that. Her head was bent low, her face hidden behind her hair. I studied her intently. It struck me that I'd been doing that a lot. "Abby, I'm in no place to judge."

She raised her head, eyebrows drawn, and turned to me, as if confused. I couldn't take my eyes off hers. Then she blinked. And it broke whatever silent communication was passing between us. "Thank you, *Blake*."

Every goddamn time she said my name, it was like a freight train running through my mind. *Why did she say it like that?* "You're welcome, *Abby*."

She smirked. She must've known I was mocking her, but she didn't call me on it. I came to a stop and tugged on her arm. "We're here," I informed her, shining the flashlight into some bushes.

"Oh." She looked around. "How can you tell?"

"I run this track at least twice a day, or night, however you want to look at it." I shrugged. "I just know."

I thought that she'd ask questions or wonder why I was out here in the dead of night while all my so-called friends were getting wasted at some cliché high-school party. But she didn't. She just made her way into the bushes, with her arms outstretched, spreading leaves and branches out of her way.

"You want me to call your phone? At least, you might be able to hear it." I shined the flashlight over her shoulder so we could see in front of her.

She laughed. Low and slow. "I don't know my number."

I came to a stop. "You don't know your own number?" *Who doesn't know their own number?* I started moving again, adding, "How do you give guys your number?"

She turned around abruptly, causing me to run into her for the second time. I grabbed her elbows to keep her upright. She straightened, pulling her hair away from her face. Then she raised her eyes. They were huge, almost as huge as the breaths she was inhaling. Looking away, she shrugged. "I don't."

"What do you mean, you don't?"

She exhaled loudly and raised her eyebrows in warning.

"Right." I nodded. "No getting-to-know-each-other stuff."

*   *   *

"So," I said, leaning against my car.

She replaced Hannah's flip-flops with her now recovered heels. "So?"

I hesitated a moment before offering, "I should probably give you a ride home."

She giggled. It was genuine, not like the annoying fake ones that spilled out of Hannah. *Why did I keep comparing her to Hannah?* "You probably should," she agreed, looking around the parking lot, "but you're not going to. I'm going to hoof it. Thank you so much, Blake, for everything. Saving me and all."

"What?" I straightened, and for some reason, a protectiveness I've never felt before kicked in. "You can't walk by yourself at this time of night." It came out louder than I'd expected. "It's not safe. I won't let you." I shook my head frantically.

She smirked. She was amused. *Great.*

"I mean it, Abby. I'm not just going to let you walk around on your own."

Her laugh cut me off, echoing through the trees around us. "Okay, okay," she soothed, settling her palm flush against my chest. My shoulders sagged in relief. I hadn't realized how tense I'd been. She dropped her hand fast. Too fast. "Sorry," she mumbled, as if I would have a problem with her touching me. She pulled out her phone. The light from it illuminated her face as she ran her tongue across her top lip.

For a second, I forgot to breathe.

She was cute. Maybe even hot.

"You okay?"

"Huh?" Fuck. I was staring.

"You zoned out."

"Oh." I faked. "Yeah, I'm . . . nothing. Yeah . . . nothing." I was going to tell her that I was just tired, but it would have been a lie.

She smiled again, that same amused smile from earlier. "You want to go for a walk? There's a restaurant open that serves bottomless coffee and all-day breakfast."

On cue, my stomach growled.

She giggled. "I'll take that as a yes."

*   *   *

It had been a while since I'd felt nervous in someone else's presence. But Abby, she made me nervous. I opened and closed my mouth at least three times, but each time, no words formed. Mustering my courage, I inhaled and began, "So I know that you—" But I stopped when I realized she was no longer walking next to me. I turned back to find her bent over in someone's front yard, her face in a rose bush. "What are you doing?" I whispered.

She shrugged and then straightened. "Stopping to smell the roses." She said it with such nonchalance, as though it was normal for someone to just *stop and smell the roses*. Once she'd made her way back to me, she asked, "What were you saying?"

What was I saying? "Just that—"

She placed her hand in the crook of my elbow and kept it there. I looked down at her, but she, too, was looking down. She didn't say a word, and for a moment, neither could I. Then I exhaled and tried to relax. She was closer now, closer than I normally let anyone be. Even Hannah. "You said you didn't want to do the whole get-to-know-you thing—and that's fine—but I kind of want to get to know you a little."

"Yeah?" she asked. "Why?"

Why? What kind of question was that? "I don't know. You intrigue me."

"I intrigue you?"

Ignoring her question, I said, "How about you tell me five random things about you?" The streetlights were closer together now, making it easier for me to see her. We'd been walking only about ten minutes before we'd hit a strip of stores.

She yanked on my arm. "We're here."

I looked around. Nothing.

She laughed. Then she opened a black door, hidden in an alcove between two stores. Not letting go of my arm once we got inside, she led me through the darkness, down a set of stairs, to a brightly lit basement room, where I was surprised to find myself in what must have been the world's most secret restaurant. Only then did she release her hold on me. As she walked ahead, my hand moved on its own to the small of her back. I had no idea why or how it happened, but if it surprised her, she didn't react. She slid into one side of the booth while I stood there like an idiot, deciding what to do. Her lips spread into a slight smile as she moved across, making room for me.

It was a silent invitation. One that I hadn't realized I wanted. As I sat down next to her, she said, "I come here often. That's one."

My brows furrowed. "One what?"

"You asked for five random things." Raising her eyebrows, she picked up a menu and handed it to me. "Two—I could eat breakfast food all day."

I sighed. These weren't really the things I had had in mind, but I let her continue.

"Three, I—"

Then a voice from above me interrupted. "Hey. You're here late."

My eyes snapped up.

He looked older than us by a few years. He wore your standard apron, but that wasn't what stood out. He was scruffy, unshaven, and had dark circles around his eyes, almost as if he hadn't slept for days. He blinked a few times and then rubbed them with the palms of his hands. "Everything okay?" he asked her.

I turned to face her.

"I'm fine," she said, voice clipped. "I didn't think you'd be on tonight." She cast her gaze downwards at the menu in front of her. But it was a tactic, a diversion from not having to look at that guy.

"Are you sure?" he asked again.

Her eyes drifted shut. Her jaw clenched. I leaned in closer. "You want to get out of here?"

"Who are you?" the waiter cut in before she could speak.

Then that protectiveness from earlier kicked in. I turned to him, my shoulders rigid and ready. I began to stand, but her arm curled around mine. "Clayton," she said quietly. "I'm fine.

I promise. I'll have the usual. He'll have the same. And two for them." She motioned toward two homeless people sitting in a corner booth on the opposite end of the room.

He shook his head but held my gaze. "Make sure she gets home safe, okay?"

"Of course," I answered.

Then he was gone.

I felt her body relax next to mine, but she didn't let go of my arm. Facing her, eyebrows raised, I asked, "Ex-boyfriend?"

"That's gross. No, more like an older brother."

I didn't question her further, just decided to move on. "Three?"

She smiled then. "Three? It feels good to have you worry about me."

She searched my face for a reaction.

"Four? I like you, Blake," she said quietly, looking away.

"Yeah?"

She nodded.

"Good. Five?"

"Five?" She smiled huge. "Tonight didn't end up so bad after all."

I smiled along with her and settled my arm behind the booth.

And that was how we stayed: with my arm behind her, itching to move closer. Even when the food came, we didn't move apart. She didn't talk much after that, so I did enough for the both of us. She wanted to know about school; I told her about sports. She asked me about home; I told her more about sports.

And then it struck me—why we were both so comfortable, here, on this one night, as complete strangers. Maybe we both had something to hide. Maybe we both enjoyed the company of someone who didn't know us well enough to judge us. Maybe we were both so sick of faking it—our breathing had somehow become natural around each other, the way it should be and not a struggle like it usually was.

CHAPTER THREE

"You ready for me to take you home now?" I asked as we exited the restaurant into the crisp morning air.

She tilted her head all the way back; I noticed her straight blonde hair flowing down to her waist as she eyed the sky. The sun had just started to come up. It had turned the atmosphere that unique shade of orange you could find only in that part of town, at that time of the morning. For some reason, the mood seemed to electrify her.

"It's perfect," she whispered, her head still thrown back.

"Yeah," I agreed. But my eyes were fixed on her, and I knew we weren't talking about the same thing.

She smiled, but she didn't speak. I wasn't sure how long she stood there, soaking up the morning light, but it didn't feel like long enough. The restaurant door behind us slammed shut, and Clayton walked out with his hands shoved in his pockets. We both turned to him. He pulled out a cigarette, lit it, and inhaled. Blowing the smoke from the side of his mouth, he jerked his head, motioning for her.

Abby's eyes flitted from him to me. "I'll be right back," she said, and then slowly made her way over to him. Initially, they spoke quietly—too quietly for me to hear—but all too quickly, their conversation grew heated. "You don't need to do this," he barked, pointing up and down at her body.

She took a step toward me, but he held her back with his hand curled around her forearm. "Fuck you, Clay. You don't know shit."

I stepped forward.

She held up her hand to stop me.

Narrowing his eyes at me, he sounded defeated when he said, "I'm just worried about you." He spoke into her ear but loud enough for me to hear. He kept his eyes locked on mine, as if to make sure I'd heard him. I had. But it only made me more confused.

About her.

About that night.

About everything.

She frowned. "I'm okay," she assured him. "You know this is just a hard day for me."

He exhaled loudly, then nodded at me as he released her arm. He spun on his heels, threw open the restaurant door, and stepped inside, lit cigarette still in his mouth.

"Let's go," she said, walking past me.

I rushed up until I was alongside her. "I take it you're not going to tell me what that was about."

She turned to glare at me. *Fire.*

"Whoa." I surrendered. "I'm not your enemy, okay?"

She relaxed, just slightly.

Jerking my thumb behind us, I added, "And to be honest, I don't think he is, either."

"Great," she said sarcastically, "someone else who thinks they know everything about me."

I stopped walking. "Abby, I don't know anything about you. That's the way you want it to be, remember? You want to give me a little insight so that maybe I don't go judging that guy at face value, then go ahead." I crossed my arms. "I'm waiting."

Her eyes narrowed, and I detected the trace of a sneer. I couldn't help but smile. "You're an ass," she snapped.

I laughed. "And you're cute when you're mad."

I would've missed the widening of her eyes if I hadn't been studying her so intently. Her cheeks darkened before she looked away. "You're still an ass." She poked me in the stomach. Then winced when her finger bent back against it. "Dude, you're like superman."

"Does that make you my kryptonite?"

She smiled then, and raised her nose in the air. With a gleam in her eyes, she said, "Maybe."

And that was when it happened.

Something changed.

A switch.

It felt like someone had taken away the gray dullness behind my eyes and splashed color into them.

Like I was seeing things in a different light, from a different life.

I swallowed, too nervous to speak.

Maybe she *was* my kryptonite.

*   *   *

She directed me to a part of town that I knew existed but had never been in before. The houses were smaller, not as well maintained as where I grew up.

"Just here," she said, pointing to one on the left. "And turn your lights off."

I did as she asked. Even went as far as turning off the engine and letting the car roll to a stop. She nervously chewed her lip. Her eyes squinted, focused on the house.

"What's going on, Abby? Are you out past curfew or something?"

She laughed quietly. "Or something."

I looked from her to the residence. My nerves formed a knot in the pit of my stomach. Shifting my gaze back to her, I asked, "Are you afraid to go home?"

Her eyes narrowed.

There it was again—that protective instinct. "Is someone in there going to hurt you?" I started to open my door. "I'll kick their ass." I was dead serious. I didn't even think about the ramifications of what would happen if I did.

As I began to step out of the car, she grabbed my arm.

She eyed me sideways. "No one is hurting me, I swear." She tried to contain her smile. "There are kids inside. I just don't want to wake them—it's early. If they wake up now, it'll throw their routine off for the entire day . . ."

"Oh." I felt like an idiot. She must've sensed it, because her hand settled on my arm when she said, "It's really sweet that you want to protect me, though. Thank you."

I wanted to tell her that it was fine and that it wasn't a big deal, but the sensation of her hand sliding down my arm made the words catch in my throat. Her hand nestled against mine, palm against palm. I watched with bated breath, waiting for her next move. When our fingers linked and curled over, I exhaled with such force that the back of my head hit the headrest. I turned to face her. She raised her eyes and locked them with mine. "You should've said something," I told her. "We could've hung out for a bit longer. I didn't need to take you home."

She shrugged. "I just thought that you'd be busy. I didn't want to take up too much of your time."

I squeezed her hand.

"Walk me to the door?"

I smiled. "Of course."

*   *   *

I wasn't even sure how it had happened, but on the way to her house, we had both silently reached for each other, linking hands like we'd done in the car.

Instead of leading me to the front door, she sat down on a swing seat in the yard. I followed her lead; I had no choice, since her fingers were still locked with mine.

I pushed away thoughts of Hannah.

"We have to be quiet," she whispered, gesturing toward the house.

I nodded and pulled her until she was as close as she could get. She hesitated, only for a moment, before she succumbed to my advances and leaned into me. I swapped the hand that was holding hers and wrapped my arm around her shoulders. I didn't even think. I just *did*. "You have younger brothers and sisters?" I asked, kicking off the ground and looking toward the house. The seat swung back and forth a few times while I studied the two-story, wooden building. It was more worn than any of the others on the street. The gutters had come loose, and the shutters were barely hanging on. The yard was overgrown, and the house obviously needed a coat of paint.

"Kind of," she replied, leaning back so she could study my face. "This is a foster home, Blake."

"Oh. So you're . . ." I trailed off.

"A foster kid?" She shook her head. "No. I mean, I was, not anymore. But they're cool. They're letting me stay here until gr—" She broke off and let out a disbelieving snort. "No getting-to-know-you stuff, remember?"

I sighed. "You don't think we're past that yet? I'm sitting in your front yard with my arm around you, holding your hand. We've walked around together, had a meal together, and driven together. That's not worth something from you?"

She pulled out of my grasp, raised her feet onto the seat and wrapped her arms around her knees. Resting her chin on them, her eyes lowered, she said, "And what would your girlfriend say if she knew that you were doing all that right now?"

"Honestly? She probably wouldn't care. As long as no one saw us, and it didn't ruin her reputation." It was the truth. What Hannah and I had was fickle, at best. I didn't love her, and I didn't think she loved me. The way I saw it, it was a show. We never spoke about it. Never dealt with it. I wasn't sure how we'd ended up the way we had, but for whatever reason, we had never bothered to change things.

"I doubt that."

I shrugged. "Doubt all you want, but I'm not lying."

"You better go," she said, avoiding my gaze.

The knot in my stomach tightened. I didn't want to leave her. Not yet. So I did what I knew best—I turned into a dick. "You're pissed at me now? So . . . when did you work out that I had a girl-friend? When I gave you her shoes? Tell me if I'm wrong, but that was before you held my hand in the car, right? And before you invited me to walk you to the door? Before you decided to sit here with me and let me be this close to you? Why do all that if you already knew and it mattered to you?"

She raised her head then, her glare intense. Dropping her shoulders, she whispered, "I just wanted one night." But she was speaking to herself. Then she swallowed loudly and repeated her words, only this time they were meant for me. "I just wanted one night, Blake. One night where I could forget myself." She wiped her cheek against her arm. She must've been crying. "The person you ran into tonight, that's not me. I wanted to lose myself. Feel something different, you know?" She shook her head. "It was stupid."

"I get it," I told her. I really did. "You wanted one night to be someone else. There's nothing wrong with that. Unless, I guess, you're running from an unchangeable reality. Then you'll be run-ning for the rest of your life. And you don't want to do that. You don't want to feel so trapped in your head that you're constantly running."

Her eyes went wide, and her mouth hung open. "Wow," she said, exhaling slowly.

I glanced at her sideways. "What?"

"You're not what I expected."

"You met me four hours ago. How can you expect anything of me?"

She kicked her legs off the seat and straightened up. "Blake, I . . ."

Her front door opened.

We both turned to it.

A little kid popped his head out. When his eyes found us, he smiled and took a step outside, closing the door behind him.

"What are you doing, Sammy?" Abby asked. "It's too early to be up, and you shouldn't be opening the door and leaving the house without a grown-up."

Sammy—maybe four—pursed his lips and crossed his arms over his chest as he made his way over to us. He climbed onto the seat, crawled into her lap, and put his arm around her neck. Then he just looked at me—more like *scowled*.

I put my hand out for him to shake. I didn't know if that was a thing that kids his age understood, but I didn't know what else to do. "I'm Blake," I told him. "And what's your name?"

He shut his eyes tight and counted to six, missing the five. Then he opened them. A smile quickly spread across his face. "I'm Sammy." He looked down at my hand and slapped it. Giggling, he turned to Abby. "Is he your friend?"

She smiled, but it was sad. "I guess."

"I didn't know you had friends," Sammy told her.

She sighed then. "You better get inside before Mary realizes you're gone."

He hopped off the swing seat awkwardly, causing it to glide backwards. And then he was gone, running up the steps to the front door, just as it swung open.

He froze.

"Inside!" A middle-aged woman whisper-yelled. I assumed that must be Mary.

He ran in, ducking under her arm while her eyes searched the front yard. When she saw Abby and me, a different expression replaced the scowl on her face.

Sadness. Sympathy. "Are you okay?"

"Yes, I'm fine," Abby replied quietly.

Mary studied me quickly, before speaking to Abby, "When you're done out here, come inside and get some clothes on."

"Yes, ma'am."

Then she, too, was gone.

Abby self-consciously tugged her skirt lower.

"Abby . . ." I said cautiously. "What's going on? Why did you want to lose yourself tonight?"

"It's the anniversary of my mom's death." She glanced up at me now. "I was having a really bad day, Blake. The kind of day where all I want to do is forget." Her voice broke. A tear fell. She went to wipe it away, but I beat her to it. I didn't remove my hand from her cheek. Not even when her eyes widened in surprise as I leaned in closer. She searched my face, begging for an explanation.

"Do you think that's what she'd want?"

She sniffed. "What?"

"Do you think that your mom would want you to try to forget her existence? Even just for one day? I don't really know you, but from where I'm sitting, you turned out pretty well . . . and if she had anything to do with that, then maybe you should try celebrating her life, rather than trying to forget it."

She let it out now—the sob that had been brewing inside her. "I'm sorry," I said in an effort to soothe her, but my words just made her cry harder. "I'm so sorry," I repeated.

She pulled back. Her hair caught in the wetness of her tears. "Where did you come from?" It wasn't a question, though. More like a thought that needed to be voiced. Then she rubbed her nose against mine.

And then it happened.

The kiss.

My eyes drifted shut. I could taste the saltiness from her tears. But the moment was over way too quickly. I was still frozen when she pulled away. Her breath brushed against my lips. Then the cold morning air replaced it. "Thank you, Blake." My eyes snapped open. She was already on the steps, walking up to the door.

I rushed over and took her hand. "What are you doing? Where are you going?"

She turned to me and placed one hand on my cheek, rose up on her toes, and kissed the other. "It's just one night, *Blake.*" There she went, using that tone with my name again. "Take care of yourself, okay?"

I blinked, confused, as she ran up the steps and into her house, closing the door behind her.

What the hell had just happened?

I sat in my car for a good ten minutes before finally starting the engine. I'd never *felt* anything like that before—that anxiety at the thought of never seeing her again. I took one last look at the house. The attic light was on. She was there, one hand raised, waving good-bye.

CHAPTER FOUR

I lifted my head and reached for the phone on the nightstand. I had no idea how long I'd been asleep, but the ringing made my head pound. I knew it was Will, because he'd put some stupid rap song as his ringtone on my phone. It drove me crazy—which was why he'd done it. "What?" I said, sitting up and letting the covers bunch at my waist.

I tried to focus my vision as I pulled the phone away to check the time. It was early afternoon, but I felt like I'd only just fallen asleep.

"Find a new toy last night? Hannah was pissed you just left."

I'd never been with anyone but Hannah, and I didn't know what made him think differently. "That's why you're calling?"

His chuckle made me squirm. "No, dick. We're all meeting at the tattoo shop. Remember?"

I rolled my eyes. We had just won the state championship the week before, and the team wanted to get matching tattoos. It was stupid. *They* were stupid.

"Yeah, man. I'll meet you there," I lied and faked the edginess in my tone as I said, "I gotta go. Hannah's calling." I hung up and threw the phone on the bed. Not five seconds later, it rang again. Hannah this time. I picked it up and rejected the call.

Resting on the edge of the bed, I let my feet drop to the floor with a thud. And then I did something pathetic. I got on my phone, pulled up Facebook, and typed in the name *Abby*. Of course I had been too dumbstruck to call my phone from hers and get her number last night, but I was sure we had to know some of the same people—and Facebook was the place to find anyone.

Only it wasn't.

I searched through four pages of *Abbys*. Nothing.

*　　　*　　　*

With the basketball season over and my "friends" being idiots, I didn't have shit to do. I tried to get some homework done, but I couldn't focus.

After lacing my sneakers and going to my wardrobe, I moved a few boxes aside on the top shelf until I felt the hard leather of the basketball. This one was new, my fifth one in just as many months. I'd tried to find different places to hide them, but my strategy didn't seem to be working. Dad had never told me, and I'd never asked, but I knew he was taking them . . . probably deflating and discarding them, just like he'd done with my ego and my dreams of playing ball.

The one thing he couldn't take away, though, was the mental escape I got from playing the game. And right now, I needed the escape. I needed to get Abby out of my head.

An hour dribbling a ball up and down the driveway killed me. I hunched over and attempted to catch my breath.

"You're dehydrated."

I lifted my eyes. I couldn't even remember the last time I'd heard her voice. I nodded in greeting. "Mother."

She leaned against the doorway of the guesthouse and took a sip of whatever her current choice of alcoholic beverage was. "Have you had anything to eat or drink today?" she asked.

Sighing, I straightened up, dropped the ball on the ground, and settled my foot on it. Then I crossed my arms over my chest and waited for her to continue with the facade of being a caring mother.

She glared at me. It was her go-to move. "What?" She raised her chin, attempting to look defiant. It would've worked if she wasn't drunk off her ass. She'd changed in the last few years since she'd started drinking. She had once been vibrant, the perfect soccer mom, according to everyone. Now she looked like ass. Her clothes were several sizes too big for her, most likely because of all the weight she'd lost recently. Her hair was a mess, and her eyes had lost the fight to fake it. She looked at least a decade older than her forty-five years.

"Just surprised you remember who I am is all."

She sighed, dropping her shoulders, and stared at the ground. "I was at your game," she said, as though it was going to make up for years of neglect.

"I didn't see you."

"I went in disguise."

I rolled my eyes. "Of course you did."

She pushed off the door frame and looked like she wanted to come to me. Maybe say something more than the few words we occasionally exchanged. "I tried" is all she said, before walking backwards into the guesthouse and shutting the door.

Guesthouse—I should probably stop calling it that, considering she'd been living there for the past five years.

"She tried," a deep voice boomed from behind me. *Great.*

I turned toward the voice, arms still crossed. "Colonel."

He eyed me up and down and raised his eyebrows. My body went rigid. I balled my hands into fists behind my crossed arms. I knew what his expression meant. It meant that my crossed arms and casual posture were no way to greet a colonel, regardless of whether he was my dad or not.

27

"You didn't come home last night."

No *hello*. No *how are you, son?* Nothing.

I opened my mouth to speak, but he cut me off. He always did. "Midnight curfew," he said. Then he paused for a beat, his jaw clenched. "I don't know why you're still messing around with that shit. Shooting a ball through a hoop won't help you when the enemy's pulling the trigger on an AK aimed at your damn head."

He spun on his heels and walked away.

"Fuck you," I said under my breath but then quickly raised my eyes. His back was still turned. He hadn't heard. Thank God. I didn't feel like an ass beating today.

*   *   *

After such amazingly heartwarming conversations with both my parents, I decided I needed to get out of the house. So I did what I always did. I ran.

Somehow, I ended up in the bushes where we'd found Abby's things the night before. I wanted to make sure that she hadn't left anything behind. It wasn't like I went out of my way. I was there to run anyway. And it wasn't like I was hoping to find something just so it gave me a reason to go to her house and give it to her. I was just . . . fuck it. Who was I kidding? I wanted to see her.

Unfortunately for me, there was nothing around. But that didn't stop me from stalking her, waiting for a glimpse of her outside her house. There were a bunch of kids playing in the front yard. Mary was there, too, sitting in the same spot that Abby and I had occupied only hours earlier.

Forty-five minutes, I waited.

I never saw her.

I drove out to the half-court I'd been going to since I was a kid and shot baskets until the sun went down. I picked up food on the way home and ate in my room, where I stayed. I didn't see either of my parents for the rest of the night.

I went to bed early, hoping to get a full night's sleep so I could actually focus the next day, but thoughts of Abby infiltrated my mind. I tossed and turned all night until my alarm finally went off. School was the last thing I wanted to deal with.

*   *   *

You know what the problem with high school is? There is way too much of it. I figured everything I needed to learn could have been compressed into two hours a day. I'd have enjoyed it a lot more if I had to devote only a couple of hours of my life each day to educating myself on the subjects I actually gave a shit about. Two hours. That was all it would take.

There was absolutely no need for lunch breaks and cafeterias, which were nothing more than a source of social awkwardness and opportunities for people like Hannah to develop and show off her hard-earned social status.

I started to pick up the apple off my tray, but she took my arm and wrapped it around her shoulders. She was speaking to Sophie, her best friend. Something about a sale on bags. Tuning her out, I decided that leaving the apple would be better than having to deal with the future conversation of how it was important that we show a level of togetherness in public settings. Hannah—on the outside—was every guy's wet dream. Perfectly straight brown hair, perfect blue eyes, perfect legs, perfect skin, perfect cheerleader body. She may have even been the perfect girlfriend, she just wasn't perfect for me.

I looked around the cafeteria and settled my gaze on a girl sitting alone at a table in the corner of the room. Our eyes locked, and I smiled at her.

She blushed and looked away.

This was my life. Everyone either had me on a pedestal or was afraid of me. Why? My hot girlfriend and the ability to shoot a ball through a metal hoop? Granted, I worked hard for the second one. The first, not so much.

The loner girl stood up and made her way to the exit. As I watched her leave, my gaze caught on a figure through the windows, sitting underneath a tree. I squinted, trying to get a better look.

It couldn't be.

She sat cross-legged, with her hair up. Her head was lowered, and it appeared that she was looking down at something in her hand. A scraping sound snapped me out of my daze. I didn't realize it was my chair being pushed back until I was almost standing.

"So you'll come with us tonight, right?" Hannah's voice sounded far away.

My eyes focused on the blonde girl sitting outside. Her head started bopping up and down. She must've been listening to music. I found myself smiling as I watched her.

"Babe!" Hannah tried to get my attention.

I blinked, trying to switch focus. Turning to her, I asked, "What?" It came out harsher than I'd intended.

Her eyes widened, and I knew I was going to pay for that later. "Will you drive us to the mall after school?"

I squared my shoulders and took a step back. The chair behind me fell and hit the floor with a loud clank. "What, Hannah? No. I'm working!"

"Babe," she pleaded. All eyes were on us. I must've been louder than I thought.

"Hannah, I can't."

I chanced a glimpse out the window. She was standing now, lifting her backpack onto her shoulders. Her head was still lowered.

I *needed* to see if it was her.

A hand on my wrist pulled me back to my surroundings.

"Babe," Hannah said again.

I looked out the window. She was leaving.

I shook my hand out of Hannah's grasp and gathered my shit. "Fuck."

And then I walked out of the room and chased after her.

Abby.

By the time I got out to the tree, she was nowhere to be seen. I searched the parking lot, the hallways, and the library. Nothing.

The moment I'd left the cafeteria, my phone had started blowing up with texts from Hannah. I didn't even bother to read them. I already knew what they'd say. The worst part was that I didn't even know if it was Abby. It could have been any number of blonde girls who walked these halls on a daily basis. Maybe I just wanted so badly to see her that I'd imagined it. I shook my head back and forth in disbelief. *What the hell was it with this girl that had made me so crazy?*

*   *   *

I texted Hannah right after I'd given up looking for Abby and apologized. I told her I hadn't gotten much sleep the night before and that I'd call her after work. I probably needed to blow off some steam, and if there was one thing Hannah was perfect for, that was it.

She was at my locker, waiting for me before the end-of-lunch bell rang.

"Just so you know, I forgive you, but you should get some more sleep." She pouted, pressing my body against the lockers with hers and moving my hand to her hip. Licking her lips and searching my face, she added, "I worry about you." She said it loud enough so that the random people walking by in the hallway could hear.

This was Hannah. All show. Then she leaned in closer, squashing her large breasts against my chest. I looked down at the

31

tight tank that barely covered them. And then I mentally compared her tits to Abby's. I started to get hard. "Fuck," I groaned. I shouldn't be having these thoughts while my girlfriend was trying to seduce me.

Hannah must've taken my reaction the wrong way, because by the time I managed to pull my mind away from Abby's breasts, her mouth was on my neck. My fingers instinctively curled around her tiny waist, drawing her closer. I waited for the moment her lips brushed mine before moving in and tasting her.

"Come over tonight?" Her voice was husky and laced with desire.

Will walked up behind Hannah, just as I pushed her away, along with any lustful thoughts. "I'm working."

"After?" She ran her finger down my shirt and into the band of my shorts.

"I'll call you."

Her lips curled. "I'll see you later." She took a step back and winked. "*Run* over to my place. We can shower together."

With a smirk on his face, Will watched her walk away. "Run over so we can shower together," he mimicked, pretending to brush hair over his shoulder. The guy was an ass, but he was funny enough and he made the long-ass school days more bearable. I turned to my locker and ignored him. "By the way," he said, his voice back to normal. "Good job on the whole flaking to get-a-tattoo thing. We waited over an hour for you." I kept ignoring him. Then I felt his hands rub harshly on my shoulders. "So who was she?" he asked, chuckling suggestively. *This kid would not let up.*

Slamming my locker shut, I turned to him. "Your mom."

He shook his head with a chuckle. "Hope she was a good time."

"That's gross."

"You're gross."

"And you're four."

His eyes narrowed. "You're being a dick."

I was. "Sorry, man. Bad night's sleep."

"With my mom?"

We both laughed.

That was as deep as any of our conversations ever went, and that was how I liked it.

*   *   *

The rest of the day seemed to drag on forever. So much so that when the final bell rang, I hauled ass out of there. On the way to my car, I checked the weather on my phone, trying to plan my next run. When I raised my eyes, all the air left my lungs.

She was a few feet ahead of me, and this time, I was certain it was Abby. I would recognize her walk anywhere. She wore an oversize T-shirt and jeans cut off just above her knees. Her outfit hid the curves that had been so obviously on display when I had seen her last. Her hair was tied up in a messy knot on top of her head, like it had been earlier when she was sitting under that tree. "Abby!" I called out, shoving my phone in my pocket and picking up my pace. She didn't turn around. "Abby!" I called again. Still nothing. I hesitated for a second before grabbing her arm.

She turned to me, and her eyes went huge. "Oh shit," she whispered. She looked shocked. Or scared. Or both.

I let my breath out with a whoosh. "It *is* you." I swallowed my nerves. *Why was I nervous?* "I was calling your name."

"Oh shit," she said again. Same tone. She spun on her heels and started walking away.

I caught up and matched her step for step. "What's going on?" Her reaction confused me. "Why are you acting like you don't know me?"

She sped up.

"Abby, stop!" She eventually did, throwing her backpack into a shitty old convertible. She fingered the door handle, but I rested my ass against the door, making sure she had no choice but to speak to me. I linked my hands behind my head and studied the sky, letting out a frustrated groan. "You go to school here?"

She shrugged but kept her eyes down. I dropped my arms. "Abby!" I tried to get her to acknowledge me again. She didn't look up, but I thought I detected the hint of a smile. My voice was flat as I asked, "Do you want to enlighten me on what's so funny?"

She giggled. God, just hearing her giggle brought back all the feelings from our time together.

"My name's not Abby."

"What? You gave me a fake name?"

"So did you!"

"What? No I didn't!"

And right on cue, Will showed up. "Hunter! You coming to . . ." He trailed off. Maybe he noticed the look in my eyes, pleading with him to fuck off. "What?" he asked me. Then he glanced from me to Abby—or whatever her name was. "Oh," he said and began to nod. "New toy?" He eyed her up and down, rubbing his hands together and licking his lips.

I wanted to punch him.

Pushing off her car, I stood between them and faced Will. "I'll catch up with you later, alright?" I didn't have time to fuck around.

He raised his hands in surrender. "Alright, man." He walked off, but not before winking at her.

I ignored the need to beat his ass and turned to her. "So your name's not Abby?"

She rolled her eyes dramatically. "And your name's Hunter?" she asked skeptically.

I shook my head. "Are you new—to this school, I mean?"

"No."

"Then how the hell do you not know who I am?"

She laughed. "Are you some kind of god who I should bow down to?"

"No." But then I replayed my words in my head—I sounded like a dick. I shook my head. "That's not what I meant."

"Sure." Amusement filled her eyes. I wanted to laugh with her, but she suddenly grew serious and took a step back.

Then the worst thing that could possibly happen happened.

"Babe!" Hannah shouted.

"Fuck."

She was at my side instantly. "I was hoping to catch up with you before you left." She rose up on her toes and kissed my cheek.

Every single part of my body tensed.

I didn't want her there. I didn't want Abby—or whatever her name was—to see us together. Not like this.

"Hey . . ." Hannah cooed. She was talking to Not Abby. "You're in my gym class, right?"

She nodded.

"Chloe, is it?"

She chewed her lip and then nodded once.

Chloe.

Her eyes met mine—conveying an emotion I couldn't decipher. And then she turned, leaned over the back door of her car, and reached for something. She held my letterman jacket out to Hannah. "I spilled soda on your boyfriend's jacket, and I offered to dry-clean it; he was just asking for it back."

"Oh," Hannah said quietly, taking it from her hands.

I stood there frozen, not knowing what to say or do. Then Hannah's fingernails dug into my forearms, and she turned me to face her. My eyes never left Chloe. Not until the wrong pair of lips brushed against mine, and her tongue invaded my mouth.

Then I heard a car start.

Pushing Hannah away, I spun around, but Chloe was already hauling ass out of there. I turned back to Hannah. "This game's getting a little old, don't you think?"

She shrugged, examined her nails, and muttered, "Call me," before spinning on her heels and walking away.

CHAPTER FIVE

Chloe

It wasn't like I was going to be late for my first day of work at the bowling alley, but I had wanted to arrive early and make a good impression. I hadn't expected Hunter to come chasing after me at school. In fact, I had expected exactly what I'd gotten from him over the last four years—nothing.

I rushed to change into the uniform that Josh, the guy who was training me, had handed me. They came in only one size: whore.

It was a tight fit, especially across my chest, and the top ended just below my belly button, leaving about an inch of skin between it and the band of my jeans. I'd be sure to order a larger size for my next shift.

I'd be working at the snack bar, which was perfect for me. I liked mundane, monotonous-type jobs that never led anywhere.

"Perfect," Josh said, eyeing me up and down as I made my way to my post. I hadn't decided if the guy was a complete sleaze or just an idiot. He looked to be around my age, but he told me he worked full-time, which meant that he was either older, or hadn't cared much for high school and had dropped out.

"I'll have to order a larger size," I told him.

"Or . . ." He paused and lifted the counter door for me. "You could keep it and make four times the tips."

"And compromise my soul?" I raised an eyebrow. "I'll be okay. Thank you for the suggestion, though."

He shrugged and led me through a doorway into the kitchen prep area and then to a separate storeroom that was reserved for staff. He told me I could keep my stuff there. Back in the snack bar, he began to show me the equipment. Just as he was about to demonstrate how to operate the coffee machine, a voice interrupted us. "Yo, Josh."

I froze.

I didn't even have to see him to know who it was. Slowly, I turned around and faced him. Blake/Hunter's eyes practically fell out of his head when he saw me. He opened his mouth, but nothing came out. Next to me, Josh laughed. "Hunter, this is Chloe. Chloe—Hunter."

We mirrored each other's reactions. Frozen. Silent. Finally, he looked away. But where he looked didn't make me feel any better. His eyes zoned in on my breasts. I crossed my arms and tried to cover them. A slow smile began to spread across his face. "You work here?" he asked.

Josh answered for me. "As of today, from three 'til nine, Monday, Wednesday, Friday, and Saturday, it'll be us three."

"Us *three*?" I choked out.

Blake/Hunter chuckled. He chewed his lip, shaking his head slowly from side to side. Then he took a big gulp of the soda he held in his hand. I pried my eyes away from his lips. I knew what those lips tasted like. And I knew that I shouldn't have kissed him, but I thought I'd never have to deal with him again. "I quit," I announced.

Blake/Hunter choked on his drink. Tugging my shirt lower, I moved to the counter and began to lift the door. A pair of heavy forearms thumped down on it. "You're not quitting," he said. He was smiling again, a smile so wide it made him look smug.

My eyes narrowed.

Josh turned to me. "Okay. I don't know what's going on between you two, but if you want to quit because of Hunter, there's no need. He works desk and shoes. You won't even see each other. And I need you here with me. I'll even go out back and check for a larger shirt."

"But you said this was the only size you ha—"

Blake/Hunter's laugh cut me off. He reached over with his hand up and high-fived Josh just as Josh was turning to walk into the storeroom, I assumed to get my new shirt.

"You guys are assholes," I yelled at Josh, but I kept my eyes on Blake/Hunter.

"My first name's Blake. My last name's Hunter," he said, leaning against the counter. His biceps flexed against his sleeves. Only then, did I realize we were wearing the same uniform. "Just so you're not confused, I didn't lie to you. Everyone calls me Hunter. I'm a jock"—he shrugged—"and my dad's ex-army, so it kind of just happened."

"Oh."

He nodded. "And your name's Chloe?"

It was my turn to nod.

"And you go to my school."

I nodded again. "But contrary to popular belief, I don't think it's actually *your* school."

He laughed then, a genuine laugh that reached his eyes, his light blue eyes. I had never known the strength of them until Saturday night. Not until he'd held my gaze and managed to tell me in a few sentences what I'd wanted to hear my entire life. It hadn't mattered that he was a stranger. Or that he had had no idea what kind of impact his words would have. He had given me more than I'd come to expect from anyone.

"You got customers, asshole," Josh said from behind me.

Blake's eyes moved slowly from me to the front desk, where a family was waiting for service. When his gaze returned to me, he winked. "Looks like I'll be seeing you around, *Chloe*."

*   *   *

Josh was right. During the six-hour shift, I barely saw Blake. Not until the lanes closed and we shut the doors to prepare for cleanup. As soon as the front entrance was locked, music filled my ears. Then I felt the heat of a body behind me. "This is when the fun begins." *Blake.*

I turned to him to ask what he meant, but he just smirked. He reached for a broom and handed it to me. "Cleanup time," he said.

I was two swipes of the broom in when the electricity cut out and the bowling alley fell into pitch-black darkness. The music was still playing, though. Blake's laugh from behind me caught me off guard. Then Josh's howl echoed through the building.

"What the hell?" I whispered.

I felt Blake's hand on the small of my back, and then his fingers skimmed my waist. "Come on," he said quietly into my ear. His lips brushed against my cheek, then he pulled away and found my hand holding the broom. "Drop it." The huskiness in his voice made me quiver.

I did as he asked. As it fell to the floor, he laced his fingers through mine. The touch was light but enough to make my head spin. The music stopped. A lone, dim light flicked on, illuminating the middle of the lanes. The song started again. Louder this time. The bass thumped, rattling the objects around us. He started to walk, pulling me with him. His hand grasped mine tighter with every step.

Josh appeared in one of the lit-up lanes, two skateboards in hand. "Come on, Hunter!" he shouted over the music. "Let's show off for New Girl."

"I have a name!" I yelled back.

"Yeah!" Josh responded. "And it's not Abby!"

My gasp was stupidly loud. I turned to Blake, but all I could see was his silhouette towering over me. "You told him?"

He squeezed my hand once. "You did lie to me. I had to check your resume, make sure you weren't lying about anything else."

"You checked my resume?" I wasn't sure if I was pissed or amused.

He laughed. "I'm just fucking with you, Chloe."

I pulled my hand out of his grasp when I was able to see where I was going. I didn't want him to think that it was okay to do things like that. Not now that we were going to have to see a lot more of each other, at least for the next three months, until graduation.

Josh dropped the skateboard in front of me. "Show us what you got, princess."

My eyebrows furrowed as I took in our surroundings. My eyes landed back on Josh. "Um. No?"

"What, are you scared?"

"What?"

Blake went over and stood next to him, arms crossed. It made his shoulders look even broader than they already were. Josh mimicked his pose. "Yeah," Blake teased. "Quit being a girl."

"Oh my God." A small giggle escaped. "You guys are idiots." I turned and started walking away, but firm hands gripped my shoulders, holding me back.

"Stay," Blake murmured into my ear. "I promise I'll be nice."

I froze, determined to push down the feelings that arose when he was this close.

With his arm around my shoulders, he sat us down on the chairs surrounding the ball return. "Just watch," he told me.

Josh—he was kind of amazing with a skateboard. I didn't know shit about skateboarding, but I knew enough to realize that he wasn't doing everyday-kid-in-a-skate-park stuff. I ignored the fact that I was sure what he was doing wasn't allowed. Skating on and between the lanes, grinding against the gutters, down the ball return machine, using his skateboard as a bowling ball and try-ing to knock down pins—I knew he could be fired in seconds—probably me, too, just for watching. But it felt familiar to me, watching him like this. Like he, too, needed a place to escape. A reason to leave the world behind and just feel free.

"You want to try?" Blake asked. I turned to find him staring at me. I wondered how long he'd been watching, but I didn't ask, just got on my feet and pulled my shirt down as far as it would go. Turned out there were no larger sizes, so I was stuck with my whore-size shirt until the manager could order me a new one.

Blake licked his lips and stood up. His eyes were pleading. I didn't know what for.

"Fine."

He grinned. "Yeah?"

"I'm warning you. I'll suck."

"At least you'll try," he replied, taking my hand again.

And I let him.

*　　　*　　　*

"You suck!" he shouted as I passed him, wobbling from side to side.

I laughed. "I told you I would!"

He jogged up next to me and held my hips, helping me bal-ance. Well, that was what I thought, until he jumped on the board, too. His legs were on either side of mine, and his fingers moved higher and curled around my waist. "It's easy," he said into my ear. "It's all about balance, moving your body with the board."

We were heading straight for a wall. "Whoa." Panic set in, and I started to fall.

He laughed and gripped me tighter. "You're fine. I got you. Just sway your body with mine, okay? We'll go slow."

I closed my eyes and let him take control. He pressed his body into mine; I followed his lead and moved forward. I felt us turning around. Feeling it was safe enough, I opened my eyes. A low laugh bubbled out of me. "It feels like we're flying." I tilted my head up and looked at him.

"Yeah," he replied, "it really does." He smiled, but his eyes were distant. Lost in another world.

Then the music cut off. Blake's foot screeched against the floor, and he came to an abrupt stop. But the skateboard and I didn't. "Shit!" we yelled at the same time. Then I was airborne. He gripped my waist more firmly and pulled me back, my legs flailing up in the air for a moment as the skateboard rolled on. I was just catching my balance when I looked up and noticed Josh behind the desk.

"What's up?" Josh's voice echoed. He was on his phone. "I'm on my way," he said, a note of panic clearly detectable in his voice. He looked over at us. Blake's hands were still on my waist.

"Hunter, man . . . I gotta jet. Tommy's in the emergency room."

Blake dropped his hands. "Dude, go!"

Then Josh was off, searching his pockets as he ran to the exit. "Fuck." He stopped and turned back to us. "I skated here." His voice broke, as though he was on the verge of tears.

"I'll take you," Blake told him. It was instant. He didn't even think twice. He turned to me and asked, "You coming?"

I didn't know why he asked me to go, but I wasn't going to say no.

Josh switched the lights on as he waited by the door. "Get your shit," Blake said. "We'll meet you at the front door."

I started toward the storeroom. "What about the cleanup?" I shouted over my shoulder.

"I got it," he answered with the phone already to his ear.

What would normally have been a fifteen-minute drive took five. Josh had the car door open and jumped out before we even came to a complete stop. After finding a parking spot and turning the car off, Blake turned to me. "Tommy is Josh's son."

CHAPTER SIX

Chloe

Josh was pacing back and forth in the waiting room when we walked in. He paused for a moment when he saw us but then continued. "They won't let me see him," he shouted to no one in particular.

Blake approached him but gave him his space. "What do you mean?" he asked cautiously.

"I mean that bitch didn't put my name on Tommy's birth certificate, so I have no fucking right to see my own son. Where the fuck is she, Blake? I'm here, so where the fuck is she when our son's in there?" He pointed at the swinging doors next to the nurses' station. "He's my fucking son!" he shouted again, this time for their benefit.

Blake took a brave step forward and put his arm around Josh's shoulders. As they headed out the door, Blake spoke quietly, with his head bent, his words meant for only Josh.

I took a seat and waited. Honestly, I felt a little out of place. And hospitals—particularly this one—weren't filled with good memories.

A few minutes later, they came back in. Josh looked a little calmer as he slumped down on the seat opposite me. Blake sat next to me. His arm rested along the back of my chair. "You okay?" he asked quietly.

"Uh-huh." I nodded. My eyes stayed on Josh. "Josh?" I asked. He looked up from the floor. He seemed to have aged a decade in the half hour since I'd watched him skateboarding so freely in the bowling alley. Then it clicked—why I had had that feeling when I was watching him. That was his escape. His hideaway from reality, where he could just be a kid again, instead of raising one. "Who's here with Tommy?"

"His grandparents. Tommy's mom's parents. I can't get hold of them to let them know I'm here."

Well, at least there was that. At least Tommy had someone.

A doctor walked in, holding a clipboard. Josh was up and out of his seat instantly. "Is he okay?"

The doctor looked up at Josh, then Blake and me. His eyes fixed on me, and I knew the moment recognition set in. I slumped in my seat and averted my gaze. "I'm sorry . . ." His voice trailed off.

"*What?*" Josh yelped.

"Oh no! I'm sorry. I mean, I just got here. I don't know who or what you're talking about. I just came in to use the vending machine."

"Oh God." Out of the corner of my eye, I saw Josh fall back in his chair.

I recognized the doctor. In fact, I'd never forget him. Dr. Ramirez was his name. He cleared his throat. I still refused to look up.

"Chloe? Is that you?"

I felt the back of Blake's fingers skim up and down my arm, but I remained silent.

Dr. Ramirez sighed. "I've been trying to contact you, Chloe. I've been sending you letters once a month. It's important that you come in and see me. Especially with—"

Glaring up at him, I tried to keep my emotions in check as I said, "Isn't this illegal—you talking about me like this in front of other people? Surely that violates patient-doctor confidentiality."

He rubbed his hand against his graying beard. "I'm just worried about you, Chloe."

"I'm fine," I said. I didn't want him talking about this—not now—and definitely not with Blake and Josh there. Blake's hand settled on the curve of my shoulder; he squeezed it lightly.

I looked down at the floor. I had nothing more to say. I heard the doctor sigh again before the sound of his footsteps faded and then disappeared.

Several seconds of silence passed. If they had questions, they kept them to themselves, and I was grateful for that.

"Chloe?" Josh said. He'd stood up and was walking toward me. He squatted down onto one knee so our gazes met. His eyes were filled with tears but clear enough that I could see the pain behind them. He took my hand in his. "I wouldn't—" His voice cracked. He cleared his throat. "I wouldn't ask if I had any other option. But you—you know that doctor and he seems to know you. And me—I need someone on my side right now. I need somebody that can help me. I need to see Tommy. I need to see my son. And I need to know that he's okay. If you could do something, anything at all, to help me, to get me closer to him . . . I'm asking—no, I'm *begging* you—please, *please* help me."

A tear fell. Not his—but mine.

I nodded, stood up, and made my way to the nurses' desk. "Can you please page Dr. Ramirez?"

*　　　*　　　*

Five minutes later, Josh was led in to see his son. I'd promised Dr. Ramirez I'd come in for a checkup. I'd lied. I'd even given him a phone number. Not mine. But Josh was able to be with his son. And that was all that mattered.

*   *   *

"That was a good thing you did."

I looked up from dumping sugar in my coffee. We were on the floor of the waiting room and had an assortment of snacks and beverages between us.

"I didn't do anything, Blake."

He shook his head slowly. "You might not think so. But Josh— he'll remember that forever."

I replaced the lid and took a sip of the coffee. It was nearly two in the morning now. I had absolutely no idea what I was doing there, but I couldn't leave, and truthfully, I didn't want to.

Blake cleared his throat and looked up at me through his lashes. "So, that doctor knows you? He's been sending you letters?"

I slumped my shoulders, heaved a sigh, and ignored his question. "What's the deal with him?"

"Josh?" he asked, then took a sip of his coffee. It must have been too hot because he cursed and sucked the skin on the back of his hand, trying to cool his mouth. I contained my chuckle. He shrugged and continued, "He met Natalie our freshman year—"

"He went to our school?"

He laughed. "Yeah . . . and I'm still weirded out that we've been at the same school for however long, and I've never seen you before."

"Go on," I said, trying to sidestep where he wanted this conversation to go.

"So, they met when we were freshman. Natalie got pregnant start of junior year, had the baby, tried to be a mom, couldn't—so she ran away. Josh has no idea where she is. She won't speak to him, just her parents. They watch Tommy when Josh has to work and no one else can. Natalie calls them every now and then and gets them to wire her money. They do, but they hate it."

"And Josh?"

"Josh's parents kicked him out of the house when they found out he got a girl pregnant. He leases a garage apartment off an old lady that loves the shit out of him and Tommy. I don't think she even lets him pay rent anymore. He maintains her yard, and she watches Tommy when she can. She's more like family to them than his own parents are. How fucked up is that? Josh stepped up to be a parent, and his own parents failed him." He paused for a moment. "Actually, everyone failed him. His parents, his girlfriend, our so-called friends."

"So you knew him in high school?"

He nodded. "Yeah. We were best friends. I mean we still are. He's kind of my reality, you know?"

I didn't respond. I didn't really understand what he meant.

"It's hard," he continued. "He leads this whole other life that kids our age are way too young to be living. But you should see him with his kid. It's like a higher power created two living individuals at different times and made them fit perfectly for each other. Josh loves that kid more than anything in the world. And when they're together, their age difference doesn't matter. Nothing matters. Just Tommy." His eyes roamed my face, and I swear he wanted to say something more, but he held back. "Anyway," he said with forced peppiness in his voice, "Josh was gonna be a pro skater. He had sponsors chasing him and everything. It was his dream." He looked away and stared into the distance. "I remember when we were kids at the skate park and everyone would just watch him. He demanded attention. He was *that* good."

"What about you? I mean, you're pretty good, right?"

"I'm good, but I'm not Joshua-Warden good."

"So what's your dream, Hunter?"

His body went rigid with the coffee cup halfway to his mouth. He tilted his head slightly, his lips apart, examining me. "I think I'd prefer it if you called me Blake."

I dropped my head to hide my grin. "Okay, Blake. What's your dream?"

He inhaled audibly, and his shoulders tensed. "Ball."

"Basketball?"

He nodded. "But it's just a dream, Not Abby."

I laughed at his nickname for me before saying, "But you're good, though, right? I mean, good enough for college?"

His smile was tight.

Then Josh's voice interrupted us. "I'm so sorry. I forgot you guys were out here."

"It's fine," Blake said as we both stood.

"He's going to be okay," Josh said.

I hadn't realized how tense I'd been until I felt my muscles relax.

"It's a horrible case of the flu, but he's going to be okay."

I felt the rush of breath from Blake and looked up at him. His head was tipped back in relief.

"Thank you, guys. I mean it. And Chloe, I can't even—"

"It's no problem. Really," I cut in.

Then his arms were around me, holding me tight. "Thank you," he said again. He pulled back. "I better get back in there. When Tommy's out of here, I want you to meet him, okay?"

I smiled. "Of course."

Then he was gone.

"Home?" Blake asked.

"Home."

Blake

I drove her back to the bowling alley, where she'd left her car. We didn't speak. She looked exhausted. "Will you be alright to drive home?"

She nodded through a yawn.

I pulled my car up next to hers. "Thanks for coming. I don't know how Josh would've handled it if you hadn't been there to come to his rescue."

She shrugged. "At least Tommy's going to be okay. That's the main thing, right?" She opened the car door and stepped out. I followed. I wasn't ready to say good-bye yet. Throwing her bag in her car, she turned back to me. "I can't wait to climb into bed and crash."

"Yeah . . ."

"Are you tired?"

I shook my head. "Not really. I'm probably gonna go for a run."

She laughed quietly. "That actually doesn't surprise me at all."

For a moment, silence filled the space between us, then she spoke. "So, I'll see you on Wednesday, right?"

"Or at school tomorrow."

"About that . . ." she said. Her eyes focused on the ground while she contemplated her next words. When she looked up, her bottom lip was caught between her teeth. "I think—" She broke off and let out a breath, then started again. "I think that maybe you shouldn't talk to me at school."

"What?"

"I just don't want people to know that you know me. I know it sounds strange, but it would just cause issues."

"What—"

"Nothing bad." She cut me off. "It's just for me. It's something I want. Please?"

"I don't get it."

"I don't expect you to. I just need you to do it, okay?"

"So, what? I see you in the halls, and you just expect me to ignore you? That's gonna be hard, Chloe." I didn't know why I was so pissed, but the thought of not speaking to her when she was *right there* made absolutely no sense.

"You've done it for four years. I'm sure you can manage another three months."

My eyes narrowed.

"Please, Blake."

I wanted to argue, but I didn't. Instead, I took a step forward and placed my hand on her hip. Her body stiffened, but she didn't push me away. "What are you doing?" she asked, exhaling a shaky breath.

"I don't know," I told her truthfully. I had spent the entire night doing everything I could not to replay that kiss in my mind. And to ignore her uniform . . . her goddamn shirt was so tight I could see every bump, every curve, every part of her.

Leaning down, I rubbed my nose against her cheek, followed by my lips. Her breath caught on a gasp, and she held it. She must have sensed it, too. Whatever this was between us. I felt her hands on my stomach as she gripped my shirt. I had her pressed up against her car by the time my lips moved to her jaw. "Blake," she whispered.

My tongue grazed across her skin. "Mmm?"

She tilted her head, inviting me to keep going.

I started kissing her neck. When she let out a soft whimper, I was certain she wanted the same thing. My hand moved from her hip, to her thigh, gripping it and lifting it off the ground so I could get between her legs. My other hand settled on the back of her head. Fingers curled in her hair, I pulled back slightly, dipping her head back so I could see her lips. Her eyes were half-hooded, and even in the darkness, I could see the lust filling them. My mouth descended, aiming for hers.

"Blake," she said again. Louder and firmer this time.

Her hands on my stomach flattened, and she pushed me away. "What?" I asked, confused as all fuck.

She straightened up, adjusting her top. She pulled it lower, which only revealed more of her cleavage. Then, her words were like being doused with a cold bucket of water. "How's Hannah?"

*　　*　　*

She got into her car without a word and drove off. Even after my dick move, I was still worried that she was too tired to drive, so I decided to follow her home. Only she didn't go home. She drove to the restaurant we had gone to on Saturday night. But instead of going into the basement, she rang a buzzer next to the door. A minute later, Clayton, in nothing but his boxer shorts, opened the door for her. They greeted each other wordlessly, and she stepped inside.

I waited half an hour, like a stalker, for her to come back out. She never did. I drove home, but I couldn't sleep. I replayed the night in my head over and over again. The thought of her sleeping with that Clayton asshole—kissing him, fucking him—I wanted to throw up.

I finally ended up going for a run. I skipped school and hung out with Josh the next day. I didn't want to see her, not when I couldn't speak to her.

Hannah called.

Eighteen times.

I never answered.

CHAPTER SEVEN

Chloe

"Busted."

I froze in the hallway and looked over to see Mary sitting on the sofa, book in hand. "Crap."

Her eyes narrowed, and it seemed that she was trying to keep her voice firm when she said, "You're supposed to be at school, young lady."

"I'm sorry. It won't happen again," I said, though we both knew that wasn't true.

Mary and Dean weren't too strict with me. We had agreed that I would graduate and that what I did after that was up to me. They knew what my plans were for afterwards, and they supported them. The only rule was that I check in enough while I was there so that they knew I was safe, and I always made sure to do that.

I slumped down next to her. She wrapped her arms around me and squeezed tight. "Did you stay at Clayton's?"

"Yeah."

"How is he?"

"He's good. Lisa's coming home from Savannah for the weekend so he's excited about that."

"Is she still enjoying it there?"

I nodded.

"And you?" she asked, releasing her hold. "How are you?"

"Good," I answered, even though I knew it wouldn't be enough.

And right on cue, "Chloe." I saw what was coming next; I'd been expecting it for a while. "You just seem to be getting more and more distant lately, and I understand that. I do. But we miss you."

"I know," I said quietly.

She sighed and changed the subject. "So how was work?" She smiled widely, in such a way that I knew she knew something I didn't.

"What do you know?" My grin matched hers. I couldn't control it. I loved Mary and everything about her. I was so, so grateful that I had ended up there, with her and Dean, when things could've turned out so much worse.

"Who was that boy that was here Sunday morning? Are you guys dating?"

And just like that my mood switched. "No, we're not dating. Honestly, I just met him that night."

"Are you working with him?"

My eyes snapped to hers. "How—"

"I've seen him there before . . . when we've taken the kids. I'm not a perv." She smirked. "But it's hard not to notice a boy like that." A part of me wanted to laugh and agree with her, but an even bigger part of me was afraid. She took my nonresponse and ran with it. "Does he go to your school?"

"I don't know. Maybe." I shrugged and stood up. "I'm going to school; I should at least show up for a class or two." I swiftly exited the room, then climbed the stairs faster than normal. If she had more questions, she kept them to herself. She knew I wouldn't want to hear them.

*   *   *

I knew my future.

I knew my fate.

And I knew that I had absolutely no control of any of it. I'd learned to accept that and be thankful for what I did have. The things most people took for granted were the things I made sure to pay special attention to: sunrises and sunsets; driving with the top down—or just driving at all; being able to wake up and know that it was safe to play outside with the kids, and, in a world populated by dictators and strewn with war zones, I wasn't surrounded by any of them. What I was surrounded by was an uncertain future. One in which I couldn't muster the courage to have hopes and dreams. Because I knew they were unattainable. That part—I could live with.

But what I hated about the uncertainty was my inability to form meaningful relationships. Not so much with guys but with Mary and Dean and all the kids that came through there. The only one I had let in was Clayton, and that was because he had been there with me, helping to build the walls around both of us.

I couldn't—and I wouldn't—let anyone else close.

So when Mary had brought up Blake, I'd frozen and I'd shut down.

Because over the years of building walls and living my life one day at a time, I'd learned to accept my fate and never hope for more than what I had. I'd never questioned the way I thought about my life.

But Blake—he made me question it.

He made me want to change it.

To change my outlook.

And to change myself.
But I couldn't.
And I wouldn't.
Because one day, sooner rather than later, I'd be gone.
And I'd leave them all behind.

CHAPTER EIGHT

Chloe

He hadn't gone to school yesterday. Not that I'd been looking for him, but his chair in the cafeteria had been empty. I'd heard his girlfriend, Hannah, telling people that he was with Josh and Tommy and that Tommy had been sick Monday night. I was glad that they had spoken and that he'd told her the truth.

He'd looked pissed when I had said that I didn't want anyone to find out that we knew each other. High school was enough of a bitch as it was. I didn't need people like Hannah as my enemy. I'd studied enough to pass my classes and moved on to the next day.

But he was there that day. Which I knew meant that I'd most likely see him at work, or earlier, as fate would have it.

I saw him when I showed up for gym class. "A special guest," Coach Riley called him. "He's here to teach us the fundamentals of basketball." Fundamentals? We were eighteen. Seniors. If we didn't know the fundamentals of basketball—living in Wilmington, North Carolina, home of *the* Michael Jordan—then it meant we didn't ever care to learn. I, for one, did not care. Hannah, however, gushed, clapping her hands when she saw him. It must've been as much of a surprise for her as it was for me.

I kept my head down the entire time, trying to be inconspicuous. Even when he stood behind me and guided me on how to hold the ball and shoot from the free-throw line, I didn't acknowledge him. Not even when I completely missed the shot and he said, "We're gonna need to work on that. What's your name?"

"Chloe," I answered, my eyes never meeting his. I turned and walked to the end of the line. He said my name eight more times during class. I knew Hannah noticed. She glared at me the entire time in the locker room. But her glare changed to a smirk after I went to put on my shoes only to discover that they'd been drenched in water. I left before everyone else. Soaking-wet shoes and all. He was outside the gym doors, waiting. He called my name, but I kept walking. He knew that was the opposite of what I wanted. He knew, and he'd done it anyway. If he'd meant to piss me off, it worked—I was done with him.

*   *   *

His car was already in the lot when I pulled up. I stepped out and yanked down on the hem of my whore-size T-shirt. My boobs almost spilled out. Note to self: Make sure to get a larger size by Friday. If not, quit.

I walked into the building with my chin up, ignoring the fact that he rose to his full height from his lazy slouch against the desk when I walked in. He called my name. I didn't care.

Flowers were waiting for me when I got to the snack bar. A huge pink balloon floated above them. The words "It's a Girl" had been crossed out with a marker. Written underneath was "Thank you." Josh walked out from the prep area and grinned. "It was all they had," he explained, pointing to the balloon. He came up and wrapped his arms around me. I wasn't expecting the embrace.

"Thank you again," he said, hugging me tighter. I hugged him back. I couldn't not.

"Switch jobs?" Blake's voice felt like a force field pulling us apart.

"Sure." Josh shrugged, lifted the counter door and walked away.

Blake walked in after him. "You're pissed at me?"

I turned my back on him, picked up the flowers and carried them to the storeroom, where I dropped my bag.

"Oh. So you're pissed *and* ignoring me?"

I spun on my heels to confront him. But he was right there, towering over me. He blocked me in with both hands, palms against the wall, on either side of my head. Looking down at the floor, I said, "So you're going to intimidate me into talking to you? That's kind of a dick move, don't you think?"

He dropped his arms and cursed under his breath. "I just don't get you."

"You don't have to get me." I raised my eyes. "All I asked was that you do the same thing that you've done for the past four years and just ignore me. Just pretend like I don't exist. But you couldn't do that. Was there a point to that little charade in the gym?"

"What is with you?"

"Nothing!" I lost it then. "I just want to get through the next few months unnoticed, like I've done my entire life, and I don't want you to ruin that for me!"

"Why? What's the big deal if people see you? If people notice you? So fucking what?"

"I don't want people like your girlfriend—" I broke off. He didn't need to know what Hannah had done.

"Hannah?" His eyes widened. "Did she do something to you?"

"No." I shook my head quickly. "No, Blake. Nothing happened."

He studied me for a second, evidently trying to decide whether to believe me or not. Then a fire sparked in his eyes. "Speaking of girlfriend," he spoke through clenched teeth. "You want to tell me why you thought it was okay to kiss me Saturday night when you knew I had a girlfriend and you had a boyfriend?"

"What the hell are you talking about? I don't have a boyfriend!"

"Oh!" He rolled his eyes. "So you drive to Clayton's house in the middle of the night, he answers the door half-naked, and just lets you in because he's *not* your boyfriend?"

"You followed me?"

"I wanted to make sure you got home safe. Don't change the subject."

"I'm not changing the subject, asshole. I told you. I don't have a boyfriend!"

"So what is it then? You guys just fuck whenever you want? No strings?"

"Fuck you."

I tried to walk past him, but he grabbed my arm. "Tell me I'm wrong." I could see the plea in his eyes, but I didn't care.

"You're wrong," I told him.

"How?"

I let out a shaky breath. "Not that it's any of your business, but I went to his apartment to sleep. I told you that I don't like going home in the middle of the night in case the kids wake up." I pried his fingers off my arm. "And it shouldn't matter. Because you and I—we're nothing. We never were, and we never will be."

Blake

There had been this party last year. It had been the party to end all parties. Some guy had come home from college and hosted it. He'd said it was open to high school juniors and seniors but only a select few. Invitations had been sent out via Facebook. You had to show the evidence on your phone before you entered. It was *that* exclusive. Hannah was thrilled when I got an invite. She didn't get one, but she was my girlfriend, so it automatically made her my plus one.

I told her that I had to help Josh out with something and bailed last minute. It was a lie. Truth was, most of my so-called friends just pissed me off. After the way Josh's life had changed with Tommy, he needed the support of his friends, but they had turned their backs on him and his kid. So I didn't really feel the need to spend my free time with a bunch of assholes, whose most important decision in life was what to drink and who to screw.

Apparently, Hannah had frozen me out for six days. I hadn't even known until she'd told me. She had come over one day, ripped her clothes off, and we'd had sex. Afterwards, she'd said she'd forgiven me. I'd asked her what for. She'd said, "For ruining my chances of making college contacts." Those had been her exact words.

Hannah and I worked because we used each other. She used me for social hierarchy. I used her for sex. It was an unspoken deal. And it had never mattered before. Not until now.

So, for six days Hannah had frozen me out, and I didn't notice.

For six hours, Chloe did the same, and it felt like my life was over.

*   *   *

"Chloe, please." I was begging, and I didn't even care how pathetic I sounded. "Can you please talk to me? I'm sorry." I reached around her, took the rag from her hands, and lifted it above my head.

She turned, eyeing it, but then her lips clamped shut and she crossed her arms.

She remained silent, so I spoke for both of us. "I'm sorry," I repeated. "I was an asshole. I shouldn't have asked to be in your gym class. I should've listened to you. It was a jerk thing to do. And I definitely shouldn't have jumped to conclusions about you and Clayton." I stopped to take a breath, then added, "I hate that you're ignoring me."

Our eyes locked. Neither of us speaking. Not with words anyway.

"It's okay," she finally said.

I let out the breath I didn't know I was holding. My arm fell to my side, and she quickly swiped back the rag.

Turning around, she said over her shoulder, "You asked to be in my gym class?"

I sat on the counter while she wiped around me. I'd started to relax the second she acknowledged me. "Well, yeah. I mean, why do you think I was there?"

She nodded her head in understanding, but the rest of her movements slowed. She raised her eyes slightly, looking unsure. "Because you wanted to see Hannah?"

The tension came back. I covered her hand on the counter with mine, pleading with her to stop and give me her full attention. I needed her to *hear* me. "Chloe, I was there because I wanted to see *you*."

She raised her head, and her eyes drifted shut. "Blake . . ." They snapped open, and a wall slammed down behind them. "You shouldn't say shit like that."

My mouth opened, but nothing came out. The words weren't there. Not yet. Swallowing the knot in my throat, I asked, "Like what?"

She didn't respond.

We spent the rest of the cleanup in silence.

No skateboards this time.

I didn't push her on what she meant because I already knew. And she was right; I shouldn't be saying shit like that. But Chloe— she brought something out in me that had never existed before. She made me want to be there. She made me want to stay. It was as if she had reached inside me, taken my heart in her hands, squeezed tight, and made it start beating again. And it did—whenever I was around her, I could feel it thumping harder, faster.

All because of her.

*   *   *

"So I have a favor to ask you."

As Josh turned the key in the lock to the bowling alley, Chloe and I both replied, "Sure."

Turning to us, he chuckled. To me, he said, "I wouldn't ask you. I'd just make you do it." Then to Chloe, he said, "Hang out with us on Saturday night?"

Her eyes went wide and then locked with mine. I grinned from ear to ear.

"Well, actually, we *need* you to," Josh added.

Slowly, her gaze trailed back to him. "You *need* me to?"

A low chuckle escaped. I was way too excited at the thought of seeing her outside school and work. I answered for him. "Yeah. You see Josh has one night a month without Tommy, and this Saturday is it." I gently shoved her shoulder. "So now you have to come hang out with us or poor Josh . . . poor hardworking, single-teen-dad Josh is gonna get all upset."

Her eyebrows furrowed, and a look of confusion took over. But behind that, I swore I saw the hint of a smile.

"Yeah," Josh said, gently nudging her other shoulder. "You have to come."

I shoved her shoulder again.

He did the same to the other one.

She took a step back. "What the hell?" She looked back and forth between the two of us.

"Come on, Not Abby. Hang out with us. I never see people my age. The last time I went to a party and someone tried to speak to me, I spoke goo-goo-gah-gah talk to them, and they thought I was high."

We all laughed.

"Fine," she said.

"Fire truck, yes!" Josh yelled, and then he was off, jogging to his car. "Oh, Chloe?" he shouted, walking backwards so he could face us. "You're driving!"

"Okay," she yelled back, and then turned to me. "Fire truck, yes?"

I threw back my head as I laughed. "He has to tone down the cussing for Tommy, you know?"

She nodded, her grin still in place.

"Are we good?"

"Yeah, Blake," she said, searching through her bag. "We're good." She took out her keys and pulled down her shirt, trying yet again to cover the inch of skin that her shirt didn't reach. "I'll see you here on Friday okay?"

It was my turn to nod.

"And I mean it about not—"

"I got it, Chloe." I cut her off. "You don't know me. I don't know you."

CHAPTER NINE

Blake

I respected her wishes, kept my distance, and pretended as though she didn't exist. Only she did. She was the only thing that existed in my mind, which made it impossible not to notice her at school. Like the time I watched her sitting under that same tree just outside the cafeteria, earphones in, head bouncing up and down with the music. Or the other time she was there, on her phone—probably to Clayton, laughing at something he said.

She even caught me staring at her once—when she was drinking from the water fountain. I swear it happened in slow motion—just to fuck with my head. My eyes fixated on her lips, dripping wet. Her tongue came out, licking them. They were red from the coldness of the water. A strand of her hair caught in the wetness. She moved it with her index finger to behind her ear, then wiped at her mouth with the back of her hand. She straightened. Then her dark gray eyes moved up, locked with mine. But she quickly averted her gaze and walked away, faster than I ever thought possible.

Chloe

For the next two days at school, he did what he'd said he'd do. He ignored me, and I ignored him. Or, at least, we did our best to try. Stolen glances, tiny smiles—they were all in play. I even failed at hiding my giggle when he walked into the fourth-period math class we'd shared all year. His eyes nearly fell out of his head at the sight of me sitting in the corner of the room. His entire body went still, hand frozen halfway up to push the hair away from his eyes. He did that a lot. Or he'd flick his head back to try to clear it from his forehead. He recovered quickly enough and gave me nothing more than a tiny nod. I tried my best not to notice, and I tried even harder not to like it.

*   *   *

Shaking my head and laughing to myself, I pulled my car into the spot outside the bowling alley. Whatever happy thoughts were running through my mind fled as soon as I lifted the hand brake and it made the squealing sound it always did. I made a mental note to get it serviced before I left.

*   *   *

"You're late," Josh deadpanned as I lifted the counter door.

I spun around and checked the clock on the wall. I was six minutes early.

Then he was next to me, nudging my side. "I'm fucking with you. I just wanted to hang out for a bit before I had to take off."

Lifting my bag strap off my shoulder and over my head, I asked, "You're leaving?"

"I'm not going far. Don't worry, Not Abby." He smiled smugly and jerked his head at Blake, who was walking toward us. "For some reason—I have no idea why—he asked management to switch him from desk to food." He raised his shoulders dramatically to drive the point home, but his smirk stayed in place.

"Fuckwad." Blake patted Josh on the shoulder.

"Shitstain," Josh retorted before turning to leave.

"Wait," I rushed over and pulled on his shirt.

He turned back around. "'Sup?"

"I got you something." Rifling through my bag, I found the toy tractor I'd brought and handed it to him. "It's for Tommy. A get-well-soon gift."

He cast his dark eyes downwards, looking at the toy in his hand. His gaze lifted slowly, first to me, then to Blake, and then to me again. A small smile formed on his lips. He took two steps toward me and wrapped me tightly in his arms, lifting me in the air. After spinning me twice, he placed me gently back on the floor, but he didn't let go. "You're good people, you know that?" he said into my ear. He pulled back slightly and searched my face. Then he licked his lips. I felt the wetness of them on my forehead but for only a second before Blake's throat clearing made him step away. Josh winked at him over my shoulder. "Later, Fucktard."

Then he was gone.

I turned to Blake. "You switched shifts?"

He shrugged. "I didn't have a say. Management decides who works where."

"Bullshit."

He tried to hide his smile.

I walked away before he could see mine.

He followed as I made my way to the storeroom to put my bag away. "So, don't think I'm an asshole, but I got you something," he said.

Placing my bag in an empty locker, I turned to him. "Why would I think you're an asshole?"

He opened his locker, two down from mine, and pulled out something green. It was the same green as our uniform. "I brought you an old shirt. Not because I don't— It has nothing to do with what you're currently wearing. I just thought . . . because I've noticed the way you dress and it just—You don't seem comfortable . . . in something like that?" He jerked his head at my chest. "I'm an ass. Never mind." He threw the shirt back in his locker, slammed it shut, and started to walk away.

"No. Wait!" I went after him.

He stopped but didn't turn to me. Not until after I watched his shoulders heave a couple times. When he finally did, his jaw was clenched tight and his eyes held an emotion I couldn't decipher. I waited for his expression to change—to switch to something that was more comforting. It didn't. Not until I felt forced to take a step back. "I'd appreciate it if you would let me wear it."

He blinked once, and the intensity in his eyes disappeared.

"Yeah." He nodded slowly, and a slight smile appeared. "It's yours."

He took the top out of his locker but didn't give it to me. Instead, he positioned the neck hole over my head and slowly pulled the shirt down—dressing me, like you would a kid. It should have made me angry or at least annoyed, but I simply put my arms through the sleeves. Then he took a step back, his gaze roaming up and down my body. The heat of my blush engulfed my cheeks. I ignored it. Just like I ignored the pounding of my heart and the lack of air in my lungs.

He moved forward until there was nothing between us. No more steps. No space. No air. *Nothing.*

And then he placed his hand on my waist.

I wanted to pull back. I wanted to tell him that it was wrong and that we couldn't. That *I* couldn't.

But I didn't do a thing.

"I like you in my clothes, Not Abby."

Then he turned around and walked away.

I sucked in a breath and held it. Then forcefully blew it out, along with any thoughts of what his presence, and what his words, did to me.

Blake

I knew that I was making it too obvious, but I just didn't give a shit anymore. I wanted to say something stupid and have her laugh at it. I wanted to do something nice and have her appreciate it. Because in the past four years that we'd been in the same place almost every day, I had never noticed her. Not even a little bit. And to me—it felt like there were four years of her life I needed to know about. Four years of not paying attention to make up for. But it wasn't just that. Deep down, I knew she was the only person in the entire world I wanted to notice me.

She leaned her forearms on the counter next to me, mirroring my position, and stared out on to the lanes. "Does Hannah ever come and visit you at work?" I looked at her. A strand of hair had come loose behind her ear. My fingers itched to touch it, but she beat me to it, turning to face me at the same time. Her eyebrows were raised, waiting. She had asked me a question. *What had she said?*

"So?"

"Huh?" I needed to get my shit together.

She smirked. "Hannah? Your girlfriend? Does she ever visit you at work?"

I straightened up. "Why do you keep asking about her?"

"Why do you keep forgetting about her?"

"Because she's not important." And as the words left my mouth, I knew I sounded like a dick. I just sighed and walked away, not wanting to get into it.

70

CHAPTER TEN

Blake

"Would you assholes hurry the fuck up?" On the other side of the counter, Josh bounced on his toes. I decided to sweep extra slow, just to piss him off. "You're a dick," he spat, and then looked to the doorway of the prep area. "Seriously, Not Abby! Let's go."

I laughed. "What's with you?"

His eyes narrowed. "Fire truck you. I get one night a month and you—" He raised his voice. "You guys are being slow on purpo—" He broke off, giving me enough reason to stop sweeping and face him. His mouth hung open. Then a smirk developed and a low whistle came from him. "Holy shit, Chloe, you clean up good."

I spun around quickly. Too quickly.

We hadn't spoken much since yesterday's shift. Once she'd brought up Hannah, the mood had shifted. Even though she had every right to mention her, I was still pissed.

"I wasn't sure what your plans were, so I didn't know how to dress." She chewed her lip and looked down at the floor. Her dress was loose but short. Too short. She cleared her throat.

My eyes snapped up. I'd been staring at her legs. "You look nice," I told her.

"Thank you."

"Can we go now?" Josh whined from behind me.

"Yeah," Chloe and I said in unison, but our eyes remained locked, refusing to budge.

"You guys are fucking ridiculous. I'll wait by your car, Chloe," Josh said as his footsteps faded.

I waited until I thought he was far enough away before speaking. "You look nice."

"You already said that."

"I did?"

She nodded.

"Maybe you deserve to be told more than once."

Her breath caught. "I'll wait at my car."

Chloe

They directed me out to an abandoned basketball court in the middle of nowhere. Apparently, that was their way of letting loose.

"There's no fucking room in this backseat," Josh complained. He sat sideways with his knees up and skateboards on either side of him. He and Blake must have planned ahead and skated to work.

Blake and I both turned around and laughed at the sight of him. "I didn't really plan on anyone ever sitting there." The squeal of the hand brake when I lifted it echoed through our surroundings.

"You should probably get that looked at," Blake said, holding on to the top of the windshield. The nights were getting warmer, and I was able to drive with the top down more often.

"I plan to."

Josh jumped out of the car, not bothering to wait for us. I only had a two door. I'd never needed room for anything more. "You know what I plan to do, Chloe?" He pointed his finger at me. I slumped farther into my seat. Blake's deep chuckle reverberated in my ears. *"I plan on getting fucked up!"*

After the third beer in ten minutes, he pulled out a Ziploc bag. I knew what it was without looking.

"He doesn't do this often," Blake explained. He sat back on his outstretched arms, next to me. We were on the hood of my car, watching Josh. "I'm not judging," I said quietly, turning to face him. "So he doesn't hear from Tommy's mom?"

"Never."

"Sucks."

"Yeah."

"And school? Does he ever plan on finishing?"

"Don't know." He dropped back and leaned on one elbow so he could face me. "He says it's hard to make plans when your future is so uncertain."

"Huh." Turned out Josh and I had more in common than I'd thought. I watched him mumbling to himself as he paced back and forth, only a few feet ahead of us.

Taking a drag of the joint and holding it, he pointed his finger between us. He didn't speak, not until he'd exhaled the smoke and taken a few steps toward us. "You know what I miss?" He handed Blake the joint and clasped us both on the shoulders. "Pussy."

Blake chuckled.

"I. Miss. Pussy." He directed his glare at Blake. "And you, *dick-face*. You get pussy whenever you want. It's as if she's an open door, and you can just walk in freely. Here, Hannah," he mocked. "Here's my cock."

"Oh my God!" I couldn't contain the laugh that escaped.

Blake took a drag, then offered it to me. I declined. If I smoked, I did it to lose myself, and I didn't want to do that tonight. Only certain nights, like the night I met Blake. "It gets worse." His words were weak as he tried to hold the smoke in his lungs.

"And you, Chloe," Josh continued. "Chloe. *Pshh*. Dumb name. I'm calling you Chlo. No. Dumb name, too. C-Lo!" He laughed to himself, but for only a second before his eyebrows furrowed. "C-Lo, I bet you're the same. You can probably get all the cock in all the world." He threw his arms out to his sides and spun around dramatically. "But not Joshua. Joshua gets no pussy." He looked back at Blake. "Hunter. Dickface. Free pussy."

"Dude, random words are not sentences."

"Fuck you, Free-Pussy Hunter." He paused. "Hunter? It doesn't even suit you. You don't hunt for pussy. It's like they scream for you!" His voice changed to match that of a whiney girl. "Take me, Hunter. Take me *now*!"

Blake's embarrassed laugh made his head fall forward and onto my arm.

Josh took the joint from his hand and walked away. "I'm Hunter," he announced, grabbing on to his junk. "What's that, tree? Oh, you want my dick? Sure! I'm Blake-fucking-Hunter. Take all the dick you want."

"Quit it!" Blake yelled. "You're making me sound like an asshole in front of Chloe. You're breaking bro code. Not cool, dude!"

Josh ignored him. Opting, instead, to start humping the tree.

"Oh my God," I laughed.

Blake looked up at me with embarrassment. "Kid's lost it."

"He's allowed."

"Yeah," he said sadly. We watched as he moved away from the tree and started pacing again. "So what about you, *C-Lo*? What are your plans after high school?"

I looked down at him. His eyebrows were raised and his head tilted lazily . . . but his eyes . . . his eyes held a depth in them that knocked all sense out of me. For a second I wanted to tell him everything. The truth about me and my future. "The Road."

Blake's eyes narrowed slightly. "The road?"

"Yeah." I turned away. His eyes had the power to wreck not only me, but also the walls I'd spent my life building. "The Road," I repeated, as if saying the words again would make him understand. Lying back, I leaned on my elbows so we were level. And I waited. I knew the questions were coming, and even though Clayton was the only one who knew my answers, for some reason, I didn't feel the need to hide them from Blake. "After graduation, I'm taking off."

"Taking off?"

"You keep repeating my words, like they're questions."

"Yeah, well, your answers aren't really answers. They're just words."

"How are answers formed, if not with words?"

"By words that form explanations."

"Explanations are the same as answers."

He laughed. "Shut up and explain." He poked my shoulder with a single finger. "Properly."

I sucked in all the air my lungs could handle and then let it out in a whoosh. "I'm just gonna get in my car and drive. No destination. No maps. Nothing. Just drive."

"For the entire summer?"

I turned to him, finding it difficult not to look at him when he was that close. "Kind of like an endless summer."

I could see the question in his eyes before his mouth opened, but before he had a chance to voice it, I cut in. "It's kind of the plan for the rest of my life."

"The rest of your life?" he said incredulously.

"And there you go, repeating my words again."

He shook his head as if clearing a thought. "I'm confused." And he looked it. Which made him even cuter. "Are you going on your own?"

I nodded.

"Forever?" His tone had changed—past confusion—into something completely different.

I nodded again.

"Why?"

"Because." I shrugged. "There's nothing keeping me here. I don't have family. I don't have any friends—"

"*I'm* your friend."

That made me laugh. "I guess. But I've known you . . . what? A week? As far as being a reason to stay, I don't think that really cuts it."

He sighed. It sounded as dramatic as it did genuine. "And you're going by yourself?"

He seemed closer, or maybe it just felt that way. The air around us intensified as I forced myself to answer. My voice came out shaky when I finally did. "Yes. Why?"

Blake

"Why?" I said back.

Her laugh was all-consuming as she pushed playfully against my chest. I fell back onto the warm metal of her hood. "You just keep repeating what I say."

I did. But I really couldn't form any other words. "I just worry about you," I said, looking up at the night sky.

It was silent for so long that I thought she'd left me. Just as I was about to turn to her, her hand swept down my arm and onto my palm. I heard her exhale right before she laced her fingers with mine. "You don't need to worry about me, Blake," she said quietly. But she was wrong. And I realized it then—that even if I tried, I couldn't help but worry. It could have been because of the way we'd met, or it could have been because she meant more to me than anyone ever had. "I don't know, Chloe," I said. "I kind of feel like someone has to, you know?" I turned to her, wanting to see her reaction.

She was already facing me; her eyes glazed with her unshed tears. She blinked quickly, letting them fall and wiping them away before I could do it for her. "You can't do that, Blake. You can't worry about me like that."

Josh's shadow fell on her. "Here, Free-Pussy Hunter." I sat up, reached for the joint he offered, and placed it between my fingers. I watched as his eyes moved down to Chloe and my joined hands. He didn't say anything. He never would. She must've noticed, though, because she tried to pull away, but I held on to her tighter.

There was no warning that they were coming. No sirens. Just the flashing of blue-and-red lights.

"Tommy," Josh said, almost as a whisper.

Why would he be thinking about *Tommy*?

He turned his back on the cop car, just as their doors opened and two uniformed officers stepped out. "Hunter, man, I can't lose him." He pulled out the bag of weed from his pocket, his hand shaking as he did. Eyes wide, he turned his head slowly from side to side. I'd only ever seen him like this once before—the day he'd realized Natalie was gone. He was scared shitless.

I could see there was no time to throw the bag in the bushes or even put out the lit joint I was holding. Without thinking, I took the bag from his hand.

Even though it all happened in a matter of a few seconds, it felt like an eternity. The joint between my fingers was pure fire in my hands. I dropped the bag onto my lap, just as a flashlight shone in my eyes, blinding me. "Hunter," the cop asked, "is that you?"

And that was when I knew it was over. My future. Whichever road I travelled—I was done. Basketball. My dad. All of it.

"Thanks, baby." Chloe's soft voice broke through the silence. She picked up the bag from my lap and took the joint from my fingers. Then proceeded to smoke it.

"What the hell are you doing?" I tried to whisper, but I'm sure it came out louder than I'd wanted.

"Whose marijuana?" the cop asked, now shining the flashlight at her.

"Mine. *Obviously.*" She took another drag. "He was just holding it for me."

"I call bullshit," the second cop said.

"Yeah?" She jumped off the hood, letting go of my hand as she did. "Clayton Wells is my foster brother. You can call bullshit all you want, or you can call him and ask him where I got this weed from."

CHAPTER ELEVEN

Blake

A cab had picked us up from the half-court and dropped Josh at his house before taking me home. Josh hadn't said a word after the cops took Chloe away. I knew he felt guilty and that it was all his fault. I hadn't even thought twice about taking the fall for him. He was my best friend, and had a shit ton more to lose than I did. Chloe, though—she hadn't needed to do any of it. In the grand scheme of things, we were nothing to her. Like she'd said, she'd known me a week.

I'd gotten in my car and driven to the station. I'd panicked when they'd started asking questions about my relationship with her. I didn't know shit. I didn't even know how old she was. So I'd done the only thing I could think of: I'd called that seedy place she had taken me to a week ago and asked for Clayton. He'd shown up fifteen minutes later. That was seven hours ago. Seven hours with nothing more than a single nod of acknowledgment when he'd walked in. He'd spoken to the cops about her and then had taken a seat opposite me—his long legs kicked out in front of him.

A few officers had greeted him by name, and I wondered how they knew him.

His loud sigh cut through the silence. My head jerked up. Slowly, he stood up and walked over to me. I didn't know what it was about him that was intimidating. I was short for a baller but tall among average people. He stood over me and glared down. "Who are you to her?" His words weren't laced with anger or confusion—it was just a question. I noticed he still looked as tired as the first time I'd seen him.

I didn't respond.

He sighed again and took the seat next to mine. "Are you seeing her? I mean, are you her boyfriend?"

"No."

"You want to be?"

I stared straight ahead. "I have a girlfriend." Though Hannah wasn't really relevant, I didn't know what else to say.

"Really? Could've fooled me. Where was she last night?"

I shrugged.

"I don't really think it's appropriate—"

I turned to face him, cutting him off. "Are you okay with her and The Road?"

His eyes narrowed. "What are you talking about?"

"I dunno," I spat out. I didn't need him telling me what was appropriate and what wasn't. "Just kind of makes you look like an asshole if you're letting her get in her piece-of-shit car on an endless fucking road trip. You can tell me what's appropriate all you like, but you know her better than I do. I'm sure you might even care about her more than I do. Just seems like a dick move, is all."

He laughed. It was loud enough that the cop at the front desk stopped what he was doing and looked up at us. Once Clayton had settled down, he leaned back in his seat and drawled, "I like you, kid."

I fucking hated being called *kid*.

"But here's the thing you may not know about Chloe . . . yet. She does what she wants. She lives her life the way she wants, and nothing and no one can stop her." He paused for a beat. "You guys go to the same school, right?"

I nodded, my eyes fixed on the floor.

"When did you start noticing her?"

My body went rigid, and my breath caught.

He must've sensed it, because he laughed again. "I thought so."

"Thought what?"

"Chloe—she likes to remain invisible. The fact that she's hanging out with you—or whatever it is you guys are doing—it means something. But just don't fall in love with her."

My eyes snapped to his. "Whoa. Who said anything about love?"

His hands went up in surrender. "All I'm saying is that you're gonna get hurt. She's not gonna be around, and she's not gonna let you in. You might as well give up now."

Maybe his words should've surprised me, but they didn't. I'd worked out enough about Chloe to know what he meant. Just as I opened my mouth to ask *why* she was like that, the cop at the desk interrupted me. "I'll tell you what, Hunter." He pointed a pen at me and smirked. "You give me the exclusive of where you plan on playing college ball, and I'll let your little girlfriend go."

I dropped my head and pinched the bridge of my nose. I was pissed and so fucking tired. I wanted her out of there. I wanted to thank her. And I wanted my goddamn bed. "Are you charging her or just keeping her for shits and giggles?"

And, right on cue, the door behind the desk opened and she stepped out. Her eyes widened when she saw the two of us waiting for her. We stood at the same time, but her eyes fixed on me. "What are you doing here?" She sounded pissed.

"Waiting for you," I answered with equal attitude.

She shook her head. "I'm sorry, that came out wrong. I just wasn't expecting you." She turned her attention to Clayton. "Or you."

He shrugged. "What am I gonna do? Let my little sis sit in the slammer?"

Her face lit up with her smile. "I wasn't in the slammer, you asshole."

"Close enough." He yanked on her arm and pulled her in for a hug. "Don't do this shit again," he said into her ear.

She nodded as they pulled apart.

"What are you doing now?" he asked her.

"Get my car, go home, and crash."

"You won't be able to sleep. The kids will be up soon."

She shrugged.

"I'd offer you stay at mine, but Lisa's home this weekend. That could be awkward."

I cleared my throat.

They both turned to me.

"Um, I know you're tired . . . and there's no one home at my house. We have lots of space . . . You can always crash there for a few hours. It's the least I could do."

Chloe

"Are you sure your parents aren't going to care?" I asked as he opened his front door.

"They won't know. Mom lives in the guesthouse, and Dad's not home." He waited for me to step inside.

I stopped in the middle of the foyer. My gaze scanned the expansive space. From the outside, I knew it was large, but I wasn't prepared for how vast it would be on the inside. "Whoa, this is, um . . . big." But it looked unlived in. Kind of like a hospital. The only personal touches I could see were military pictures of a man—I assumed, his dad—and some war memorabilia on the mantel in the living room. There was absolutely nothing at all that said a family lived there. No family photos hung on the walls, and there were none of Blake anywhere. No proud trophies on display. Nothing.

"I guess," he said, taking my hand and leading me upstairs to his bedroom. "I'd describe it as empty."

I stopped in the middle of his room and looked around. "This is, um . . ."

"Big?" he finished for me.

"No." I dropped my bag and turned to him. "I was going to say empty."

He glanced around the room. "I guess."

"But this is your home, right?" I kicked off my shoes and slowly made my way to the side of his bed.

"Yeah, of course it's my home. Why?"

I pulled back the covers and sat down. "I mean your *permanent* home. You've lived here for years, right? So why don't you have anything personal in here?"

"What do you mean?"

"I just expected it to be different. You're good at basketball, right? Where are all your team pictures? All your trophies? Your jerseys?" I shrugged. "Aren't you proud of your accomplishments? Or your parents—they aren't proud of you? Mary—she even keeps the kids' participation ribbons. I just thought—"

A low laugh bubbled out of him. But then he stopped—he must've noticed the look of pity on my face. "It's just a room, Chloe. I come home, and I sleep in the same bed every night."

"I don't know," I said, moving down the bed until I was under the covers and my head rested on the pillow. "I guess I just grew up in foster care . . . moved around a couple times . . . Those places were houses, not homes. I'd give anything to have a room I could call my own."

He cursed under his breath and moved to draw the curtains closed. "I'm an asshole, Chloe, I didn't even think."

"It's fine," I said through a yawn. "Are you gonna sleep for a bit, too?"

"Yeah, I'll be downstairs. Just come—"

"Wait." I sat up. "You don't have to go. It's your bed."

He hesitated for a beat, until I pushed down the covers as an invitation. He smiled, and I could see any fight he had left was gone. I waited for him to settle in before I spoke again. "Thank you for waiting for me. You didn't have to do that."

"Why did you do it—take the fall for us? You didn't have to do that, either."

I turned onto my side. The bed shifted as he did the same. We were face-to-face, only inches apart. "I didn't want you to get in trouble. Josh has Tommy. You have your entire future ahead of you."

"And what do you have, Chloe?"

"I have the *now*."

I could see that he wanted to persist, but he just frowned and stayed silent.

"They're not pressing charges, Blake. Don't worry."

He nodded. "That's good."

"I'm wired now."

"You want me to take you to get your car?"

"Do you want me to go home?"

"No," he said quickly.

I laughed. "Can I ask you a question?"

"Anything."

"Where's your dad? And why does your mom live in the guesthouse?" He blinked once, his eyes searching mine for a long moment. Long enough that I suddenly regretted asking. "You don't have to tell me. I'm sorry if it's too personal."

"No. It's not that." He reached out and settled his hand on my hip. My eyes drifted shut, but I didn't remove it. After taking a deep breath, he continued, "My dad goes hunting with some old friends the first weekend of every month. That's where he is now, or at least that's what he tells us. The truth is he has a mistress. My mom lives in the guesthouse because she probably knows about it and hates her life. She's a big-shot author. You know those romance novels with a bunch of white people almost kissing? Most of them are hers. She'd rather live in the world she creates in those books than deal with what's in front of her. She's also an alcoholic, so I guess living in the guesthouse makes it easier for her to not have to justify her actions or behavior to anyone."

I felt I had plenty of reason to feel sorry for myself, but at least I had people that cared for and supported me, even when I didn't deserve it. "I'm sorry."

"Hey, it could be worse. At least I *have* parents."

I smiled, but it was sad. "Mary and Dean are good people. They take care of who needs taking care of. I'm eighteen now, they don't even have to let me stay there anymore. I'm lucky, really."

"Maybe. Or maybe they just know how lucky they are to have you."

I tried to hide my smile. "You're not at all what I thought you'd be like."

He laughed and pulled me closer. "You've been thinking about me?"

My cheeks warmed with my blush. "You know what I mean. It's . . . never mind . . ." I buried my face in his chest.

"What, Chloe? What were you going to say?"

I raised my eyes to meet his. "You and Hannah. I get the whole high-school-jock-and-cheerleader thing, but you just seem above all that, you know? I guess it just doesn't make sense to me why you're with her. Well . . . apart from the fact that she's ridiculously beautiful." I stopped myself from saying anything else. "I'm sorry,"

I said quickly. "I shouldn't say stuff like that. I don't even know her. I'm being mean."

His hand on my waist gripped me tighter while his gaze roamed my face. His eyes met mine with that same intensity I'd seen before. "I think *you're* beautiful."

My heart tightened at his words, but I couldn't let him see that. So instead, I laughed and pushed his chest. "Shut up!"

He fell onto his back but recovered quickly, wrapping his arms around me and pulling me closer. I didn't care that it might have been wrong, and I didn't think he did, either. Alone, in this room, we could be who we wanted to be. No faking. No hiding. Just us. "Oooh," he teased. "Chloe . . . What the fuck is your last name? I'm the worst friend ever."

"Thompson," I chuckled. "And I forgive you."

"Well, you did give me a fake name. What the hell was that about?"

I laughed and shook my head. "Blake, will you do me a favor?"

"Anything."

"After we wake up and we go to get my car, will you come over and have dinner with us? Dean—he goes to all the games. And maybe you could hang out with the kids . . . shoot your touchdowns?"

He laughed. This beautiful, boyish, carefree laugh. "Shoot my touchdowns?"

"What?" I asked, playing along.

"You're not kidding?"

I bit my lip, trying to contain my smile. "What?"

"You're just cute, is all. Fire truck, yes. I'd love to meet them and shoot my touchdowns." He pressed his lips to my forehead. "Now sleep, my beautiful little stoner."

*   *   *

"HUNTER!"

I knew who it was before my eyes snapped open. Within seconds I was out of his hold, out of his bed, and out of his house. "Shit shit shit." I didn't have time to see Hannah's reaction, and I sure as hell didn't want to be there to witness the aftermath. *What the hell was I thinking?* "Shit," I said, louder this time. Pulling my phone out of my bag, I tried not to trip as I ran down his driveway. I'd never been to this part of town before, and I had no car—*and* my phone had just died in my hands.

A door slammed.

Turning around, I glanced at the front door expecting Blake. But no one was there.

"Is everything okay?" I looked back down the driveway and saw a middle-aged woman walking toward me. Her hair was dark, as dark as Blake's. She had the same light blue eyes as him, too.

"I'm sorry, Mrs. Hunter. I didn't mean to disturb you."

She laughed once, stopping a few feet in front of me. "No one's called me that in years, dear." Then she looked from me, to the house, and to the car parked near the front door. "Is that Hannah?"

I nodded, trying to keep the tears at bay.

"Do you need a ride somewhere?"

I nodded again, but then I remembered what Blake had said about her drinking. "Uh. No, thanks. I'll walk."

I turned to leave, but she grabbed my arm. "Sweetheart. I'm not—what Blake has probably told you. I've been sober for six months." She pulled her keys from her pocket and showed me her six-month-sobriety-chip key chain. "I promise. I would never endanger someone else's life."

The front door opened, and Hannah's deathly loud shriek made my mind up for me. "You can't just have other girls sleeping in your bed, Hunter!" Blake's mom must've seen the answer on my face, because she had already gotten into her black Bentley and was reversing down the driveway toward me.

"Where to?" she asked once I'd opened the passenger door and slumped down in the seat. I ignored Blake standing in his doorway, glaring at us. And I ignored Hannah in front of him, waving her hands in his face, trying to get his attention.

"I don't really know. It's this abandoned basketball court, but I have no idea—"

"I know the one," she broke in, smiling slightly as she pulled out onto the road.

*　　　*　　　*

"He and Josh used to come here all the time when they were kids," Mrs. Hunter said, driving onto the middle of the court, next to my car. "I haven't been here in forever," she mused to herself. Then she turned to me. "Are you his new girlfriend? Friend?"

"I'm nobody," I said flatly. It was the truth, despite the stupid second in his room when I had let myself believe otherwise.

"It didn't seem like that to me. You seemed pretty scared when you saw Hannah." I opened my mouth to respond, but she raised her hand to stop me. "It's okay. I'd have been scared, too. She seems like a bitch."

I laughed. I couldn't help it. Her words were as surprising as the woman who'd voiced them.

"I don't have a clue what Hunter sees in her," she said.

"You call him Hunter, too?"

She rolled her eyes. I could see them even though she was looking straight ahead, past the windshield. "Military husband. I should've stopped it when he was a kid. It made my son sound like a soldier, you know? Someone that's trained to take orders. *Blake* ..." She frowned. "Blake ..." she repeated. "I love the name Blake."

"Maybe you should call him that or talk to him about it . . . or just talk to him . . ." I trailed off. It wasn't my business, and I shouldn't have said anything.

She turned to me, smiling again. "I don't think *Blake*—" She paused and grinned wider. "I don't think Blake would consider you a nobody, Chloe."

"How did you—?"

"Your mother and I were sorority sisters. I was a senior when she was a freshman and moved into the house, but I got to know her and your Aunt Tilly well enough. They were sweet, caring, genuine girls. I heard that your mother got pregnant and had you a few years later. And then when she passed . . . I was there at her funeral, and your aunt's, too. You were what? Eight when your aunt died?"

I nodded.

"I'm sorry—for what it's worth. Are you . . . ?"

"I'm fine." I wiped my eyes and prayed that my voice would come out even. "You can't tell Blake. You can't tell anyone. Please, Mrs. Hunter." I ended in a sob. I hated that I had. But what I hated more was when strangers spoke to me about them. When they'd had the experience of sharing a piece of them that I would never know.

"I'm sorry." Her voice broke. "I didn't mean to make you sad. This is your life, sweetheart. I won't tell a soul."

I buried my face in my hands, trying to compose myself. She pulled me into her and let me cry on her shoulder. "I'm sorry," I told her. "I'm such a mess."

"No, you're not. You're just a girl who misses her mom. We're all allowed to cry for that."

I pulled back and wiped my nose. "Blake—he misses his mom, too."

"He told you that?"

I shook my head. "He describes his house as empty. I'd say that's pretty damn close."

She nodded slowly.

"He thinks you're still drinking. I'm not going to tell him you're not, but maybe you should. Maybe that's one secret that should be shared."

I opened the door to get out, but her words stopped me.

"Will I be seeing you around? Are you going to be spending some more time with Hunt—I mean, Blake?"

I *almost* said yes. After he'd waited all night for me at the police station, then held me in his arms as we'd fallen asleep . . . the way we were both so comfortable in our own world. But I just couldn't let it happen. "No," I finally told her. "But it was really nice meeting you, Mrs. Hunter. Thank you for giving me a memory of them."

*   *   *

"Sammy counted to ten today, including the five," Mary said. She was sitting next to me in the swing seat and gave a push to get it going.

"That's awesome," I said through a yawn. It was four in the afternoon, and I'd been home for over an hour, but I was still exhausted.

"He asked for you as soon as he did it. He wanted to show you."

I smiled, looking down at the ground.

"You're welcome to stay here as long as you need, Chloe. You know that, right? No one's going to kick you out."

"I appreciate that, but I'm still leaving after graduation."

"Oh okay. I just thought maybe you might have changed your mind."

"What would make you think that?"

"Oh, I don't know. Maybe the tall, dark, and handsome boy pulling up to the curb—" She nudged me with her elbow.

My head whipped up, and I spotted Blake's car. He was just stepping out.

Mary continued, "—stepping out of his car with . . . what's that? Flowers? Ooh, I hope they're for me . . . and a bottle of wine, maybe? Now I really hope that's for me. And his eyes look up—jeez, his eyes. And then he sees us. Oh, that smile . . ."

"Okay, Mary." I stood up. "Thanks, but I don't need your commentary."

Her laughter faded as I walked down the path, meeting Blake halfway. "What are you doing here?" It came out harsh, just how I intended.

"Wow." His eyebrows rose. "Someone's pissy when they're tired."

I let my shoulders relax but not my guard. "Seriously, Blake. What are you doing?"

"You invited me for dinner," he replied slowly, as if I were crazy.

"That was before all that shit with Hannah! You can't—"

He pushed past, ignoring me. "You must be Mary?" I heard him say. I turned to them. He offered her the flowers. "These are for you."

Mary thanked him before pulling him in for a hug. She smiled huge, giving me a thumbs-up behind his back.

Shit.

He was going to *charm* his way in. Mary was still gushing when the front screen door slammed open against the planter box next to it.

"Who the hell is this kid with his arms around my wife?" Dean yelled, a wide smile on his face.

Blake and Mary pulled apart, finally.

I stepped forward. "Dean, this is—"

"Blake Hunter!" He couldn't contain his excitement. "Well, well." His gaze moved to me. "Ain't that something?" Then to Blake, "Come on in, son! Welcome to our home."

*　　*　　*

Mary left and went to the store. Apparently, Blake's presence was enough reason to cook a fancy meal. I could tell Dean was a little embarrassed by the house when he showed Blake around. He must've known the type of lavish lifestyle Blake was accustomed to.

Our furniture was old and worn and nothing matched. But they had been used, well lived-in, and I had a feeling that Blake preferred what he was seeing to what he had. It wasn't until Dean showed Blake his high school–basketball trophies and pictures that I detected a sense of pride in his voice. I left them alone and went to the kitchen to make us drinks.

"You're pissed?" His voice came from behind me.

I kept pouring, my eyes fixed on the seven glasses on the counter in front of me.

"You're really good at the whole ignoring thing." His hand clamped down on my wrist while the other removed the pitcher from my hand. "Did I do something wrong?"

I had to laugh. "Your—" I cut myself off and lowered my voice. "Your girlfriend walked in on us sleeping tog— Not *sleeping*—"

His chuckle broke through.

"You know what I mean, and it's not funny, Blake."

He set the pitcher on the counter and held my hands, turning me around, and bending his knees to look me in the eyes. He still had a smug smile on his beautiful face. "First, we weren't doing anything wrong." We had been, but I let that slide. "Second, *my girlfriend* walked in on us *not* doing anything wrong. If you should be mad at anyone, it should be her." He straightened up, but he didn't let go of my hands.

"That's ludicrous. I can't be mad at her. She didn't do anything! She caught her boyfriend in bed—"

"So really . . . you have no reason to be mad at *anyone*?"

My eyes narrowed.

He laughed again.

I wanted to stay mad, tell him that he was being a dick and that he was wrong, but I just couldn't. Not when he was this close, laughing that same boyish laugh from last night. "You're an ass."

"Maybe." He shrugged. "But you like me, regardless."

*   *   *

"Is he your *boooooy*friend?" Amy teased when we were back out in the yard. Her cap fell forward over her little seven-year-old head and covered her eyes.

"No. And stop being a child," I joked back.

Then Dean chimed in. "Yeah, Chloe, is he your *boooooy*friend?"

Blake's chuckle was enough to make me turn and glare at him. "No, Dean," I retorted, my eyes never leaving Blake's smug face. "Hunter has a girlfriend." His smile fell. "She's the head cheerleader and the hottest girl in the entire school," I sing-songed.

That shut everyone up.

*   *   *

We sat on the porch steps outside and watched the kids while Mary and Dean cooked dinner.

"Are all these kids . . . ? I mean, are they all adopted?"

I glanced at him quickly, but he was gazing at the kids playing. Amy and Sammy were attempting to build a fort with branches and a bed sheet while Harry, the eldest at fourteen, was screwing around on a shitty old skateboard. "They're all fostered. Mary and Dean haven't adopted any of them yet. At the moment, they're trying to get approval for Harry, so that will hopefully happen soon. But, no. Sammy, the youngest, he's only been around for a few months. Amy has been here for over two years now."

"Dean and Mary? They don't want their own kids?"

"They can't."

"Oh," he said quietly.

"Yeah . . ."

I watched him as he looked around the yard. It wasn't much, and the garden wasn't maintained like his was, but no one had the time for any of that. "What—?" He cleared his throat. "What happened to their parents?"

I sighed. "Another time, maybe?"

"Okay," he answered. But his tone was sad.

"Blake?"

"Mmm?"

"We're fine. We're happy. Are you worried about something?"

He sniffed once, but his eyes never left Harry on the board. "What happens to them? I mean, if no one wants them?"

I tried to laugh. Tried to find a way to soothe his worries. "They become me."

His eyes snapped to mine. And I saw it then—a side to Blake I doubted he shared with anyone. This sad, vulnerable boy who cared. Our eyes stayed locked and the seconds felt like an eternity. The thumping of my heart against my chest began to ache. But I couldn't look away. I couldn't fight it—what it was that was happening to me. To us. To my entire world.

"Blake . . ."

He blinked once, breaking the connection. Then his gaze moved to Harry again. "Dude," he yelled, standing up and walking toward him. "You almost had it that time. That was awesome! Do it again."

I'd watched and listened to Harry enough to know he was attempting a kick flip. He did it a few more times while Blake circled, one arm crossed over his chest and the other with his hand on his chin. His eyebrows furrowed in concentration as he took in Harry's form. "Is it cool if I try to help you out a little?"

"Sure." You couldn't have wiped the smile off the boy's face if you'd tried. The other kids stopped what they were doing and made their way over so they could watch. I joined them and stood next to Blake. He'd winked when he'd seen me coming. I wondered for a second what the hell he was doing there, hanging out with my broken family and me. But it was only a second before I decided that I just didn't care.

"So I think if you move your left foot back a little and put your right foot on more of an angle, you'd be good."

Harry's eyes narrowed in concentration as he looked from Blake to me. I encouraged him with a nod of my head.

The cheers he got when he nailed the trick were so loud Dean came rushing out the front door. His body visibly relaxed when we told him what had happened. "Wash up," was his response. "Dinner's ready."

I watched the kids run up the porch steps while we trailed behind. "That was really nice, Blake, you helping Harry like that."

"It was nothing."

"It meant something to him."

He put his arm around my shoulders and brought me closer to him. "Did it mean something to you?"

"Yes."

He kissed my temple, longer than what was necessary but shorter than what I wanted. "Then I guess it means something to me, too."

CHAPTER TWELVE

Blake

It took two minutes for me to devour my plateful of food. The others were still going, slowly chomping away while entertaining themselves with conversation.

"You can have seconds," Chloe whispered up at me.

I looked down at her plate. Her food looked untouched. "It's okay."

The scraping of a chair got my attention. Dean leaned over, grabbed my plate, and proceeded to fill it with a little of everything from the smorgasbord on the table. Three different varieties of pasta, steak, chicken, salad, everything. "You're a growing boy," he boomed, setting the plate back down in front of me. "You need to eat."

"Thank you," I said quietly. I was a little uncomfortable and out of my element. "It's been a long time since I've had a home-cooked meal . . . and we never really sat down at a table like this."

"Your parents don't feed you?" Mary asked.

"Um . . ." The words caught in my throat. Looking around the table, I decided that my self-pity wasn't valid, not in this situation.

"His parents are busy," Chloe answered.

"You speak for me now?" I joked, looking down at her.

She smirked, her eyebrows raised in a challenge.

Then Dean chimed in, "Get used to it, Hunter. That's what gir-*rrr*lfriends do."

She dropped the knife and fork on her plate, the sound of it almost as piercing as her frustrated grunt. "He's not my—"

My phone rang, interrupting her. Will's stupid rap ringtone. I fumbled for it in my pocket, trying to silence it. "Oh yeaaahhh!" Sammy yelled, hopping off his seat.

"Don't drop that booty booty!" the other kids sang, their hands moving up and down above their heads.

"Oh no," Chloe said through a laugh. "This is not good."

The ringtone continued to play. Sammy was standing to the side of the table now . . . *twerking.* I started to laugh, but then the ringing stopped.

"Again," Sammy whispered, his ass sticking out midtwerk. I chuckled as I searched everyone's faces. The kids just smiled. Mary shook her head, giggling to herself. Dean nodded enthusiastically. "Do it." It almost sounded like a dare.

Then I turned to Chloe. "Don't even think about it," she warned, but she was smiling, too.

The music filled the room the instant I tapped the screen. Amy and Harry got up and started dancing. "Do it!" they yelled at Sammy. Sammy smiled from ear to ear.

Then his shirt was off.

"No!" Chloe laughed.

And then his shorts were gone.

Mary's giggle turned to a guffaw.

"Always with the clothes off!" Chloe yelled over the music. "Dean. Do something!"

Dean slowly stood up, a stern look on his face.

I turned to Sammy, now completely naked. His tiny body shaking from side to side. *"Drop that booty booty!"*

"You bet your ass I'm going to do something." Dean turned his back to Mary . . . Then right as the chorus hit and the kids' singing got louder, he stuck his ass out and copied Sammy's dancing.

"Oh my God!" Chloe pushed her plate aside, folded her arms on the table in front of her and dropped her head on them.

I stroked her back and laughed as I took in the sight of her family. Even Mary got up and joined in.

Leaning down, I whispered in her ear, "What's wrong?"

"They're crazy," she whispered back as if her answer should have been obvious.

I leaned in closer so she could hear me. "They're not crazy, Chloe." I shifted my eyes and continued watching them. "They're kind of perfect."

I swore I heard her say, "You're kind of perfect," but when I glanced back to ask her to repeat it, she was sitting up in her seat, all emotion gone.

*   *   *

"My cheeks hurt from laughing so hard," she said as she led me up to her room.

It had been Dean's idea that she show me. I'd almost high-fived him on the spot before I'd remembered that he was kind of like a dad to her and it would be a little inappropriate. I'd wanted to spend time with her alone since I'd arrived.

She opened a narrow door on the second floor that exposed an equally narrow staircase, leading up to what I assumed was the attic. "So this is it," she said, standing in the middle of the tiny space and motioning her hand through the air. There was a bed with a nightstand on one side pushed up against the corner, a desk, and one of those temporary wardrobes, which had a few clothes hanging in it. And about two feet of free space. The room made mine look like a mansion.

Her laugh pulled me out of my daze. "I know it's not much, but I survive."

"I know that . . . but you can't take one of the bedrooms downstairs?"

She shook her head. "The kids have them."

"They can't share?"

"They can, but they have nightmares sometimes, so Mary likes them to have their own space."

I nodded, but I found it hard to imagine what life was like there. I glanced quickly at the tiny window, the only one in the room, the one she had stood behind and watched me leave from the first night we met.

"You should be careful. You're gonna hit your head on the ceiling."

I looked up at the beam a few inches in front of me. "Shit," I breathed out. "You're lucky you're short."

She laughed at that.

"So, my mom—" I took a step toward her, hitting my head on the beam.

"Oh my God," she squealed. "I just warned you."

Pressing my hand against my forehead, I tried not to curse. "I know."

"What is wrong with you?" She grasped my forearms and pushed me back until I felt her bed behind my legs. "Sit!"

I sat.

"Let me see."

I let her see.

"You're such a baby. There's barely a lump."

"You're mean."

"Cry to your mama."

Then her face fell, and she frowned.

"Speaking of my mom . . ." I raised my eyebrows in question. She stayed silent.

I reached into my pocket and pulled out my keys to show her my new key chain: Mom's six-month-sobriety chip. "She came and spoke to me when she got home."

She looked down at the object in my hand, and her frown turned to a smile. "Really?"

I nodded, my eyes fixed on her lips. "Yeah. She said that *you* gave her the courage to talk to me. Apparently, she'd been wanting to for a while, but she was afraid of how I'd react. She thought I hated her."

"And you don't?"

"No," I sighed. "I really don't. I think that I was disappointed in her. And it may have made our relationship worse because I think she should've at least seen how I was feeling. That's what I told her. But no, I don't hate her. Honestly, I kind of miss her."

Her smile widened.

"She didn't go into too much detail, though. She said she needed time, but hopefully soon. There's a family thing at her AA meeting coming up. She asked if I wanted to go. I don't know if I'm ready for that. It seems like a big step. What do you think?"

"Me?"

I laughed. "Yeah you."

"I don't think I know your mom or your relationship well enough—"

"But you know *me*," I interrupted. "And your opinion matters to *me*."

She chewed her lip, her gaze looking past me, into the distance. "I don't know," she said so quietly I almost missed it. "It's your *mom*, Blake. I know that I wouldn't walk away from an opportunity to get closer. Maybe this way you can stop missing her?"

It took a few seconds for me to find the words. "Thank you, Chloe. I don't think you actually realize how long it's been since my mom and I have had a decent conversation. One car ride with you and it's . . ." I shrugged. "It's just nice."

Chloe

I continued to chew my lip and looked down at him.

"I'm sorry," he said softly. "Did I say something to make you uncomfortable?"

I shook my head.

He spread his legs and pulled me forward by the fabric of my dress until I was standing between them. "Are you sure?"

"Yes." No. He hadn't *said* anything. His presence alone was reason enough to make me nervous.

"What's going on?" He sounded concerned. Maybe it was because I was no longer able to form complete sentences. I had to do something to take my mind off the fact that we were in my room. Alone. With his hand on my hip, gripping me tighter with each passing second.

I couldn't look into his eyes. Or at his lips. Especially not his lips. So I zoned in on where the lump was beginning to form on his head.

"What are you thinking?" His voice was hoarse.

Then I made the mistake of looking into his eyes. *Fire.*

I cleared my throat. "It's hot." I tried to pull away, but his grasp on my hip intensified. His other hand settled, gentle but firm, on my bare thigh. I sucked in a breath and held it, waiting for some sense to be knocked back into me.

"Chloe," he said with the same huskiness in his voice. He let his head fall forward onto my breast. The warmth of his exhale spread across my skin. I tried to swallow, but the lump in my throat prevented it. My hands raised of their own accord. I laced my fingers through his hair. He pulled back slightly and looked into my eyes.

"Chloe," he said again. He removed his hand from my thigh and curled it around my neck, pulling me down to his waiting mouth.

I let out the breath.

Game. *Over.*

But he didn't kiss me. He just kept pulling me down, farther and farther, until he was lying on the bed, and I was on top of him. He moved the strap of my dress off my shoulder with his teeth. I let my head drop into the crook of his neck. Then his lips were on my shoulder, skimming the skin lightly, moving so slowly, up to my neck. His tongue darted out, leaving a trail of wetness behind. Then his mouth was on my jaw. Soft. Slow. His fingers tangled in my hair, and he pulled slightly until I lifted my head, and we were face-to-face. He rubbed his nose across mine, then pulled my bottom lip between his teeth. I moaned, breaking the silence that filled the room. He didn't stop with the small, torturous kisses. Not until, finally, his tongue swept between my lips.

My teeth clamped shut. My breath caught. I was scared. I was so frickin' scared of what it meant to have him there, doing what we were doing.

"Please let me kiss you," he begged.

And I couldn't stop myself. The moment my mouth parted for him, he was there. His tongue brushed against mine. But it was different. I'd made out with guys in the past, but never sober. It wasn't just that, though. *He* was different. He wasn't at all what I'd imagined. His kisses were slow and passionate, yet controlling. He demanded so much attention, from his kiss alone, that I forgot who I was. Who *he* was. And who we were together. I couldn't bring myself to fight him anymore. I let my body relax into his.

"Holy shit," he moaned into my mouth, deepening the kiss. He thrust up. Just once. But enough that I could feel his hardness pressed against my stomach. He pulled back quickly, searching my eyes. Contemplating. Then just as fast, he flipped us over so I was on my back, and he was on top of me. "I'm losing control," he mumbled.

My chest rose and fell with every short breath. I was gasping, trying to level my breathing. But he kissed me again, and I knew I was losing control, too. He shifted onto his side but never stopped kissing me. His hand lay flat on my stomach, the heat of it matching the heat between my legs. And then it moved. Lower, until it settled on my thigh, past the hem of my dress.

He pulled away, allowing us both to catch our breaths. "You're so beautiful, Chloe," he whispered. My eyes drifted shut. He kissed my lips once. Then his hand moved higher. I felt the material of my dress slipping upwards. "I want you so damn bad."

I parted my legs. I wanted him, too. I wanted him everywhere. His mouth moved to my neck, sucking lightly, while his hand moved higher until it was where I wanted it. His single finger brushed the space between my legs, over my panties. I knew I was wet. He moaned into my skin—he knew it, too. His mouth sucked harder while his fingers pushed the material aside. The cold air hit my wetness. Then a single finger slid up, and then painfully, slowly, down. My body tingled all over. I'd never experienced this before. Not when I was sober. A clear head magnified the intensity of what I was feeling. Not just physically. Then I felt his finger slide slowly inside me. My back arched off the bed. I refused to open my eyes when I felt the throbbing ache begin.

His lips moved up to mine. "Chloe," he said against them.

I panted in response. Then he paused and pulled away. "I'm sorry, Chloe," he whispered.

My eyes snapped open. "What?"

"I can't . . . I need to break up with Hannah before—"

Then a door opened downstairs. It sounded far away, but it wasn't.

I forced myself to look away, trying to compose myself. The footsteps on the stairs got louder.

"Shit!" I pushed him away, stood up, and adjusted my dress. He did the same, adjusting his hard-on trapped in his jeans.

"Hey, Blake, come shoot some baskets," Sammy said from my doorway.

Blake opened his mouth to speak, but I did it for him. "Blake needs to go home now," I said. "Say good-bye, Sammy."

"Five minutes?" he begged, his eyes pleading.

I inhaled deeply. "I'm sorry, Sammy, but Blake's leaving now. I'll come out in a bit and play, okay?"

"Okay." His footsteps faded as he walked back down the stairs.

"Chloe." Blake reached out, but I pulled away, taking a step back.

"This is exactly what I didn't want."

"Chloe," he repeated, quieter this time. "What are you talking about?"

"You and me . . . us . . . This can't be a thing." I pushed back my sob before speaking. "I can't be what you want, Blake. I'm sorry. Can you just leave? Please?"

I could tell he didn't want to go, but he turned and left without another word.

I watched him get into his car from my window, with tears streaming down my face. It was too much. I never should have let him get so close. Now he was willing to change his life for me, and I couldn't do the same for him. No matter how much I wanted to.

CHAPTER THIRTEEN

Blake

I'd left Chloe's last night and done what I'd told her I would do: I'd broken up with Hannah. It had been easier than I'd thought. Especially when she'd told me that she'd been fucking Will for the last six months. I could lie and say that I cared, but I just didn't. And apparently, neither did she. "You're the asshole, and I'm the girl with the heartless ex-boyfriend who dumped me for no good reason. Everyone's going to take my side," she'd said.

I'd gone running after that. I'd gotten home and tried to sleep, only to push the covers off, put my sneakers back on, and bail. I'd been unable to get Chloe out of my head.

Which was why I was currently at school, walking to my locker in a complete zombie state.

A roar of laughter pulled me out of my daze. I strolled over to where a crowd had formed in front of a bay of lockers. Since I was taller than most of the other students, I was able to see what everyone was looking at. The word *Whore*, spray-painted bright red on a locker.

"Excuse me." The crowd parted. I knew her voice before I saw her face. And when I did, I wished I hadn't. She brushed past me, her head down.

I tried to get her attention with my hand on her arm. "Chloe."

She yanked it away. "It's fine," she mumbled, never looking up from the floor.

My fingers straightened, releasing their hold. The sadness in her tone caused an ache in my chest. Then she looked up at me, her glazed eyes locked with mine. Silence fell, or it could have just been in my head. She opened her mouth, but nothing came out. She just shook her head and walked away.

I followed her out to the parking lot, but by the time I got there, she was already in her car driving away.

I wanted to follow her and make sure she was okay, but Hannah was waiting for me at my car, which was odd because classes hadn't even started yet. She must've known I'd be pissed about Chloe and would want to take off. Which meant that she knew what had happened to Chloe's locker, even while she was out there, waiting for me to show up. I wanted to believe that it hadn't been Hannah's doing, but seeing her standing there, with a smug smirk on her face—there was no doubt. "You're a bitch."

"And your new girlfriend's a whore."

"Fuck you."

*　　*　　*

My tires spun and screeched as I sped out of the school parking lot.

By the time I pulled up to the curb outside Chloe's house, I had calmed myself down. I wanted to see her. No. I *needed* to see her. Only her car wasn't there. And neither was anyone else's. There was only one other place I knew to look, but she wasn't at Clayton's restaurant, either. I pressed the buzzer to Clayton's apartment, and he appeared in the same disheveled state, the way I'd always seen him.

"She doesn't want to see you."

So she was there. "Maybe she can come down and tell me that herself."

He raised his hands above his head and gripped the door frame. The muscles in his arms and shoulders bulged. He was a few years older than me, but I was taller. I wondered for a moment if I could take him, just long enough so I could run up to his apartment and see her. I looked over his shoulder, hoping for a glimpse of her, but all I saw were stairs.

He moved his head, blocking my view. "I don't know what happened, but something obviously upset her. If you care about her at all—just give her some time. Some space. Okay?" He didn't sound pissed, more like concerned. But he also didn't wait for my answer before closing the door in my face.

Chloe

Skipping school was easy when you didn't have parents that cared. Skipping work was also easy, although I might lose my job, considering I hadn't even been there two weeks. I didn't care. I didn't need a job. I had money. The money I earned from the bowling alley was just going into a bank account for the kids so they'd have something from me when I left. The only thing that was hard—and that I couldn't ignore—were my feelings for Blake.

I was falling for him.

Which was why when I pulled up to the house on Thursday afternoon and saw the kids in the driveway, skating around on new boards and wearing all the safety gear a kid could handle, my guilt increased tenfold.

"Where did all this come from?"

The kids stopped immediately. Mary stood up. "I don't know," she said, stopping next to me and putting her arm around my shoulders. "Damnedest thing. We got home, and it was all laid out on the porch. The kids' names were attached to each set. Whoever got it must know the family well and care enough to buy the protective gear."

I shrugged out of her hold and turned to her. "Yeah," I agreed, pushing through the lump in my throat. "Maybe a little too much."

*　　*　　*

"Maybe he's just doing it to get in my pants."

Clayton's laugh grated on my nerves. "Sure, Chloe. If that's all he wanted, then why break up with his girlfriend? Why not just score with you and keep it a secret?"

"I don't even know if they broke up. It's just what I heard from all the jerks who were standing around my whore-painted locker, laughing at me."

"So you haven't spoken to him about it?"

"No!" I huffed. "What am I supposed to say to him? That he did it for nothing? That I can't be the girl to replace her? That he'd have had better luck just *scoring* with me and moving on?"

He chuckled under his breath.

"What's funny?"

He shook his head, his eyes wide, but his smile stayed in place.

I slumped down onto the sofa and watched him set two coffees on the table.

"I don't know." He sat down next to me. "Seems like he cares about you."

"That's the problem, Clay."

He laughed again.

"You're not helping."

"Fine. He's a jerk. An asshole. How dare he show any sign of caring? Or friendship? What a dick. Did I say he was a jerk? We should go egg his car."

I narrowed my eyes at him.

He hid his smile by taking a sip of his coffee.

I rolled my eyes and scanned the walls of his apartment. He didn't have much. A single bedroom, a bathroom, a tiny kitchen, and the living room, where we both sat. My eyes caught on a picture, framed, resting right above the TV. I'd never seen it there before. "Does Mary know you have that?" I motioned to the photo before standing up and walking over to it. It was of him and me, sitting on the porch steps, I was smiling at the camera. Clayton was smiling at me. That same sad smile I'd known ever since he had moved into the house. I wore one of those paper party hats on my head. It was my thirteenth birthday. I remembered it because Clayton had given me so much shit about being a teenager.

I had been with Mary and Dean only a few weeks when Clayton had joined us. We were both withdrawn and quiet, and somehow, that attracted us to each other. He'd never had a mom, I'd never had a dad, and that was the basis of our early relationship. Soon after I'd moved in, I'd told him about my life, about losing my mom and my aunt. Clayton—even though he was young at the time himself—had known enough to keep his secrets until I was old enough to understand them. When I was twelve, he'd told me about his past. And that had been when Clayton had become my *hero*. Because despite the fact that I'd lost everyone close, I had been loved, and I was left with those memories. The love, and the laughter, and the joy of my family. Clayton—he was left with nothing but nightmares.

He cleared his throat, standing behind me now. "No. I stole the album and got a bunch copied, then returned it. She never knew. She'd kick my ass if she knew I'd taken it."

I laughed. He was right, she would.

"Mary and Dean are amazing people, huh?" There was something about his tone. A sadness I recognized but hadn't heard in a while.

I turned to him, but his gaze was still on the picture. A slight smile graced his face. "Are you okay?" I asked.

His eyebrows furrowed before he looked at me. "Of course. Why?"

I shrugged. "Nothing," I said, even though a part of me didn't believe him.

Sighing, he sat back down on the sofa. "I'm just tired, Chloe. Don't take it personally. The shifts are taking their toll. Lisa being away in college and barely having time for phone calls. You—with this whole Blake thing—"

"It's not a *thing*."

"Are you sure? Because I never thought I'd see the day when I had to start turning boys away for you." He grinned now, the amusement evident.

"I'm positive," I assured him, then changed the subject. "Did I wake you when I showed up?"

"No," he said quickly, though I knew it was a lie. My expression must have shown it, because he added, "Yes, but it's no big deal."

I grabbed the cushion from behind me and set it on my lap, patting it twice as an invitation. He didn't hesitate, just set his mug down on the coffee table, rested his head on my lap, and kicked his legs up, settling them over the arm of the sofa. His eyes slowly drifted shut while I ran my fingers through his hair. "This is nice," he said.

"Yeah."

"It's been a while."

"Yeah, you stopped having nightmares after a while—actually, right after my thirteenth birthday—and you didn't need my help anymore." I knew why he'd stopped having them, but I didn't want to bring it up.

It was silent for a moment before a chuckle escaped him. His eyes snapped open.

"What?"

"Remember you used to sing to me while you did this? I tried to deal with it for like, a week, but then I couldn't take it anymore. Your singing voice is *ass.*"

"Shut up!" But I was laughing, too.

"Seriously, Chloe. You sound like a dying cat whose claws are being scraped down a chalkboard."

"I'm not that bad!" I got another cushion and started hitting him with it. "If you don't shut up, I'll start again."

"Oh shit. Please don't."

I started hitting him again, harder this time. He let me get a few good shots in before pulling the cushion from my grip. He threw it, hitting our picture on the wall. He got up quickly to straighten it before resuming his position.

"It wasn't that bad, actually. In fact, I want to hear you again. What was that song you used to sing?"

I remembered the tune; Mom used to sing it all the time. Looking back now, the words held more meaning than I had ever realized. A lump formed in my throat, but I spoke through it. "Eric Clapton. *Tears in Heaven.*"

"That's right." His mind seemed to be somewhere distant. He blinked hard, bringing himself back to the present. Then his eyes bore into mine. "Sing it?"

"Clayton, I can't—"

"Please?" And there was that little boy I grew up with. The first, and only, person I'd ever let love me after my mom and aunt died.

"Okay."

His eyes seemed heavy as they drifted shut.

And I started to sing.

I sang through the giant knot in my throat, the memories of my mother and of Clayton filling my mind.

Clayton lay still, his eyes closed. I watched his handsome face, void of emotion. His eyes were red when he finally opened them at the end of the song. "I love you, Chloe."

"I love you, too, Clay."

CHAPTER FOURTEEN

Chloe

The squeal of my hand brake made everyone turn and look. The yelling and laughter stopped, and the smile on Blake's face faltered for a second. He quit skating and held the basketball under his arm, then did that flick thing with the skateboard to hold it upright. The kids tried to copy him and failed.

"Hey, hon." Mary waved from the swing seat as I got out of my car.

I waved back before making my way over to Blake. "What are you doing here?"

Sammy answered for him. "He's playing skateball. You wanna play?"

I looked down at him. "No, I'm good, thank you." Then to Blake, I asked, "So?"

His shoulders sagged. He released the ball, letting it bounce away. No one bothered to chase it. "I can leave. I'm sorry," he said quietly, looking down at the ground.

He got only a few steps before Sammy grabbed his arm, pulling down on it in an effort to stop him from going any farther. His helmet fell forward and covered his eyes, but he adjusted it quickly and said, "No. Stay, please. If she doesn't want you here, she can leave."

Silence.

My voice came out hoarse. "It's fine." I smiled at Sammy, then faced Blake. "You can stay." I turned quickly and walked toward Mary, too afraid to witness his reaction.

I tried to listen while Mary chatted, but I couldn't take my eyes off Blake. I watched the way he moved on the board . . . The way he'd stop to help the kid . . . The way he ran to Sammy the second he fell off the board to inspect his scraped knee . . . The way he laughed and joked with Dean . . . The way he winked at me and nodded once, as if thanking *me* for letting him be there.

And I knew it then. He was absolutely everything I had never let myself dream of having.

"Dean! Amy has little-league practice," Mary shouted.

Dean looked at his watch and grumbled.

"It's okay." I stood up. "I'll take her, Dean. You keep playing."

Amy ran up the steps to get her gear while I walked over to Blake. "Are you going to be here when I get back?"

He looked at his watch and frowned. "I have to leave in an hour to watch Tommy."

"Okay."

He grabbed my arm and gently pulled me closer to him and looked in my eyes. "Are we good?"

"I don't know yet," I told him truthfully. "Maybe."

He let out a breath. "Maybe's good enough."

Blake

Skateball was exactly what the name implied. Basketball on skateboards. Josh and I had made up the game when we were ten, combining two of our favorite things. We'd thought we were so smart.

We'd even talked about how much money we could make as pro skateballers.

I stood in Mary and Dean's kitchen, laughing to myself as I turned on the tap to fill Sammy's water bottle.

"Do you have any of your own brothers or sisters, Blake?" Mary said from behind me.

I tensed at her question, wondering why she would ask something like that. And then it dawned on me—I'd been buying them gifts, showing up unannounced, hanging out with them for no real reason. *Of course, I was overstaying my welcome.* I shook my head. "No. I'm sorry. I'll go now."

"That's not what I'm saying. Stay as long as you want." She pulled a container of ice cubes out of the freezer and proceeded to drop a couple in each of the water bottles. "It's just that you're very good with them, is all."

"Oh. Thanks, I guess."

"Did something happen between you and Chloe?"

I tensed. I had known the moment was coming, but I didn't know whether it would be with her or Dean, and honestly, I didn't know which one I'd prefer.

I couldn't lie. "Yes, ma'am."

"The last time you were here for dinner? When you went up to her room . . . something happened?"

"Yes, ma'am." But then I paused, thinking about how that had sounded. "No. I mean—we didn't sleep together . . ."

"Okay . . . That's not really my business, though. What is my business is the fact that she locked herself in her room and cried most of the night."

I gripped the edge of the sink and let my head fall forward. "Shit."

"It's probably not your fault, Blake."

"To be honest, I still don't really know what happened. I thought things were going well—and then she kind of just shut down."

It was silent for a moment before Mary finally sighed. "How long have you known Chloe?"

"Not long." I raised my head and stared out the window above the sink. It was the first time I'd noticed that they had a backyard. But it was overgrown. Unusable.

"So you haven't known her long . . . but she means something to you, right? I mean that's why you're here?" It came out as a question, but she wasn't asking. Not really. "Chloe—she's built walls around herself—ones that it took Dean and me years to break past. It hasn't been easy. But you, Blake . . . I don't know . . ."

I didn't know what to say, so I stayed quiet. She continued, "She's never invited anyone to the house before. It was kind of a big deal that you were here."

I turned to her now, surprise clear on my face.

She nodded. "Yeah. You're her first real friend. That's what I'm assuming you are—friends?"

It was my turn to nod.

"Good. That's good . . ." I could see the contemplation on her face; she was planning her next words carefully. "Chloe's mom died when she was five. Breast cancer."

Even though I knew that her mom had passed, I didn't know *how*. I tensed and waited for the pounding in my chest to settle.

"When her mom passed away, she went to live with her Aunt Tilly. They were twins, her mom and her aunt. Her dad was never around. He bailed after finding out about the pregnancy. Tilly didn't have kids of her own, so it was perfect . . . for a while. But then a few years later, she passed away, too. Same disease."

I swallowed down the lump in my throat as I tried to picture Chloe. Her life. Everything that she had had to go through.

"So by the time she came to live with us, death was no stranger to her. After a couple of years, neither was cancer. She got obsessed. Fixated with it. She spent all her time reading books, searching online, learning everything possible about it." She stopped to clear her throat; her voice came out shaky as she added, "She was withdrawn, not just from us but from the other kids here and at school. Then one day, she came home with a huge smile on her face. Something in her switched over that day. She announced to Dean and me during dinner that night that she was over it. She said that she was going to live her life to the fullest, take in the world and everything it had to offer. We thought it was great." She sniffed and wiped the tears that were falling too fast. "But then she said that when *she* died of cancer, she didn't want to leave anyone behind. She actually said, 'You are not allowed to love me. No one can.'"

I turned and leaned against the counter behind me. I needed something to hold me up.

"Can you imagine, Blake? She couldn't have been more than eleven at the time. And she'd decided that cancer was her future. And the saddest part is that she didn't let that part ruin *her*. She was scared for the people around her."

I rubbed my eyes, trying to hide the fact that I was close to tears. Then I cleared my throat. "So that's why she's . . ."

"Invisible?" Mary nodded slowly. "She's good at what she set out to do . . . experiencing the world and all that. She never takes anything for granted. But she does it alone, and it's sad, because she's so easy to love."

I nodded. I wasn't sure why. Maybe because I knew she was right, that falling in love with Chloe would be effortless.

"I'm sorry," she sniffed. "I'm a mess. I just love her. And I want the best for her. So if that's having you in her life, I'm going to support you, and you'll always be welcome here. But if you cause her pain, if you're the reason she's in her room crying at night, then I guess . . ." She trailed off. She didn't need to finish her sentence. I knew what she meant.

"Anyway . . ." She perked up and inhaled deeply. "Let's see who ends up the champion of basketskate!"

"Skateball," I said and attempted a smile.

*   *   *

The house was empty when I got home, which didn't surprise me. Neither did the army-issued footlocker sitting in the middle of my bed.

See, you'd think that my dad—being as proud as he was—would want to brag about his army days. That he would want to tell me stories about his time in Panama and the Gulf War. But he didn't. He didn't speak about it at all. Not to me and not to his small circle of friends. If he talked to other vets, I didn't know about it. This was his way of talking to me. Maybe not *to* me as much as *at* me.

Normally, I'd just push it aside. Throw it under my bed and deal with it another day.

But today wasn't like other days. After hanging out with Dean and the kids, something in me had switched. My decision about my future had always been about what I wanted versus what I thought I had to do. Now? I had no idea what I wanted.

"Fuck it," I said under my breath, and sat on the edge of the bed, dragging the footlocker over so it was next to me. I unhinged the latch and lifted the heavy metal lid. His dress blues were folded perfectly at the bottom, his Bronze Star Medal still attached. He had never told me how he'd earned it, but then again, I'd never asked. On top of all of that was a letter-size envelope with the U.S. Army logo on the corner and a sticky note attached. *September 30—MEPS,* was all it said.

MEPS—*Military Entrance Processing Station.*

September 30—*enlistment day.*

CHAPTER FIFTEEN

Blake

I knocked on Chloe's door. Mary answered and tried to contain her smile. "Blake, what are you doing here?"

All of a sudden, I panicked. It had seemed like the greatest idea in the world when I had thought of it. Now, though, I kind of felt like an ass. "I'm here to clean up your backyard."

"What?" She let out a disbelieving laugh, just as the street filled with cars. The sound of doors opening and closing and the familiar ruckus of a group of teenage boys filled the otherwise quiet neighborhood.

I shoved my hands in my pockets and shrugged. "Well, me and the rest of my team . . . and the JV team."

Her eyes widened as they all started to walk up her driveway. "What kind of teenage boy wants to spend his Sunday weeding a neglected yard?"

"A teenage boy whose coach ordered them to. Plus, it's for extra credit." I waited for her to give me the go-ahead, but she didn't. Suddenly, I was nervous as fuck. Maybe I'd overstepped my boundaries. "I just thought the kids would like to have some extra space to play . . . It was stupid. I'm sorry."

I turned to leave but she gripped my shirt. "No way," she said. "You don't get out of it that easy. Come in!"

*   *   *

My eyes kept wondering around, looking for any sign of Chloe. I didn't want to ask Mary, because I wanted her to believe I wasn't there for Chloe. My reasons for being there were genuine, but that didn't mean that seeing her wouldn't have been a bonus. We still worked together, but it hadn't been the same since that night in her room. I still had no idea what had really happened, but I didn't want to push it. I was more than happy with a little Chloe rather than no Chloe at all.

The boys and I worked in the yard for an hour before the sun started baking us. I'd sent out a few of the guys to get some drinks and ice and coolers, but I was dying. I didn't want to disturb the family too much, so I quietly walked in through the back door to get a drink. Mary was already there, making a pitcher of iced tea. She smiled when she saw me. "Wash up. I'll pour you a fresh glass."

"You're my hero," I joked, looking around again.

"She's up in her room. Hasn't been down yet."

I nodded; I was a little worried about her reaction to me being there.

Mary handed me the cold iced tea just as I turned the tap off. She gazed out the window and watched the rest of the guys at work. "Dean will be so happy when he gets home."

"Yeah? He's not gonna be mad?"

"Why would he be mad?"

I turned so my back was against the counter. "I just don't want him to think that I'm doing his job or something."

"Honey, Dean has a job. He works six days a week and provides for our family. So what if we don't have the nicest house on the street?" She shrugged. "So what if he doesn't spend his time away from that job weeding the yard? I could get a job. I've offered, but he doesn't want me to. He says that being a mom, taking care of our family, that's more than enough work. And when he has any spare time, he spends it with Chloe and the kids. It's important to *him* that we do everything we can so that the kids know we're here for them." She took the glass from my hand, refilled it, and handed it back. "So no, Blake. He won't be offended. He'll be enormously thankful."

"Good. Because I wanted to put this in the yard when it's done . . ." I reached into my pocket and pulled out the page I had ripped out of the Toys "R" Us catalog. But before I could show her, Chloe walked in.

"Who the hell are all those guys in—" She froze midstep.

My eyes nearly fell out of my head.

She was wearing a white bikini top. Tiny shorts. Nothing else. She was even hotter than my imagination had given her credit for. She was tanned, which surprised me, because she didn't seem to be the type to be out there working on her tan—or whatever the hell it was chicks did.

"What are you doing here?"

She had a mole on her right breast. It was tiny. Right above where the bikini covered. Then her arms blocked the view.

My eyes snapped to hers. I was staring at her tits. *Holy shit.*

Her face flushed red as she clamped her mouth shut, trying to hide her smile.

I cleared my throat. "Um." That was all I could get out.

"He's clearing the yard for us," Mary answered for me.

"You and whose army?" she asked, smiling openly now.

Mary giggled. "I'll be in the living room if you need me."

I never took my eyes off Chloe. She watched Mary leave the room before stepping closer to me.

"Blake?"

"Uh?"

"I didn't know you were coming today, I made plans with Clayton."

I couldn't stop staring at her breasts.

"Blake!"

My eyes snapped to hers, and I shook my head, clearing the thoughts that were running wild in my mind. And then I laughed, because I didn't know what else to do. She was driving me *insane*. "It's okay," I told her. "You'd just be a distraction anyway. Go. Leave."

She chuckled and walked away.

I stared at her ass.

"Holy shit," I mumbled.

"Blake," Mary said, walking back into the kitchen. "That's kind of my daughter you're drooling over."

I wiped my mouth. My cheeks burned. "Sorry."

She laughed.

I was glad she found it funny. My dick sure as shit didn't.

Chloe

"I don't think this is it, Chloe."

I looked down at the picture in my hand. Mom and Aunt Tilly as teenagers, hanging out with their friends by a lake . . . or a river. The picture had faded and creased over the years, so it was hard to make out. "Yeah, I don't think it is, either." I tried to hide the sadness in my voice, but Clayton could always tell.

"I'm sorry," he said, walking up the rocky embankment toward me. He pulled me to him and wrapped his arms around me.

"It's okay," I hugged him back and spoke into his chest. "I'll just keep searching. We'll find it next time."

He squeezed me tighter. "You bring any food? I'm starving."

*   *   *

"Mary called."

I quirked an eyebrow.

That made him laugh, but only for a moment, before he sighed and set his sandwich on the rug we were sitting on. "You know I've never been one to give you advice or judge you or try to make you think that what you're feeling is wrong."

He was right, which meant that whatever he was about to say held a certain significance. I watched as his eyes roamed my face, searching for something that probably wasn't there. Clayton had been through a lot in his life. His eyes—to me—always held a familiarity to them. A sense of home, if ever I had one. Despite how much he'd grown up the past few years, his eyes always reminded me of the kid who I was first introduced to.

I dropped my sandwich, faced the river, and brought my knees up to my chest. "Out with it," I told him

"I just worry about you, Chloe."

I rolled my eyes.

"I know you're rolling your eyes."

I turned to glare at him.

"You think I need to see you to know what you're doing? That's ass, and you know it."

"Whatever."

"All I'm saying is that I worry. I worry that you're not getting the best out of your life."

I went to interrupt, but he raised his hand to stop me.

"Just let me speak, please?"

I nodded but kept my eyes on the glistening water.

"I get why you do what you do . . . why you shut yourself off from the rest of the world and the people around you. But I'm scared for you. I'm scared that maybe you'll do it, and it will all be for nothing. Maybe you'll live to be a hundred."

"There's a fifty-fifty chance I carry that gene, Clay."

"I know that. And *you* know that I know that. But that's a fifty percent chance you don't carry it, Chloe. And even if you do—it doesn't necessarily mean cancer, and it might not get you as young as it got them. It might come a lot later in your life. It might not happen at all. Don't you think that means something? That *has* to mean something. And the fact that you refuse to get checked . . . I mean . . . things have advanced since your mom—"

"What's your point?" I didn't want to hear what he had to say. I'd heard it all before. From Mary, from Dean, from the counselors they'd made me see when I was eleven.

He sighed heavily and moved closer so our sides were touching. "I'm just saying that maybe you're missing out. Maybe if you open your eyes a little you'll see that it's not all bad. Maybe it's okay to let someone in. To let them understand you. Maybe Blake—"

My breath caught.

He didn't let it stop him from continuing. "I don't know Blake, but neither do you. It's just—from what I can see—he cares about you. More than you probably know. And I don't know what's happening between you two, but he's trying. I know he's the first guy—or person really—that you let in, even just for a little bit. But maybe you should try . . . Just *try*."

The lump in my throat ached as much as the pain in my chest. I wanted him to stop talking.

He threw an arm around my shoulders and pulled me to him. "I dunno, Chloe. You had a mom who loved you. An aunt who took you in. Foster parents and siblings who adore you. You have a guy interested in getting to know you. If you take all that in, and the life that you've built for yourself, maybe it's worth it. Maybe it's worth that fifty percent chance at *living*."

I released the sob I'd been trying so hard to contain and dropped my head into my hands. And I cried. I cried for my mom. My aunt. And I cried for Clayton—because he'd never had any of those things.

"I love you, Chloe. I'm so glad and so honored to know you. To be a part of your life. My point is that maybe others deserve that chance, too."

Wiping my tears on his shirt, I whispered, "I can't, Clay." I looked up at him. "What would you do if you were me . . . if you thought your time was limited? Would you purposely hurt the people you cared about?"

He shook his head slowly, his eyes penetrating mine. "No, Chloe, that's the absolute last thing I'd ever want." He kissed my forehead. "But I'm glad we had this talk."

I sniffed and nodded into his chest. "Me, too."

*   *   *

By the time Clayton pulled onto my street, it was early evening. Boys were walking down the driveway and into waiting cars. Some were loading mowers onto the beds of trucks. There had to be more than twenty of them.

"You coming in for a bit?"

Clayton nodded as he stepped out of his car. "I'll just come in and say hi real quick."

We walked to the end of the driveway and through the gate into the yard. I heard Dean's voice before he came into my vision. "Holy shit, kid! This is amazing."

I froze.

The entire yard had been cut back; the grass was short enough that you could actually walk on it. It'd been years since I'd seen it this clean. But that wasn't what caught my attention. It was the giant play set that'd been built in the corner of the yard. I'd only ever seen such things at playgrounds.

Sammy stuck his head out the window of the upper level of the playhouse. "Chloe! Clayton! Come look!"

Blake and Dean quickly turned to us.

"It's pretty great, huh, Chloe?" Dean said in awe.

I couldn't take my eyes off Blake. His hands were in his front pockets. A slight smile on his face, almost as if he was embarrassed by Dean's praise. His eyes moved to Clayton next to me, and he jerked his head in greeting.

Sammy's childish holler broke through the silence. "Guys! What do you think?"

I glanced up at him. His smile was so big it was infectious. "It's amazing, Sammy! It really is."

Clayton cleared his throat. "Hey," he said, speaking to Blake. "You want to show me the playhouse?"

"Yeah, man," Blake replied and started to walk away.

I grabbed his arm before he could get far. "You staying for dinner?"

He smiled. "You inviting me?"

I shrugged.

"I guess I have no choice then."

Blake

Clayton led me to the playhouse and up the ladder. I knew he wasn't interested in seeing it, but the thought of what he really wanted made me nervous. We sat quietly, waiting for Sammy to tell us everything he loved about the new yard. After a couple minutes, Dean came out and got him so he could wash up for dinner. "You staying?" he asked Clayton.

He shook his head. "I gotta take off. Blake will just be a minute."

It felt weird, him speaking for me. My nervousness escalated, and I wondered what it was about him that I found so intimidating.

"You could be her change, Blake."

That's it. That's all he said, before climbing down the ladder and heading out of the yard to the driveway.

You could be her change.

I had no idea what that meant, but I knew that I wanted it.

*   *   *

Mary sighed loudly at the dining table. It wasn't the first time, and I wasn't the only one who noticed. "What's with you?" Dean asked. "You've been edgy all day."

She seemed to bounce in her seat as she replied, "I don't know. Something's off. I feel like I'm forgetting something."

Dean eyed her sideways before facing the kids, lifting his hand, and moving his index finger in circles next to his ear.

"She's not crazy!" Sammy yelled through a laugh.

Mary smacked her palms flat on the table. "I can't handle it." Then she waved her hands in the air. "I'm getting my diary." She stood up, shaking her head as she left the kitchen.

"Crazy, I tells ya," Dean whispered jokingly. The kids laughed, but I noticed Chloe stayed silent next to me, her eyes fixated on her untouched plate.

Then Mary walked back in, diary in one hand, the other covering her mouth. Her eyes glazed over with tears. "Oh honey . . ." she said sympathetically, looking straight at Chloe. "I'm so sorry I forgot."

"It's fine," Chloe answered.

Mary sat back down. "It's not fine. I always remember your mother and aunt's birthday. I'm so sorry."

Shit.

Mary added, "Did you and Clayton have any luck finding it today?"

Chloe shook her head.

"Honey." Mary tried to get her attention.

She finally looked up from her plate.

"I'm sorry. Not just for forgetting, but you know . . ."

Chloe nodded slowly but jerked her head toward the kids, sending a silent message.

Mary smiled, but the smile was sad. Then she sucked in a breath and faked a peppiness in her tone as she said, "So I caught Dean in the bedroom, watching himself twerk in the mirror."

The kids' laughter filled the room. Chloe just looked back down at her plate.

I leaned in close to her ear and whispered, "Are you okay?" She turned her head and looked up at me with such sadness in her eyes that I swear my heart actually broke. "Can I do anything?"

"No." She tried to smile but failed. Then I felt her hand reach for mine under the table. "You're already doing it."

*   *   *

"See?" she said, pointing to a picture. "There's a river or a lake behind them, but we can't find where it is."

"Do you mind?" I asked, taking the photo from her hands.

"Not at all."

I scanned the picture quickly. "Holy shit, Chloe. You look just like them," I said, before pulling out my phone and snapping a picture of the photograph, then handing it back. It wasn't a lie. She did. Only younger and more beautiful. I kicked off the ground, setting the swing seat in motion.

Her smile was genuine. "I just want to find the place before I leave."

I ignored the tightening in my chest and placed my arm behind her. "So, you're still leaving?"

She looked up at me. "Of course. Nothing's changed, Blake."

I sighed, remembering Clayton's words. *I could be her change.* "So . . . Mary told me about the cancer."

"I know," she said quietly, averting her gaze. "She told me that she did."

"I just think—"

"Don't, Blake," she interrupted. "Don't do that. Don't think about it, and don't think *for* me."

I wanted to press further, but I didn't want to push her. And I had a feeling that with her, if you pushed enough times, she'd push back. She'd push hard enough that one of us would fall off the edge and whatever delicate thing we had would be over. And that was the last damn thing I wanted. "So your plan's still The Road?"

She nodded. "And what about you? What's your plan?"

"I don't know," I said truthfully. "I thought I did, but a lot has changed lately."

"Like what?"

"I got a scholarship to Duke."

She gasped, her smile wide. "That's amazing, Blake! Basketball?"

"Yeah," I said quietly.

Her brow furrowed. "But you're not happy about it?"

"No, I am," I said quickly. "I've always loved basketball. Ever since I was four and my uncle got me one for Christmas. The fact that I'm good at it . . . That's a bonus."

"But?"

"But my dad's army. His dad was army. His dad's dad was army. So that's what I've been raised to believe my future is. *Army.*"

"Does your dad know about the Duke scholarship?"

I shook my head. "No. Only Josh and Hannah. Hannah . . . she knew about shit with my dad, and she kind of used it as blackmail." I laughed once, thinking about how petty it was. "She said that if

I ever tried to break up with her she'd tell my dad about the scholarship. That's pretty much why I stayed with her as long as I did. And I know that it's not important, Chloe, but I just think that you should know that I didn't love her."

She nodded slowly, as if she understood, but all she said was, "So it's basketball or the army. What are you going to do?"

I sighed and rubbed my hand across my jaw. "You know, until I met you, I thought this decision was the hardest thing in my life. I thought it was make or break. Life or death. With the pressure from my dad . . . the expectations of my teammates and my coaches . . . I put so much pressure on myself that it was all I could think about. I felt like I was drowning in it. Some days I still feel like that." I paused for a beat, before adding, "The night I met you . . . when I was out for a run . . . I was trying to escape it. That's what I do when I feel like things are too much and I don't want to feel them anymore. I run. But now, I see things differently. I actually have a choice, and there's nothing life or death about it."

Her eyes snapped to mine, and she must have known what I'd meant. I was talking about her.

She looked away when her eyes started to glaze. I changed the subject, because the last thing I wanted was to upset her. "I signed the letter of intent for Duke. The truth is I've always wanted basketball, and not just the game, but Duke specifically."

"So go to Duke," she said, as if it was the answer to my problem.

I waited a moment, forming my thoughts before adding, "But there's also a huge part of me that *wants* to enlist. Meeting you, Mary, and Dean—it's kind of . . . I don't know. It's made me want to do something more with my life. It's made me want to make a difference, you know? My dad is right in a sense. Being able to shoot a ball through a hoop isn't going to do anything to improve the world. Joining the army—being part of a team, waking up every day and knowing that you have a purpose, a reason—there's something satisfying about that. Something special, you know?"

She laughed quietly and shook her head.

"What?"

"Every time I think I know you, Blake Hunter, you just keep surprising me." Then her mouth was on mine. But it wasn't just a kiss; it was more. Her lips didn't move. Her tongue didn't search. And just as quickly, it was over. She settled back in the crook of my arm, with no answers or apologies. Which was perfect—because I didn't want or need either of them.

CHAPTER SIXTEEN

Chloe

I knew something was about to happen, even though there were no physical signs. The hair on the back of my neck stood up, and my palms began to sweat. Butterflies formed in my stomach, and the beating of my heart thumped faster, harder—and even though I was staring down at the floors of the familiar hallways of high school—I knew that when I'd lift my gaze, something was going to *change*. And then I looked up—and the beating of my heart stopped for a split second. The boy with the messy dark hair and the piercing blue eyes was watching me—a hint of a smile on his beautiful face that was enough to kick my heart back into gear. But then he turned around and walked away—not for him—but for me. Because he knew that was what I wanted, and I knew that he only wanted me to be happy.

Blake Hunter—he was my *change*.

*　　*　　*

"I saw you at school today," he said, coming out of the food-prep room. I had my back turned; leaning my elbows on the counter, I was looking out at the lanes, trying to act cool, as if being around him didn't set my heart racing.

"I know. I caught you," I joked, straightening up and spinning around.

"You think it'll be busy tonight?"

"I doubt it. There was only one person here on Monday, and I'm pretty sure he only stayed for the hot dogs."

He laughed.

"What?" I asked, leaning my back against the counter.

"Chloe, he didn't stay for the hot dogs. He stayed for your tits."

"What!"

He chuckled lightly, moving in closer to nudge me with his elbow, only he didn't shift back. He just stayed there. Far enough from me that we weren't touching, but close enough that I knew he wanted to.

"Well, he's not here now, so I guess they weren't worthy of his return."

"I beg to differ."

I leaned back slightly, trying to see his face. "Are you being a pig?"

"Yes," he admitted freely.

*   *   *

A single swipe of the broom, and the lights were off.

"Skate time, you little punks!" Josh hollered.

We didn't waste any time. When his hands weren't on me, his eyes were.

"You staring at her like that doesn't make her yours," I heard Josh tell him.

"Shut up, asshole."

That made Josh laugh.

"Shit. I gotta go." I tried to brake on the board but couldn't, so I just jumped off, letting the board hit the wall in front of me. "Oops."

Blake got up from his seat and picked it up. "I'll walk you out."

*   *   *

"So I guess I'll pretend to not be seeing you at school tomorrow?"

I smiled as I threw my bag onto the passenger seat. "That would be perfect."

I tugged on his shirt until he stepped forward. I threw my arms around his waist, and he drew me closer to him, with his hand on the back of my head.

"Good night, Blake."

He kissed the top of my head. "Good night, Not Abby." I started to pull back, but his hold on me tightened. "Do you want me to follow you home? Make sure you get there safe?"

I laughed into his chest and attempted to remove myself. He let me this time. "You're always trying to save me."

"Yeah, well, you've already saved me."

*   *   *

You look extra beautiful today.

That was what the note in my locker said. Red ink on torn white paper. I read it again for the millionth time, and each time it left me with the same feeling. *A change was coming.*

But it wasn't the change I expected.

When my teacher stopped next to me in class and told me I had to go to the principal's office, I knew something was wrong.

And when the uniformed officers just outside the principal's door came into view, I knew it was bad.

Classes were in progress. The halls were empty. Each step toward them got harder, heavier. My heart thumped faster, louder in my ears. "Miss Thompson?" one of them asked.

I used the wall behind me to keep me upright. "Yes?" I think I said. The walls closed in, and everything else disappeared.

"Would you like to talk somewhere more private?"

I shook my head. It felt as heavy as my feet only minutes ago. Or was it seconds? I didn't know. I couldn't tell.

"It's about Mr. Clayton Wells."

The bile rose; I swallowed it down. My eyes stung. "Shut up!" My head pounded. I covered my ears with my hands. "Don't say it." I pressed them firmer. I didn't want to hear another fucking word.

"We're so sorry for your loss, Miss Thompson."

Blake

I walked down the empty halls, with a stupid smile on my face, remembering how she had felt in my arms when we'd said good-bye last night.

But just like that, my smile was gone.

"No," she gasped, her hands pressed against her ears.

She slid down the wall. I wasn't aware how I got to her. Or that I was even there. Not until she looked up with tears streaming down her face. "Blake?"

I was on my knees, holding her while she cried into her hands. "It's okay," I whispered to her, then louder to the cops, "What happened?"

Before they had a chance to answer, the bell rang. "Take me home," she cried.

I got her to my car as fast as I could.

*   *   *

She cried hysterically the entire way to her house. Each sob had the same effect as a vise surrounding my heart. I didn't bother to ask her what had happened. I just gripped her hand tight as it rested on her lap.

The car hadn't even come to a complete stop in her driveway before she was out the door, up the porch steps, and in the house.

I followed.

"Did you know?" She was yelling at a wide-eyed Mary, sitting in the living room with Sammy. He had a paintbrush in his hand with an art smock on. His hand was frozen midstroke on the paper in front of him. He looked scared. Hell, I *was* scared. "Did you?" she yelled again.

Mary's eyes narrowed, but they didn't move away from her. "Sweetheart," she said. "I don't know what you're talking about."

"Clayton! Did you know that he was depressed again? Did you know he'd gone back to using?"

"What?" Mary asked, the shock clear on her face. "I didn't." She took a comforting step toward Chloe. "Honey, you have to tell me what happened."

"He killed himself, okay?" she screamed, her face scarlet. "He fucking killed himself!"

Fuck.

Silence.

The only sounds in the room were heavy breaths and the ticking of the clock coming from the kitchen.

Tick.

Tock.

Tick.

Tock.

Then Sammy's little voice. "What?" His face contorted. A cry escaped. "What's that mean?"

I turned to Chloe, but she was gone, her feet thudding up the stairs so fast there was no sound separating her steps.

"Go with her." Mary took the brush from Sammy's hand and tried to hold back her tears. "Now, Blake."

*　　　*　　　*

She had a small suitcase on her bed, already half-filled with clothes. I sat down next to it and watched her for a moment. I couldn't speak. I didn't know what to say. *What the hell do you say in this situation?*

She wouldn't stop crying. Her cries came out louder, more uncontrolled. She threw more and more into the suitcase. Once it was filled, she flipped the lid and began to zip it shut. Then my sense kicked in. *Where is she going?* I panicked and grasped her wrist, stopping her from sealing her bag. "Chloe, stop. What are you doing?"

"I'm leaving. Fuck graduation. Fuck this place. I don't want to be here anymore. Not without him."

My stomach dropped. *She can't leave.* "You can't leave."

"Why?" The word echoed off the walls in her tiny room. "Give me one good reason, Blake!"

I had a reason, but I knew it wasn't enough. Not even close. Still, I told her, "Because I'm not ready to lose you yet."

Her eyes snapped shut. Her head fell forward, and all the fight she had in her disappeared. "He's gone, Blake."

"I know. I'm so sorry."

Then she looked up. Her eyes locked with mine, holding so much pain, anger, and sadness that I felt it, too.

Her pain was my pain.

"He's gone," she said again.

I pulled on her wrist until she was between my legs, and my arms were around her waist, holding on to every single piece of her. "He's gone," she repeated. But it was different this time.

It was final.

"I know, baby, and I'm sorry."

Her arms went over my shoulders, bringing me closer. Then she curled into a ball on my lap. "Will you just hold me, Blake?"

She cried until she fell asleep in my arms. I moved her so she was under the covers and her head rested on the pillow. And then I made my way downstairs.

Dean was home now. The kids were at the neighbor's house while Mary and he took some time to gather their thoughts. I didn't know much about Clayton, but I assumed they had fostered him, too.

"Hi, Blake." Dean's forced smile was overshadowed by the solemn tone in his voice.

"How is she?" Mary asked from next to him.

"She's asleep."

Dean nodded.

"Is it okay if I stay with her tonight?"

He nodded again.

* * *

"I thought you'd left." She sat up, letting the covers bunch at her waist.

I stood just inside her doorway, awkwardly, not knowing where to go. "I wouldn't leave without telling you."

"What time is it?"

"Just past six."

"Are you going now?"

I shook my head.

She moved the covers down on one side of the bed as an invitation. Then she waited until I'd shrugged out of my jeans and gotten in her bed before lying back down. "Blake Hunter, you're always saving me."

I stayed quiet.

She sighed loudly. "Thank you for my note."

"You knew it was from me?"

She moved so her head was in the crook of my arm. "No one's ever called me beautiful but you." I wanted to tell her that it was a shame. That she deserved to be told a million times over, but she spoke before I could get it out. "Will you stay with me tonight?"

"Of course." *And all the nights after that.*

She settled in, her arm and leg resting on top of me. It was quiet, but I knew she was awake. I knew she was thinking.

"Do you want to talk about him—Clayton? Maybe it might—"

"What do you want me to tell you?"

"Tell me anything and everything, whatever you want."

Chloe

Clayton's dad had physically and sexually abused him when he was a kid. He'd hid it from everyone until he was ten. That was when his teacher had begun to notice certain things about him: He was closed off and never tried to make friends with the kids. He'd jump at loud noises and shrink into the corner when there was too much going on. His clothes were too small, worn at best. They'd smell so bad that some days his teacher had found clothes in the lost and found for him to change into. One day, she'd asked him to change in front of her. He'd told me he'd kind of known why she had, but he'd been too young to really comprehend the events that would follow once she'd seen the bruises and cuts all over him. The cops had been called.

And then his dad had killed himself.

I guessed some assholes could live with being a pedophile and raping little boys, just as long as nobody knew about it. Apparently, the death of his father had been a guilt Clayton had carried with him well into his teenage years.

By the time he'd turned sixteen, he was using. Pot at first, then, too quickly, heavier stuff. He'd kept it from me—just like he'd kept the fact that he was depressed and those drugs were his form of an upper. Dean and Mary had known and gotten him help when he'd agreed to it. It was strange, that when he was with me, it'd never showed. But when I looked back on it—I could see signs. Like how he'd frown when watching the kids or go days without speaking to anyone but me. Or be gone all weekend and nobody knew where he was.

When he was eighteen, he'd moved out, and things had gone from bad to worse. We'd tried to help him, but he'd kept us all at arm's length, not wanting us to get involved in his mess, and concealed his secrets. He'd been in and out of jail, hadn't been able to hold down a job or make money unless he was dealing, had barely spoken to or seen the family, unless it had been me. He *always* had time for me. It hadn't been until a year and a half ago, when he'd met his girlfriend, Lisa, that things had begun to look up.

Her parents happened to own a restaurant in town that they were about to shut down. They'd offered him the work for six months, to see if it was worth saving. To him—it had been like being offered a second chance—one that he'd taken seriously. He changed the hours of operation, opening only at night through to brunch. He'd had trouble sleeping at night, so it had been perfect for him. And perfect for them. Soon enough, his girlfriend's parents had welcomed him into their family, just like Dean and Mary had. And he'd needed that. He'd needed to know that he'd still been loveable; at least that was what he'd told me. And Lisa—she was great. She'd seen through his bullshit and seen the same person that I had. She was one of the few people who knew about his past, and had loved him, regardless. When she'd gone off to college in Savannah, a good four-and-a-half-hour drive away, they'd known it would be tough, but they'd promised to make it work. It had meant a lot of phone calls and coming home to visit when she could. And it had meant Clayton spending a lot of time on his own, time that I should have been there.

I should have seen it. I should have noticed him struggling. He'd always been able to know how I felt before I even realized it myself, but I'd been unable to do the same for him. He'd kept his feelings hidden so that I would never have to feel his pain. He'd always put me first, put everyone else first. He'd found a way to care for Mary and Dean and all the kids, even when he'd had no idea what it felt like to be cared *for*.

His past, his depression, the drugs—none of that was really who he'd been. To me—he would always be Clayton—the quiet boy who'd so easily become my best friend. *My hero.*

CHAPTER SEVENTEEN

Blake

"Blake."

Something nudged my foot.

I waited a moment, trying to get my bearings. And then I remembered where I was and what had happened.

"Blake," she said again.

When I opened my eyes, I expected to see her in bed next to me. But she wasn't there. And it wasn't Chloe who was saying my name.

It was Mary.

"Where's Chloe?"

"She left early; she wanted me to come in and tell you that you should go to school and not wait around for her."

"Oh" was all I could say.

"She just needs some time, Blake. It's not like she doesn't appreciate that you're here for her."

"I know that." I shrugged. "I just wanted to see her. That's all."

She smiled warmly before leaving the room.

Chloe

His arms had felt nice around me.

I'd never felt the warmth of someone's embrace before.

Not really.

Not before Blake.

Those clouds kinda look like Blake.

I brought the joint to my lips and inhaled deeply, blowing circles as I puffed out continuous, single, tiny breaths.

A lethal cocktail of recreational and prescribed pills—the cop's words replayed in my head, over and over. But Clayton—he'd been smart. He'd known what the fuck he'd been doing. He'd *wanted* to die.

"I hope you're happy, fuckhead," I said aloud, ignoring the prickles of grass in and around my back. I was at an abandoned baseball field close to home. This was where Clayton and I had used to come and talk shit—a place where we'd pretended to have dreams. He was also my first kiss—right there—in that patch of grass. It had been gross, but he'd said that it shouldn't be with some random guy I met at a party, just because he told me I was pretty. He'd said he wanted it to mean something. And it did. Even now, he's the only guy I had ever kissed who meant something to me.

Before Blake.

"Have you seen my mom? My aunt Tilly?" I squinted at the sky, the sun so bright it made my eyes water. But I didn't blink. I wanted to feel it. I wanted to use it as an excuse for these endless, goddamn tears. "What's that?" I raised my heavy hand—or at least it seemed heavy—and cupped my ear. "No? You haven't seen them? Then what the fuck was it all for, Clayton? Was it that bad here?"

I stopped myself and let out a sob. "I'm sorry," I cried to the sky. "I didn't mean that. I know you had your reasons, and I'm sorry that you couldn't talk to me about them. I'm sorry that you felt like there was no other way." I sat up and let the sob consume me. And when I was done—not just with the crying but with the entire joint—I got in my car, drove to the liquor store in the next town over, and bought a bottle of vodka.

I spent the night in my car in a constant cross-faded state.

Emptiness.

Perfection.

*   *   *

I woke up in the backseat, sweating like a pig. Moaning, I reached for my phone in the console; twenty-four missed calls. I didn't bother to check whom they were from. Instead, I climbed back into the driver's seat, turned the key in the ignition, and drove back to the abandoned field.

And then I started all over again.

*   *   *

Clayton had introduced me to weed. He'd said that I would probably encounter it sometime, and just like my first kiss, he'd wanted to be the one to show me. He'd told me that I shouldn't smoke often, but if I ever felt like I needed to, he had to be there so he could stop me when I wanted to fall too deep. Too far.

But then I'd have bad days, like the anniversary of my mother's death. Days where the pain was so unbearable, I wanted to forget all about it—about her and about my chances. But it wasn't limited to just that one day a year. The older I got, the more pain I felt. And the more I wanted to forget.

The weed-booze mix was perfect when I wanted to lose myself. It was my nirvana.

The Road had been my master plan since I was thirteen. Not just because I wanted to see and appreciate the little things the world had to offer, but because I thought it would be easier not to feel for anyone—and vice versa—if I was never in the same place long enough to develop any meaningful relationships.

But the longer I stayed, the harder it got.

Like when Sammy had introduced me as his sister to his pre-K teacher. Or when Harry had asked me for advice on relationships and I hadn't had the answers. For a second, though, I'd let myself think about it, and what it would be like to actually have a relationship or to fall in love. To have someone who loved me, regardless of my future. Regardless of the cancer. And regardless of how much of my life I could possibly give them. I'd thought about having kids. Raising them. Maybe fostering some, like Mary and Dean. And then I'd thought about how they would be at risk. And that at some point, that risk could take their lives. And all because I was selfish and wanted something for myself: a white picket fence, a beautiful husband, maybe with dark shaggy hair and perfectly clear blue eyes. And kids. Lots of kids.

See?

Selfish.

At some point, I'd wanted more than just the emptiness inside of me. And one night, when I'd been walking past a house party and had seen a bunch of kids flowing out the door and onto the front yard, I'd gotten it.

I didn't remember his name. I didn't remember what he looked like. All I knew was that we'd had sex, it'd hurt like a bitch, and that he'd used a condom.

Blake

I'd tried calling Chloe no less than a million times, give or take. She'd never answered. When I went to her house, Mary and Dean said she was out, and that they'd tried phoning but had gotten the same response. They said not to worry, that she'd disappear for a while when things got to be too much for her but she'd always come back fine. I asked if I could wait for her there. They both gave me a sympathetic smile but agreed. I waited on her porch steps for three hours. She never showed.

Then my phone beeped with a text. It was from Will: *Your new girlfriend's looking hot these days*, and he'd included a picture of Chloe leaning against a wall. Her eyes were shut, makeup a mess all over her face. She had a bottle of something in her hand, but her grasp was loose, as if she was about to drop it.

I knew where the party was because everyone at school had been talking about it all week. I got in my car and sped the entire way there.

The volume of the music increased tenfold when I opened the door. I was already scanning the room for Chloe before I'd even fully stepped inside. "Hunter!" Sophie, Hannah's best friend, was walking over to me. She plastered her body onto mine and wrapped her arms around my neck. I was trying to pull her off me when I caught sight of a mess of blonde hair and the tiny girl it was attached to.

She was coming out of the hallway, with one hand resting on the wall next to her, helping to keep her balance. Her head was down as she stumbled into the living room. She took another step, but her ankle twisted from her stupidly high heels. Will was there to catch her fall. And then she raised her head, her eyes half-hooded. She tried to straighten up with Will's hand on her waist. She curled her arm around his neck and brought his face to hers.

My gasp was so sharp it surprised even me. The assholes around him cheered while he handed them his beer and pressed her up against the wall—not once breaking apart from their kiss. I wanted to move. I wanted to get him the fuck off her. But my feet were leaden, planted to the floor. His hand on her waist moved lower, past the hem of her short dress and onto her bare thigh. Then he gripped the back of it, pulling her leg up so his dick could get closer to where I was sure he wanted in. Another round of cheers; but they were drowned out by the rushing of blood in my eardrums. He pulled back slightly; whatever he must've said to her seemed to deserve high fives and pats on the fucking back. He dropped her leg, grabbed her hand and then led her down the hall.

Fuck. No.

I finally pried Sophie's arms from around my neck and put one foot in front of the other. It was slow, my movements still getting accustomed to their apparent weight. By the time I'd made it to the hallway, every single muscle in my body ached from the tension. But my mind—my mind was clear. I pushed open every door possible, ignoring the screams or "fuck offs" I got when I interrupted something. I didn't leave until I was sure it wasn't Chloe in the room. By the time I got to the last door, my rage was all consuming. The door was locked, but I just kicked it down. Will's mouth was on her breast, and his hand was down her panties.

Within seconds, I had pulled him off her and punched him twice in the face.

I wanted to kill him.

"What the fuck is your problem, Hunter?" He held his now-broken nose between his thumb and fingers. Blood poured from it and down his arm.

"What the fuck is my problem?" I yelled, yanking my arms away from whoever the fuck was holding me back. "You enjoy taking advantage of girls who are too wasted to know what the fuck is happening?"

"Fuck you! Get off your fucking pedestal! She's the one that wanted it. She asked me to come in here!" He accepted the cloth that someone held out for him and placed it on his nose.

I looked down at the bed, but she wasn't there. "Chloe," I breathed out.

"Dude, that girl left." I wasn't there long enough to find out who'd said it.

I was out of that house faster than I thought possible.

A surge of relief washed over me when I saw her. She was folded over, with her head in the bushes at the end of the driveway, puking. I stood behind her, holding her hair out of her way.

"It's okay, Chloe," I said, rubbing slow circles on her back.

She threw up three more times.

By the time she was done, she was weak and struggling to stay upright. When she finally straightened up—wiping her mouth and lifting her eyes as she did—the expression on her face turned my insides to stone. "What the fuck are you doing, Blake?"

"Wh—?"

"You have no right to get in my shit like that. You have no right to burst into rooms, acting like a fucking superhero!"

"Chloe, you need to calm down. You're beyond wasted, and you're talking shit."

I grabbed her arm so I could give her a hug and try to soothe her. She let me.

And then she cried into my chest. "I'm sorry," she sobbed.

I started walking us to my car. "I know, Chloe. It's okay."

She apologized four more times on the way to the car and then twice more once we were inside. By the time we got to Josh's apartment, she'd passed out.

"What the hell happened?" Josh asked, wiping the sleep from his eyes.

"She's wasted."

His eyes rolled so high, I almost wanted to punch him, too. "Okay, Captain Obvious."

"What the fuck do you want me to say?"

"I don't know, how about . . . how the fuck did she get like that in the first place?" He paused a second and narrowed his eyes at me. "Did you *help* her get like this?"

"No! She was like that when I found her."

He sighed, and opened the door wider for us. "Put her in my bed. I'll take the couch."

CHAPTER EIGHTEEN

Chloe

A doorknob turned. Footsteps. My eyes snapped open. I was a little groggy, but apart from that, I was fine. No pounding head, no need to puke. "Hey." Josh was next to the bed, looking down at me with a huge grin on his face. "Morning, Chucky."

"Chucky?" I took the glass of water and aspirins from his hands and downed them both.

"Yeah. You know . . . because of all the times you chucked last night."

"Oh." Heat crept into my cheeks. "I'm sorry."

He shrugged. "All good. Made me feel like a kid again. Come out when you're ready. I have someone I want you to meet." He started to walk out of his room. "I set some clothes at the end of the bed. I didn't think it was appropriate for me to strip you down and change you last night."

"Fair point."

"Yeah. And Hunter would probably kick my ass," he said, before closing the door behind him.

*   *   *

After showering and putting on the sweats and shirt Josh had set out, I made my way to the living room. Tommy was on the floor, playing with blocks, while Josh was in the kitchen. Blake was nowhere to be seen.

"So you must be the famous Tommy I've heard all about." I got down on my knees and watched as he stacked one block on top of the other. "Josh, how old is Tommy?"

He came out of the kitchen with two coffees in hand. I'd never been so happy to see coffee in my life. "Nine months and three days, why?"

I stood up and accepted the coffee but kept my eyes on Tommy. "How long has he been sitting up for?"

"Twenty-six days," he said proudly, motioning with his head to the sofa. He waited for me to seat myself before taking the spot next to me. "Why?"

"Dude. Your kid's a genius. Stacking normally comes at around fifteen months."

"Yeah?"

I nodded.

"Huh." He looked down at Tommy, but his smile faded. "Who would've thought two high school dropouts could produce something like that?" There was sadness in his voice, completely separate from the boy in the bowling alley or the boy that talked shit and got high.

"Josh?"

His gaze slowly moved from Tommy to me.

"You know what you're doing is beyond extraordinary, right? You're a great dad—and an amazing person. You gave up your chance at being an irresponsible kid and took all of this on . . . and you did it on your own."

"He's my son." He shrugged. "There was no question. It wasn't like I had a choice."

"You're wrong."

His eyes narrowed.

"There were a lot of choices, Josh. You could've given him up for adoption. You could've handed him over to his grandparents. You could've not had him at all. You could have just walked away. But you did none of those things. You went from being a kid to a man overnight. No one forced you to do it. You chose to. And I see how proud you are of him, and he's going to know that. When he's older, he's going to see that."

His eyes glazed over as they went back to watching Tommy.

"He's going to grow up knowing that. And when he's old enough to understand—when he knows about your struggles and everything that you gave up for him—he'll be proud of you, too. And you should be—you should be proud of yourself."

He sniffed once, his eyes still trained on Tommy. I knew he was trying to hold back, but it was clear he needed to hear these words, because maybe no one had ever told him before. Maybe he had never realized the impact he had on other people, not just me. And not just by his actions but also by the type of person he was. "You made that choice, Josh. Whether you realize it or not. You chose to stand up—to be the strength that you and Tommy need. And Tommy's mom . . . She's going to regret it—"

He sniffed again and wiped his eyes on his forearm.

"She's going to regret missing out on this. Not just Tommy. But you, too. I'm sure she already does."

He cleared his throat with a grunt and used his palms to rub his eyes. He inhaled a few calming breaths before turning his gaze back on me. "And what about you?" he asked.

I looked back to Tommy, his little eyes so concentrated on the blocks in front of him. "What about me?"

"I think you should give Blake a chance. He cares about you."

My gaze dropped to floor.

"He shouldn't," I whispered.

"Chloe," he said quietly, tapping on my arm. I refused to look up. "If you don't care about him like that, then you need to tell him. It'll *ruin* him, but you need to be honest with him."

At his words, a piece of me shattered. All my self-control, the walls I had built, all of it—broken. I felt the tears prick behind my eyes, but I held them back and faced him.

Truth time.

"It'll be nothing like the hurt I cause him if I let him in, Josh."

He cleared his throat. "I'm sorry," he said, "but I don't understand what you're saying."

So I told him.

I told him about the cancer. My mom and my aunt. I told him about foster care and Clayton. I told him about the chances. I told him everything. He listened to every word, without interrupting me.

"I'm scared," I continued. "I'm scared that if I let anyone in and I die . . . I'm gonna hurt them when I leave them behind. And I don't want to cause that type of pain for anyone. My foster parents, and brothers and sister, and Blake . . . especially Blake . . . because I think I care about him the most."

He nodded slowly. "So you just take off? Not form friendships? Relationships?"

"Yes."

His eyes narrowed as he searched my face. "I get that, Chloe. I really do." He cleared his throat. "It's not the same. But I feel like that sometimes. I mean, having Tommy, that's a lifelong commitment. If I ever want a relationship, I have to make the right choices, not just for me but for him, too. If I ever do end up meeting someone, they need to know that Tommy will always come first. Forever." He paused and stared off into the distance. "But you and Blake are completely different."

"What do you mean?"

"I mean, you as a kid, you lost your mom and your aunt, and I'm sorry for that, but you had no choice. They were your family, and you were a kid. Blake—he's old enough to make his own decisions. If he wants to spend time with you—that's his choice. But you have to let him make it."

The front door swung open, and Blake stood motionless, box of diapers in one hand and formula in the other. "Hey," he said, his gaze moving between Josh and me, before finally settling on me. "Are you ready to go home?"

I nodded.

Blake

"Are you okay?" I asked her once we were in the car.

"Yeah," she said through a sigh. "I'm just a little embarrassed."

"Why?"

"Just the way I was last night, and the way you saw me, and the way I acted."

"It's okay. I get it," I told her. "Listen, I know that you have a shitload to deal with. More than any eighteen-year-old should ever have to. And tell me to fuck off if I'm overstepping, but next time you feel like you need to lose yourself—going out, getting beyond wasted . . . screwing around with guys—I dunno." I shook my head slowly. "I just worry that it's dangerous. I know that you don't want people close, but that's happened. People care. People worry. It's not just you that behavior affects. If you feel like that again, you can come to me or Josh. We'll always be here, but if you wait until it's too late, like it was last—"

"Okay," she interrupted. "I get it, Blake. I promise."

When I pulled into the driveway, Sammy and Amy were there playing skateball. Even after last night's events, I found myself smiling.

Sammy ran to the car. "Blake's here!" he screamed.

I wound down my window and returned his fist bump. "Hey, bud. Who's winning?"

"Amy." He rolled his eyes. "But I think she's cheating because she can count to eleventy-three. I can only count to twelve." Then his eyes went huge. "Wait here," he said excitedly. "Don't go anywhere okay? Just wait right here."

"Okay."

"Promise? Say you promise," he said, a seriousness consuming his little four-year-old face.

"I promise, bud. I'm not going anywhere."

He grinned and ran up the porch steps. "Amy! Let's show Blake what we got."

I turned to Chloe. "What's up with Sammy? He got a little intense there for a second."

"Yeah. He has a fear of people leaving him. His parents left him at a movie theater. They said they were going to get popcorn and never came back."

"Who the fuck—?"

"I know. The world is full of fucked-up people, Blake. But you can't let it change your perspective on life."

Sammy and Amy came barreling down the steps, wearing matching basketball jerseys.

"Is that our school jersey?" Chloe asked.

"I still don't understand how you don't know these things."

"Look!" Sammy yelled, stopping in front of the car. He waited for Amy to stand next to him. "Ready?" he asked me.

"Go for it!"

Sammy grinned from ear to ear. "One. Two. Six."

Then they both spun around to show me the back of their jerseys.

Hunter 23.

"Holy shit."

Chloe smiled and squeezed my hand. "Maybe you should remember this next time you think that shooting a ball through a hoop doesn't serve a purpose."

CHAPTER NINETEEN

Blake

Josh told me that Chloe was taking a personal day off work, so when she walked up to the snack bar, I was surprised. "What are you doing here?"

"Good to see you, too."

I laughed. "I just thought something might be wrong, that's all."

She shook her head, and leaned on the counter. "Actually, I came to ask you for something."

"Anything."

"Clayton's funeral is tomorrow." She smiled sadly. "It's a closed ceremony. Just the family and Lisa and her parents."

"Okay?"

"You can say no . . ."

"You want me to watch the kids or something? Whatever it is, I'm there."

She shook her head. "I was actually wondering if you'd come with me. It would mean a lot if you were there," she mumbled quickly, "and I know you didn't really know Clayton, but you would've liked each other. But I'm not asking you for him. I'm asking you for me, because it'd be nice to have you there. It's during school, and it's not fair for me to ask you to skip, but the kids and me, all of us, *we*—"

"Chloe. Of course I'll go. You didn't even have to ask."

She smiled. A real smile. One that I hadn't seen in days. "Thank you, Mr. Blake Hunter. Number twenty-three. Starting shooting guard. Made varsity freshman year. MVP last three. Leading scorer in two divisions. All-frickin'-American."

I couldn't help but grin. "You researched me?"

"Yup," she said proudly. "So two thirty?"

"I'll be there."

Then she turned and walked away, nudging shoulders with Josh as she did.

"You staring at her like that doesn't make her yours."

"Shut up, asshole."

Chloe

"Are you going to stay for dinner?" Mary asked Blake, while he held his car door open for me after the services.

"Yes," Sammy answered for him.

Mary laughed. "That's settled then."

She started to walk away. "Actually," Blake's word rushed out. She stopped and waited for him to continue. "I was wondering if I could take Chloe somewhere for a few hours . . . if that's okay?" He looked nervous.

"You can ask her yourself."

"Oh yeah," he said, a blush creeping to his checks as he turned to me. "Is it okay . . . ? I mean . . . would you like to go somewhere with me for a little bit?"

I nodded.

"Okay then, let's go."

*   *   *

"Are you okay?" I asked him.

He glanced quickly over at me. "Yes. Why?"

"You just seem nervous."

He didn't respond.

I took that as my cue to keep quiet.

We drove about twenty minutes out of town. "Where are we going, Blake?"

"We're nearly there."

That didn't answer my question, but I let it go.

He pulled over on the side of the road in what seemed like the middle of nowhere, unclipped his seat belt, and turned to me. "I'm not going to kill you," he said through a smile. "I know your whole jogger theory, but I swear I won't hurt you." He trained his gaze on me, then he reached up, laced his fingers in my hair, and held the side of my head. He leaned in slowly, and my eyes drifted shut. I licked my lips, anticipating the contact of his lips against them.

But they never came.

I opened one eye first, then the other.

He was staring at me, his eyes dark and intense. Then he leaned in, placing a soft kiss on my lips. "Ready?"

*   *   *

We walked on a hidden path in the woods for five minutes before he took my hand and stopped. "I'm going to have to blindfold you now."

"You're actually going to kill me, aren't you?"

"Yes," he said, feigning disappointment. "You ruined the surprise with your smart-ass comments."

I laughed, but then he pulled out a blindfold. "You were serious?"

"Trust me. It'll be so much better this way."

I closed my eyes, an invitation for him to go ahead.

He led me, my eyes covered, one of his hands holding mine with the other on the small of my back, for another two minutes. "Okay," he said. "Ready?"

I nodded.

I felt his breath against my forehead as he removed the blindfold. When my eyes adjusted to the light, all I could see was him in front of me. "My surprise is you?"

He smiled huge and stepped aside.

Then I saw it.

And a million emotions went through me.

I laughed.

I cried.

I hurt.

I healed.

"Blake . . ." Because it was all I could say.

I dropped to my knees.

"This is it, right?"

I bit my lip to stop the sob escaping. But the tears—I let them flow freely. I couldn't speak, but it didn't matter. There were no words for what he'd just done.

"The picture of your mom and aunt, this is it?" he asked, squatting down to my level.

I nodded. I didn't think—I just threw my arms around his neck and pulled him into me. He lost his balance but steadied himself with one hand on the ground.

"Blake," I cried, and then pulled away. I placed his hand against my heart so he could feel the impact this had had on me. *"You brought her back to me."*

* * *

I wasn't sure how long we spent there, on the lake, while he held me and I cried. He didn't console me or tell me things were going to be okay. He didn't shush me or ask me to talk it out. He was just there in that moment with me. It was perfect. *He* was perfect.

*   *   *

"How did you find it, Blake?"

He glanced at me, one hand on the steering wheel while he drove me home.

I added, "I've been trying to find it for years. Ever since Clayton—" A lump immediately formed in my throat at the mention of his name. "Ever since Clayton was old enough to drive, we spent days looking for it. You've known about it for a week. One week, and you found it. You found it for *me*."

"I just looked—every day—and most nights." He shrugged. "I skipped school yesterday afternoon and went home to get the maps I'd collected. Mom was home. She saw me leaving the house and asked what I was doing. So I told her." He glanced at me again with a slight frown. "I hope that's okay?"

I nodded and gestured for him to continue.

"She knew what I was talking about right away. She said that your mom and your aunt—they were sorority sisters?"

"So she's been there?"

"Yeah, she said that it was their spot."

I sank deeper into my seat. "I need to thank your mom."

"No." He shook his head. "We actually need to thank you, Chloe, for bringing us back to each other. Somehow, somewhere along the way, my mom and I lost each other. But you—you brought us back, and we're thankful for that. We're thankful for *you*."

*   *   *

160

It was dark by the time we got home, but the lights were still on. He didn't make a move to turn the engine off when he pulled into the driveway. "My mom wanted to give you this," he said. "She told me to give it to you when you were alone."

I took the envelope from his hand and ran my fingers across my name, scribbled across the front in red ink. "What is it?"

"Just something from her and something from me."

I started to open it, but his hands covered mine, stopping me. "Wait until you're alone," he said. He'd leaned in closer; the heat of his breath brushed against my cheek.

"Okay," I whispered.

*   *   *

Pictures.

So many pictures.

Of my mom. Of my aunt. All through college. Some of Blake's mom with them, but mainly just of them together. Laughing and smiling. It was as if they had given me a time machine, and through these pictures, I was able to see into their lives. Into their emotions and into their happiness.

Tears fell, and they didn't stop. Not even when I got to the last piece of paper. It wasn't a picture, though. It was a letter.

My fingers shook as I unfolded it.

Once.

Twice.

Red ink.

Dear Not Abby,

It's strange, right? A handwritten letter . . . Mom says they're more personal. And you deserve that—something personal.

I don't know if you have ever gotten a personal letter. I want to be your first. I want to be a lot of things for you. But I don't know how to do that.

I wish I knew how to do that.

But I wish even more that you'd show me.

Nine weeks until graduation.

I'm already missing you.

My beautiful, beautiful girl.

CHAPTER TWENTY

Blake

"You look like ass," Trent—the team's center and all-around dumbass—said, leaning on the locker next to mine. "Have you even been sleeping? You haven't been at school much. Is it because of Will? Everyone said that you broke Will's nose. He's been nursing it like a little bitch. Is that why you haven't been at school? Because you're avoiding him? He's probably going to be in the cafeteria now. I don't know if you want . . ."

He kept talking, but I ignored him, too busy looking over his shoulder at the blonde girl slowly making her way toward me. She looked up from the floor and caught me watching, a hint of a smile on her face. I thought she'd look away, turn away, but she didn't. She just continued walking closer, and closer, until she was next to me.

"Hi," she said, awkwardly fiddling with the strap of her bag.

"Hi."

"Hi." I think Trent threw his hand out, but I couldn't be sure; I was too busy locking eyes with Chloe. "I'm Trent," he said.

"Hi, Trent," she replied, but she didn't break our stare.

"O . . . kay . . ." He backed away slowly, leaving us alone. Alone—in our own little world—where it was just she and I and nothing else mattered.

"Hi," I said again.

Her smile widened.

"You're talking to me at school?"

She nodded. "Do you have plans for lunch?"

I slammed my locker shut and answered, "Yes."

"Oh." She finally broke our stare and dropped her gaze.

I threw my arm around her shoulders, leading her away from the lockers and down the hallway. "With you, you silly fire-truck head."

She stopped in her tracks. "Did you just call me a silly fuckhead?"

I laughed. "I guess I did."

"Fire truck you," she said as I opened the door that led to the school parking lot.

"Where to?"

"I'll drive."

*   *   *

If she saw the kids at school gawking at us, she didn't mention it. She drove with the top down, sunglasses on, and a smile on her face. She pulled into the abandoned basketball court that we'd gone to the night she'd ended up at the police station.

Her hand brake squealed when she pulled at it. Grimacing, she noted, "I need to get that checked before I leave."

My heart clenched. Sometimes, I forgot that she was leaving. So I told her that.

"I actually wanted to talk to you about The Road," she said.

"About the fact that you're *not* going to leave?" I knew I was grasping at straws.

"No. About what we—you and I—do in the meantime. While I'm here."

"Okay?"

"I have a proposition."

My eyes lit up, and a smirk took over. "I like the sound of that."

Her brows drew in. "Are you being a pig?"

"Yes."

She sighed and rolled her eyes dramatically. This was the best version of her. The version that acted her age and wasn't carrying the weight of her future around. Then she looked at me and turned serious. "We only have nine weeks, Blake."

"I know this," I said, my tone matching hers.

"So will you be my *friend*? For nine weeks? And after that, I'm gone. I'm leaving, and I don't want you to think you might change that, because you won't."

Friends.

Nine weeks.

Her words replayed in my head. Nine weeks wasn't long enough. Surely, even if she was gone, we could still talk. Phone, emails, letters. "But—"

"Nine weeks, Blake." Her gaze dropped. "That's all I can offer you."

"I'll take it. I'll take anything you give me."

Then she leaned in and pressed her lips to mine. She kissed me once. Softly. But it was enough to cause my heart to beat faster. She started to pull back. I panicked and lifted my hand to her head to keep her there. She smiled against my lips, but I refused to open my eyes. I refused to let go of this moment. "Are we friends that kiss?"

She giggled, her mouth still on mine.

I took her bottom lip and sucked lightly. "So what is this, then?"

"A thank-you for your letter."

I opened my mouth wider, trying to deepen the kiss. "I'll write you a thousand fucking letters."

She chuckled into my mouth, but my tongue sweeping against her lip made her instantly stop. "You don't need to write more," she whispered, and then pulled away.

I allowed it this time.

She sat back in her seat and looked through the windshield. "That one letter said enough."

I sat back, too . . . and tried to hide my hard-on.

Seconds of silence passed.

"I've never made a shot from the three-score line."

"The what?" I laughed.

She turned to me with a confused look on her face. "The three-score line. You know . . ." She motioned to the faded lines on the half-court. "That semicircle line. I brought a ball from home so you could teach me." She reached in the backseat and produced a basketball. "Teach me?" She pouted.

Christ, she was beautiful.

Beyond beautiful.

I stared at her for a moment, taking in every single detail of her face. Then I let my body relax and my mind wrap around the idea that I had her for nine weeks. *Nine amazing weeks of Chloe.*

"Shit," I joked as I took the ball from her hands and got out of the car. "I can't believe I have to put up with you for another nine weeks. This is gonna be hell."

"Fire truck off."

Chloe

Even though I'd told Blake that he didn't need to write any more letters, every morning I'd open my locker, and there'd be a note. White paper. Red ink. Always red ink. Some were funny. Some were sweet. Some were a little dirty. I kept them all, locked away in a box that I'd be sure to take with me when I left. They were *mine*. Forever.

CHAPTER TWENTY-ONE

Chloe

Ever since the day I'd taken him to the half-court and told him that we could be friends until graduation, we'd spent basically every second together. He picked me up for school, and we went to work together or just hung out afterwards.

As graduation had gotten closer, so had he. He was touching, feeling, holding all the time. Even at work. I'd told him that he shouldn't—that *we* shouldn't—but he'd said that it was his choice. His burden to bear when the day arrived and I'd be gone.

"I have absolutely nothing to offer you," he said, his head in his fridge. "I have beer, pastrami, and cheese." He closed the refrigerator door and turned to me. "And water. I have water."

I laughed and jumped off the kitchen counter. "I guess I'll take the water."

"Good choice." He opened a cabinet and pulled out a glass, then proceeded to fill it with tap water. Then he did the same for himself.

His eyes locked with mine as I drank the entire contents of the glass, trying to relieve the dryness in my mouth, which occurred whenever he looked at me the way he was.

When I was done, he took the glass from my hand and placed it in the dishwasher, then picked up his gym bag from the floor and walked to the laundry room. I followed and watched as he emptied the bag and loaded the washing machine, switching it on before turning to me.

"You're so domesticated," I joked.

He laughed. "Yeah, I had to learn the hard way. Turns out kids don't want to hang out with you when you wear the same clothes three days in a row because your parents forget to do your laundry."

I pouted. "Well, at least you'll make some woman very happy one day."

He sighed and dropped his gaze. Then he reached over my shoulder and closed the laundry-room door behind me. Both his hands were on my hips, gently pushing me until my back hit the door. "Chloe," he said, his mouth descending and making contact with my bare shoulder. "I could make you a very happy woman right now." He pulled back, raising his gaze to mine. He chewed his lip, waiting for me to speak, but I couldn't.

He smiled slowly, before moving in and kissing me. The touching, the hand holding . . . they were all constant, but the kisses weren't. He lifted me off the ground until my legs were around him. My hands gripped his hair as he kissed me harder, lifting me and moving us until I was sitting on the washing machine. He began to kiss along my jaw and down my neck. He grabbed my ass and pulled me closer to him, so I could feel him between my legs. Then his hands moved higher, under my shirt and onto my waist. His lips moved back up until they were on my mouth again. Kissing me softly, slowly. He pulled back quickly, searching my face. "Chloe?" It came out as a question, and I knew what he wanted.

"No, Blake," I told him.

It was the first time he'd brought it up but definitely not the first time I'd thought about it. Sex with Blake wouldn't just be sex, no matter how much we'd try to convince ourselves otherwise. Sex, Blake, the experience, the emotion . . . I knew without a doubt that it would be the one thing that could make me stay. And I didn't want to do that to either of us.

"I know." He frowned before pulling away, holding my hand, and helping me to hop down.

He swiftly exited the laundry room mumbling something about needing to shoot hoops to get his mind off it.

Blake

"Chloe. I don't wanna sound mean or anything . . ." I watched as she used both hands to bounce the basketball in my driveway. "But I've been trying to teach you how to dribble for weeks now, and you're just like . . . beyond uncoordinated. I feel like I've failed at life."

She laughed. "Shut up!" She bounced the ball twice; the second time it hit her foot. She yelped as the ball rolled away toward the guesthouse. Mom opened the door just as it stopped at her feet.

She waved. "Hi, Blake."

"Hey, Ma." I nodded toward the ball and clapped my hands, a signal for her to throw it back.

"Oh," she said, surprised, then bent over and picked it up. She looked at it a moment, her eyebrows furrowed in confusion.

"Just pass it," I shouted.

"Okay, Blake. Calm down."

She lifted the ball in her hand and slowly moved it over her shoulder. It looked as though she was about to throw it, but she changed her mind last minute. Instead she placed both hands on either side of it and lifted it over her head.

I stood with my fists at my waist. I tilted my head, wondering what the hell she was doing.

But suddenly she dropped it—right onto her head. She squealed and ducked as it fell away from her.

I laughed. "You and Chloe should start a team. Call it Team T.U.L—The Uncoordinated Losers!"

"Hey!" Chloe shouted from behind me. "We could totally take you. Both of us against you? No competition!"

"Yeah?" I asked, watching her walk over to me. "I'd like to see you try."

She stopped in front of me, her arms crossed and her eyes narrowed. Then she smiled, an all-consuming smile. "Mrs. Hunter," she yelled over her shoulder. "Blake just challenged us to a game." She looked over at my mom. "Get your sneakers on and come play!"

*　　*　　*

A minute later, Mom joined Chloe and me in the driveway.

They stood next to each other, their arms at their sides, looking ridiculous. "Do you need me to remind you of the rules?"

Chloe rolled her eyes.

Mom shrugged. "Maybe."

I held the ball to my side. "Rule one: Travel—"

Chloe stepped forward and pushed my arm, releasing the ball from my grip. She squealed when she got hold of it.

I laughed. "Maybe I should have started with fouls."

She awkwardly dribbled in her spot a few times but stopped when I towered over her. "Your move, Chloe."

She squealed again and threw the ball in the air, aiming for absolutely nowhere.

"Got it," I heard Mom shout.

I turned around to see her chasing the ball. Once it was in her hands, she tried to dribble and move at the same time, but it was too much for her.

"Pass it," Chloe said, now standing under the ring.

I just stood there, watching them, I guess, *attempting* to play.

Mom didn't pass. Instead, she just walked the ball over to Chloe, who then tried to shoot.

Nothing but air.

"You guys are the worst," I laughed. "I've never seen anyone so awkward!"

Mom stopped and started to laugh. "You think this is awkward? You should see me dance. I'm like Taylor Swift, all over the place."

Chloe screamed with laughter.

We played for a good half hour. Well . . . I played; they just stood around shouting and calling me names.

"Time out," Mom called, her hands resting on her knees and her body bent over, as if she was trying to catch her breath. I don't know why—she hadn't even been running.

"You got one minute. Max." I set the timer on my watch and eyed Chloe as she made her way over to Mom. When she was close enough, Mom covered her mouth, I assumed to whisper something to her. As I got my water bottle from the side of the driveway, I pushed down the thoughts of how good a time I was having and how nice it felt to watch Chloe and my mom together. Laughing, joking around, getting along. When the timer went off and I looked back at them, Mom was looking down Chloe's shirt. "What the hell!" I shouted.

Chloe laughed.

"Time's up!"

"Settle down, Blake," Mom yelled, then whispered something else to Chloe. Chloe shook her head, her smile wide. Mom rested her hands on her hips. "Come on, Chloe. It's our only hope."

Chloe lifted her gaze and locked it with mine. She shook her head again and groaned, "Fine." Then she took off her shirt.

My jaw dropped.

My hands had touched her bare skin, the curve of her hips, and her tiny waist, but I'd seen her body only once, when she was in a bikini, and that had been for only a minute. But that was nothing compared to seeing her like this. Up close. So close her sports bra–covered breasts were just under my nose.

"Blake?" she whispered.

I struggled to take my eyes off her chest, but I finally made it to her face. She had her hair tied up in a messy knot on top of her head, like she often did. But a few strands were stuck on her neck and on her face . . . and a little sheen of sweat covered her arms and her stomach, her chest, her breasts . . .

"Blake," she repeated, and I trailed my eyes back to hers again. She pouted before she said, "Give me the ball?"

I shook my head and hid the ball behind my back.

She pouted again. "Please?" she whispered. Then a hint of a smile broke through.

"Are you trying to seduce me into giving you my ball?"

She snorted with laughter.

Then I felt the ball being smacked out of my hands from behind. "Yes!" Mom shouted.

I laughed and watched as she bounced it once, then took five tiny steps toward the hoop. "That's travelling!" I shouted.

Chloe ran toward her. "I'm open!" she yelled dramatically. Of course she was open. There was no one there. Mom ran the ball over and handed it to her.

Chloe stopped in her spot and dribbled it twice. I strolled slowly over to her. She stopped bouncing the ball when she saw me coming. I stopped a few feet in front of her. She squealed and ran away, trying to dribble at the same time. "That's travelling and double dribble. Do you need me to go through the rules again?"

She just laughed and tried to shoot. She missed. Completely.

I started to jog over to the ball, but Mom shouted my name. "If you touch that ball, you're grounded."

I threw my hands in the air. "What the hell? Who's setting these rules?"

I ignored her and picked up the ball, but before I could straighten up, Chloe's arms were around my neck and her legs around my waist. "And this is definitely a foul!" I successfully completed a layup with her on my back.

"You're cheating!" she shouted.

Mom walked over and handed Chloe the ball.

"If we get this, Mrs. Hunter," Chloe yelled, "then we win."

"How do you win?" I said, adjusting her more comfortably on my back. "It's sixty-eight to nothing."

"Shut up, Blake."

I laughed.

"I wanna slam it!"

I laughed harder. "Slam-dunk it?"

"Whatever!"

I walked us to the hoop and adjusted the lever until the post dropped and the hoop was as low as it could possibly go.

I *guess* you could say that she dunked it. Whatever it was, it made her and Mom squeal. "WE WIN!" Chloe shouted.

"No, you've scored once."

"Shut up, Blake!" She gripped her legs tighter around my waist and fistpumped the air. "*We are the champions . . .*"

I shook my head and laughed again.

"Do you hear that, Blake?" she said in my ear. "That's the crowd cheering my name."

Mom cupped her hands around her mouth. "CHLO-E! CHLO-E! CHLO-E!"

"It's sixty-eight—" I started.

174

"What part of WE WIN do you not understand?" Chloe cut in. "I can't believe I won the Super Bowl!"

I lost it in a fit of laughter, almost dropping her.

"I need a victory lap!" she squealed.

I gave her a victory lap around the driveway. She kept her hands raised in triumph as she made a speech thanking everyone but me for training her. Mom kept on chanting her name.

On the second lap, I froze.

So did Chloe.

So did Mom.

"Hunter," Dad said, nodding his head. He narrowed his eyes at Chloe.

I carefully released her until her feet were on the ground, but she didn't step out from behind me. "Colonel," I replied.

His eyes moved to Mom. "Celia. Nice to see you upright and coherent."

She didn't respond.

"Who's your friend, Hunter?"

I didn't answer him. But Chloe stepped to my side, her voice mousy when she said, "I'm Chloe Thompson, sir—Colonel—sir. It's nice to meet you."

"Right." He nodded. "You might want to put a shirt on, young lady. My house isn't a strip club."

I wanted to punch him, but Chloe held me back.

And with that, he turned and walked away.

"Asshole," Mom said. "I'm sorry, Chloe. Don't pay him any attention. He's a miserable old bastard."

I turned to Chloe, but she was looking at the ground. "Hey . . ." I drew her into me and hugged her.

"Can you please take me home," she said into my chest.

I rested my cheek on the top of her head. "You don't have to go."

"I know, but I should."

I looked at my mom. She was watching us with a frown on her face. I held more tightly on to Chloe. Mom mouthed, "I'm sorry." And I knew she wasn't just talking about Dad, she was talking about Chloe and how much she obviously meant to me. And she was sorry that soon it would all be over.

Chloe pulled out of my hold and made her way over to her shirt, silently shrugging it on before going to Mom and hugging her good-bye. Then she walked to my car and waited for me to catch up.

"You want to go somewhere and hang out?" I asked her as we pulled out of the driveway.

"No. I just want to go home," she said, looking down at her lap.

"Sure?"

"Yeah, Blake, I'm sure."

*   *   *

After dropping Chloe off, I didn't really feel like being in the house with my asshole dad, so I went out to the guesthouse.

"How long?" Mom asked, handing me a drink and sitting on the couch opposite me.

"Four weeks."

She frowned. "I'm sorry, Blake."

"I don't know what to do, Ma. I'm just not ready to let her go."

Mom sighed. "Just ask yourself this: If you could describe your days with Chloe as black or red, what would it be?"

I smiled, remembering how she used to tell me about red- and black-letter days. Black-letter days had negative impact. Like when you got news of someone's death. A red-letter day was the opposite of black. A positive experience or something *unexpectedly phenomenal.*

"Red," I told her. "Definitely red."

CHAPTER TWENTY-TWO

Chloe

"How did it go?"

Dean grinned. "Great." He ruffled Harry's hair. "It's official. Harry's ours. He's stuck with us for life now."

Harry contained his smile and tried to move away from Dean.

"That's awesome, Harry."

"Yeah." He shrugged. "I guess."

"So. I was wondering if you still had that big gear bag from when you did karate last year?"

His face fell instantly. "Yeah, why?"

"I don't have a bag big enough for when I leave. I was wondering if I could have it?"

"It's in my room," he bit out. "I'll go get it."

And then he left the kitchen, thumping loudly up each step to get to his room.

"What's with him?" I asked Dean, just as the sound of a door slamming shut echoed through the house.

"I think you should talk to him, Chloe. I think there's a lot he's not telling you."

*   *   *

I knocked twice on Harry's door before entering. A single step in, and a bag was hurled at my head. I ducked right in time to avoid being hit. "Whoa. What's going on with you?"

"Nothing." His nostrils flared, and a snarl appeared. "Just take the bag *and fuck off* already."

My eyebrows pinched as I took in his state. He stood at the foot of his bed, with his hands fisted at his sides. "Dude, what the hell?" I stepped farther into his room. I wasn't going to let up until I knew what was going on.

"Seriously, I don't even care about you right now. You're leaving in a week, and you've barely been around. You're always out with that Blake jerk, or he's always here. He's not even part of the family. You know that, right? *We* are. We're your family." His voice broke, but he kept going, his tone getting harsher with every single word. "Do you even think about me? I've been here for years. You're *my sister*. Not his."

Before I could speak, Harry added, "You know what? I know about you—and about your mom's cancer, and your aunt, too. I know that Mary and Dean asked to adopt you, and you told them no. And I don't get it. Mary and Dean—they love you." He paused for a beat. "*I* love you, Chloe, and you don't even care."

I blew out a breath and took a seat on his bed, physically weakened by the impact of his words.

"Don't!" he yelled, pulling me off his bed. "Don't even think about getting comfortable in here. I don't want you here. Just like you don't want me. One week, Chloe. One week, and you're gone." His hands were firm against my back as he pushed me through his door and out of his room.

I turned to him just as his hand curled around the edge of the door.

His face was red, fueled by his pent-up rage. "So just do it, Chloe!" He was screaming now. "Just do what you've always wanted to do and fuck off! And don't ever come back!"

I opened my mouth to speak, but my throat closed up. My face was wet from the tears I hadn't known were there.

"Harry," I whispered.

But he didn't hear me. He was too busy slamming the door in my face.

I'd been so closed off, so blinded by the walls I'd built that I hadn't even realized how Harry felt. He'd called me his sister. He'd told me that he loved me.

And all it had done was give me more reason to leave.

"I'm sorry," Dean said from the bottom of the stairs. He didn't offer any more condolences. He just walked away. And I knew why—because he agreed with Harry.

*   *   *

"I've been so selfish," I told Blake. We were in my car, with the top down and the seats reclined, looking up at the clear night sky. It had taken only eight weeks, but I finally had scored from the three-point line. He'd celebrated as if he'd just won a state championship. But his celebration had died quickly when I'd told him that I needed to cut back on spending time with him so I could be home more.

"What do you mean, you've been selfish?"

"Harry hates me."

"What?" he laughed.

"I'm serious, Blake."

He must've known it, too, because he sat up, pulling the seat with him, and turned to me. "What are you talking about?"

"He hates me," I repeated, my words strained as I held in my sob.

"What? Why?"

"Because I'm leaving."

He sighed heavily. "Then he has a point."

"Blake." I glanced up at him, but the sadness on his face was too heartbreaking, and I had to look away. "You're not helping."

"I don't know what you want me to say, Chloe. That I think it's great that you're leaving in a week?" He reclined his seat back down and continued to stare up at the sky. "I'm not going to lie to you. And you shouldn't lie to yourself, either. You had to have known there'd be this kind of reaction."

"You don't understand, Blake. He was yelling at me. He told me to fuck off and to never come back!"

"Quit sulking," he said. "I'm sorry that he spoke to you like that, and that your feelings were hurt. But I'm not sorry he said it. Maybe you need to know that what you're doing—The Road—it's not just your journey to take. Your plans affect everyone. And I know that you did your best to keep people from caring about you—or whatever—but you're pretty hard not to care for. You're pretty hard not to *love*." He paused and cleared his throat. "*Really* hard not to love."

My eyes drifted shut. I tried to settle the thumping of my heart before I spoke. "Lucky you don't love me."

He didn't say anything, just reached over, took my hand, squeezed once, and never let go.

Blake

I had barely stepped foot in the house before Dad's voice filled my ears. "You have a meeting with the recruiter at Fort Bragg after school tomorrow."

I squared my shoulders and raised a hand to my head, saluting him. "Sir. Yes, sir!"

He looked up from his position on the couch in the living room. His hands tightened around the glass of what was, no doubt, whiskey in his hand. "Don't bring that fucking smartass attitude with you tomorrow, Hunter. You're not playing a useless game on a basketball court. This is real life. This is your future."

*   *   *

Chloe had offered to come with me on the hour-and-a-half drive to the army base, but I'd told her not to. She'd just be sitting around doing nothing, and after what she'd told me yesterday about needing to spend time with her family, it would have been selfish of me to agree.

Officer Hayden, the recruiting commander, was in his late twenties. He'd done three tours in Iraq before deciding to stay home with his wife and kid and "settle" as a recruiter. He said that my dad and he had spent a good chunk of time on the phone while my dad basically ordered him to show and tell me exactly what he wanted me to hear. Hayden laughed about it, said that he encountered army dads on a daily basis but none as extreme as mine, which didn't surprise me at all.

He skipped the formalities of Dad's standards of the meeting, like showing me around post and introducing me to what career choices I would have if I chose to enlist. He said that after talking with my dad, he'd figured I'd heard and seen it all by now. Instead, he took me to his home on post and introduced me to his wife and his little girl. I didn't know why we'd ended up there, but I wasn't going to argue.

He set out two deck chairs in his front yard, facing both his house and the American flag that flew proudly in front of it.

"Why do you want to enlist?" he asked, his eyes never leaving the flag.

"I don't know."

"Well, that's a shit answer." He kicked his legs out in front of him, getting more comfortable. "Do you want to do it for you or your old man?"

"I don't know," I repeated. I was getting edgy because I hadn't expected questions. I had come there to keep Dad off my back and had expected a standard run-of-the-mill meeting. The same ones I had been through the past two years. No one had asked me any questions before.

Hayden sighed. "My old man, he works at a cardboard factory. Has ever since he was sixteen—same job his entire life. He's sixty-seven and every day he wakes up at four in the morning, drives to work, puts on his gloves, and does the same old thing . . . makes cardboard boxes."

"So?"

"So, that's his job, Hunter. Making boxes."

I rubbed my jaw, confused by why he was talking about his dad's work. "There's nothing wrong with making boxes, sir. It's an *honorable* job."

"You think so?" he asked, looking back at the flag.

"Yes. The world needs cardboard boxes. His job serves a purpose. There's *honor* in that."

A slight smile appeared on his face. "Is that what you want out of this? You want to serve a purpose?"

"I don't really—"

"My mom's never had a paid job. I have three brothers, seven nieces and nephews. My dad has always supported the family on his cardboard-box-factory wage." He paused for a beat. "I've only ever seen him cry once. You want to know when?"

"Sure."

"When I told him I was enlisting." He was silent a long moment before he cleared his throat and added, "I remember him getting off his chair and walking to me, then wrapping me in his arms. He said, 'I'm proud, son. You're doing something with your life,' and he used the same word you just used. He told me that what I was doing was honorable." He laughed once. "What he didn't know was that I was an eighteen-year-old-punk and wanted to enlist purely because I wanted to shoot shit."

I kept my mouth shut, not wanting to tell him that I thought he was stupid.

He laughed again, louder this time. "I know what you're thinking. That it's stupid . . . my reason for enlisting."

"A little, yeah."

"Obviously, my perspective has changed," he said quietly. "But that's the difference between you and I, Hunter. I enlisted for a stupid reason. You're considering enlisting because you want to serve a purpose. You probably think it's honorable, right?"

"I guess."

"But like you said, you could work in a cardboard factory, and you would serve a purpose. You would be doing something honorable."

My gaze dropped to my lap as I took in his words.

"Your dad," he continued, "he's kind of intense. The way he acted had me intrigued about you, so I looked you up. High school basketball star, right? Division I college prospect . . . set for the NBA?"

I exhaled a shaky breath and shut my eyes; the weight of his words coming down on me full force. "That's not relevant."

"No?" he asked, the surprise at my response evident in his tone.

I shook my head.

"Hunter," he sighed. "I'm not here to convince you to join the army, even though that's my job. The choice you make has to be yours. It's not something you want to regret ten, twenty, thirty years from now. I'm just going to say that the army, hell, the *United States of America*—we'd love to have someone like you on our side. We'd be *honored* to have you serve our country."

CHAPTER TWENTY-THREE

Chloe

"I have a confession." Josh stood in front of us and took a swig of his beer. "That day, when you came into work for the first time and that stuff happened with Tommy, I called Hunter the next day and told him that I thought you were hot and asked him if he thought I had a chance."

My jaw dropped. Blake's chuckle tickled my ear.

We were back at the abandoned basketball court, or half-court, as Blake had corrected me. He leaned against the back of a bench with me in front of him. His arms were wrapped tightly around my waist as he rubbed my stomach under my shirt with his thumb.

"What did he say?" I asked Josh.

"He basically pissed all over you and marked his territory."

I laughed.

"It's true," Blake murmured in my ear.

"I can't believe you're leaving." Josh removed his cap and dropped it to the ground. Then he ran his hand through his dark hair. "Everyone fucking leaves me. Natalie . . . my own goddamn parents. Everyone. The only one that hasn't is Hunter, and that's 'cause he pretty much hates the world."

Blake stood a little taller, gripped me a little tighter. "A, I don't hate the world. B, Natalie's a bitch." Josh flinched but remained silent. "C, your parents are assholes. And D, you're above all that shit."

Josh's eyes went wide before he shook his head and asked, "So have you decided yet? August 19, Duke orientation, right?"

Blake tensed for a moment before dropping his hands and letting me go. I took a step forward, unsure of what was coming.

"What about it?"

"I'm just saying . . . it's not that far away." His eyes moved to me. "Has he told you what he's doing?"

"No," I said quietly, looking at the ground.

"I haven't decided." Blake moved to the side and farther away. "I still don't know what the fuck I'm going to do." He sounded pissed. "Is that okay with you, Joshua? Do I need to check in?"

"What the fuck's got into you? I was just asking."

Blake stepped toward him. "You weren't just fucking asking. You were pushing."

I stayed put, too afraid to move or speak. They were face-to-face by then, glaring at each other. I had no idea what had set it off. Maybe it was the beer, or maybe it all just needed to be said.

Blake's hands fisted, and he added, "You don't think that decision weighs on me every day? I know time's running out. It's *my* goddamn choice, and I can't make it."

"Why?" Josh lifted his chin. "How hard could the choice be, Hunter? It's basketball, or it's the army. Two choices. It's not like you have a kid to think about. Or bills or rent to pay. Or someone else's future to worry about. There's not a single, fucking thing keeping you here."

Blake eyed me quickly before shoving Josh hard enough that he fell back a step. "Fuck you."

"No, Hunter, fuck you." He pushed him back. "You have months to make up your mind. In fact, when did you sign that letter of intent? November, right? It's fucking June. I'm too buzzed to work out how many months that is—but it's too fucking many. Quit being a pussy and decide."

"Fuck off, Josh. You don't know shit." He shoved him again. Harder this time.

And then Josh snapped. He launched himself at Blake, and they fell to the ground. Punches were thrown. Insults exchanged.

I panicked. "Get off him, Blake! You're being a dick."

They froze, simultaneously turning their heads to glare at me. Blake stood. Followed by Josh.

Blake slowly covered the distance between us, his eyes narrowing with every step. I swallowed and took a step back. For the first time since I'd met him, I was scared.

"You wanna take his side?" he said. "That's great, Chloe. Maybe you should have played this little game with him instead. Then he'd be the one having to deal with you leaving. Not me."

My heart sank.

"Dude." Josh stood next to him with a hand on his chest to stop him from moving closer. He was our barrier—something I never thought I'd need. Not against Blake.

I held back the tears threatening to fall. "I'm sorry," I squeaked out.

He shook his head. "You wanna know why I can't decide? Because I can't think of my future without you in it. *Four days.* We have four days together, and then, you're gone. And it might seem like nothing to you, because you've had years to accept it. But I can't, Chloe. I just can't."

Josh pressed his hands more firmly against Blake's chest. "I think that's enough."

Blake pushed Josh's hands away but kept his eyes on me. "Fuck this," he spat. Then he turned around and walked away.

"Blake." I started to go after him, but Josh stopped me.

"Just leave him. He just needs some time."

*　　*　　*

Blake came back ten minutes later. He walked to the cooler, got a few beers, handed one to Josh, who thanked him, and gave me one. Then he sat behind me, his legs on either side, and wrapped his arms around my stomach again. "I'm sorry," he whispered in my ear.

"Me, too," I told him.

Then Josh spoke up. "Remember that time when we came here, and I tried to grind along the bleachers?"

Blake laughed. "The first time we came here and smoked?"

Josh nodded. "That was so fucking bad. I was tripping so hard."

Blake laughed harder.

"What happened?" I asked

"Well, C-Lo," Josh started. He pointed his beer at Blake, and Blake returned the gesture. "We were what? Fourteen?"

"Thirteen, I think," Blake answered. "Fuck, we were such cocky little punks."

That made me laugh.

Josh continued, "We smoked, like, two puffs of weed, and we were gone—"

"Josh thought he was Superman," Blake cut in.

Josh rolled his eyes. "Okay, kid-that-wore-a-cape-to-school-for-a-month-in-third-grade."

"What?" I laughed. I tilted my head to look up at Blake, but he was already watching me.

His eyes danced with amusement when he said, "I also believed I could shoot lasers out of my eyes."

"Oh yeah!" Josh yelped. "Squinty!"

Blake threw back his head and laughed.

"The entire school called you Squinty for months. I fucking forgot about Squinty."

"Tell your story, asshole." He took a swig of his beer and winked down at me.

*　　　*　　　*

Josh told his story—about when he'd tried to grind on the edge of bleachers but failed. He'd fallen off the side of the railing, but his pants—which they admitted had hung way too low, almost at their knees, but they'd thought was so fucking cool at the time—had gotten caught on a bar at the end. It had made him flip over the edge of the rail, but he'd caught himself by throwing his arms out over his head.

"He was stuck there, upside down, with his pants down to his ankles," Blake said through his laughter.

Apparently, he'd been there for so long his face had started to turn red. But the best part was that somehow Josh had managed to knock out two of his teeth. Probably from the board, but really, they had no idea. So there'd been Josh, hanging upside down, off the edge of the bleachers, for who knows how long, with his pants down—and Blake, also high, had been so busy laughing at him that he'd been unable to even grasp the concept of trying to help him down.

"He was rolling around on the fucking ground, pointing and laughing at me!" Josh yelled. "My mouth was full of blood from my knocked-out teeth. And I kept trying to spit it out, but I was flipped over the edge, and high, and had blood rushing to my head, and my balls were sore from being so cold."

"Help me, Hunter! Help me!" Blake mocked in a feminine tone.

"What happened?" I couldn't stop laughing. "How did you get down?"

"Some guy walking his dog saw us and called an ambulance," Josh said.

"Why the fuck didn't he just get you down?" Blake yelled.

"Why the fuck didn't *you* just get me down?" Josh retorted.

"What happened?" I was laughing so hard my sides hurt.

Josh answered. "So the guy called an ambulance. It took them forever to get there."

"It was, like, two minutes, you pussy," Blake said.

"Fuck you, *Squinty*. It felt like forever." Josh's eyes moved to me. "So the ambulance gets there, and the dudes help me down, check my teeth and shit, and then they asked us what'd happened."

Blake laughed again and pulled me closer.

"And?" I placed my hands over his and linked our fingers. "What did you tell them?"

"This is so fucking bad." Josh shook his head. "Hunter and I looked at each other, and I don't even know what happened . . . I think we were both so paranoid from the weed that we thought we couldn't tell them the truth."

"What did you say?" I needed to know.

"Hunter here—" He stopped, unable to speak through his cackle. When he finally calmed down, he continued, "Hunter said that vampires came and tried to attack us! We tried to fight them off, but they got me, hence the blood, and then they hung me off the end of the bleachers as a warning to the werewolves that they'd been there!"

We all roared with laughter.

I looked up at Blake, with teary eyes. The good kind. "Vampires? Werewolves?"

He just shrugged and said, "*Twilight* had just come out."

*　　*　　*

"Where to next?" The cab driver asked as he started to reverse out of Josh's driveway.

Blake pulled me so close to him that I was almost on his lap.

"My house, I guess." I looked up at him, but he was looking out the window, his mind somewhere else. "Blake?"

His gaze dropped to mine. "Huh?"

"The cab. My house or yours first?"

His eyes fell shut. When he opened them, they were glazed and red. He was holding in tears. "Stay with me tonight?"

And that was all it took.

I'd known it was coming. And I'd known it would be soon. But I wasn't prepared for it. I wasn't ready for the moment where my mind caught up to my heart and the walls I'd built crumbled.

I wasn't ready to admit that I'd fallen in love.

*   *   *

Without a word, he took my hand and led me up to his bedroom. I stood in the middle of his room while he went through his dresser and pulled out a shirt. He didn't hand it to me like I'd expected. Instead, he set it on his bed, turned to me, and slowly slipped my dress over my head. I stood in front of him, in the darkness of his room—lit only by the moon outside—in nothing but my bra and panties.

And I'd never felt more beautiful in my life.

My eyes drifted shut. I waited for him to touch me. For his hands to follow where his eyes had roamed. But it never happened. The touch never came. Then the soft material of his shirt covered me. His voice came out in a whisper: "I like you in my clothes, Not Abby."

*   *   *

190

He waited for me to get into his bed before following. Then he pulled me into him—the heat of his bare chest against my back. His hold was tight. So tight I almost couldn't breathe. But that was fine—because in this moment, all I needed to breathe was Blake.

His nose skimmed along the back of my neck, moving my hair to make way for his lips. His kisses were soft and slow, but they were also commanding. His hand moved under my shirt and flattened against my stomach. Then his palm crept higher. And higher. "Blake."

"Mmm?" The wetness of his open mouth, followed by his tongue, made me shiver.

"What are you doing?"

"I don't know," he said. The frustration, the plea, the need in his voice was enough to make me turn in his arms. Once we were face-to-face, he continued, "I feel like I need to—no, *we* need to—do something so that you don't forget me."

I reared back. "You think I could forget you?"

He dropped his gaze, but he didn't speak.

"So you want to have sex?"

"No," he said quickly, lifting his eyes to meet mine. "I don't know. *Yes.* I just want you to remember me."

My chest tightened at his words. "Would you forget me?"

"Never."

"Then what makes you think I'd forget you?"

"Because that's your goal in life, Chloe. To be forgettable."

"That's not fair, Blake."

He sighed. "Maybe not, but it's the truth."

I let his words sink in and settle before I spoke. "I've had sex, Blake."

His eyes narrowed.

"With lots of guys."

His lips thinned to a line.

"And I don't remember them."

"So what are you saying?"

"I'm saying that it didn't mean anything. Sex. It probably never will."

He leaned his forehead against mine. "I wish I was enough," he said quietly.

"Enough?"

"I wish that I could ask you to stay, and that it would be enough. That *I* was enough."

I wanted to tell him that he was. He was more than enough. But it wasn't just about him. It was about me, too. It *always* had to be about me, and the people I'd leave behind.

He took my silence as an answer. Sighing, he leaned in and placed a chaste kiss on my lips.

I kissed back, lingering longer than he'd probably expected.

His fingers on my back curled, gripping the shirt.

"You know what I've always wanted? What I never let myself dream?" I said against his lips.

"What?" he whispered.

"To meet a guy that wanted to kiss me. Not because it would lead to sex, but because he felt like he would die if he couldn't. I want to fall asleep, kissing someone, and for that kiss to be enough, to be *everything*. Just kiss. Sometimes when I'm with you, that's all I want. I want to kiss you like my life depends on it." My voice cracked, but I kept going. "If I could dream the same dream a million times over, it would be you—you would be my last kiss, my last breath."

"Chloe," he sighed.

And then he kissed me.

He kissed me with everything he had.

Every piece of him.

Like his life depended on it.

We never broke apart.

Not even when fatigue set in, and we struggled to move.

Or when fatigue won out, and we fell asleep.

Not even when I dreamed that the cancer had won, and I was dying.

And that Blake Hunter—he was my last dying breath.

CHAPTER TWENTY-FOUR

Blake

Her eyes fluttered open, and a slow smile spread across her face.

"Hey, beautiful."

"You know what I love?" she said groggily.

"What?"

She skimmed her fingers over my nose. "These little freckles, right here. They don't come out often. Sometimes in the sunlight. Barely ever indoors. But they're out now. I bet it's just for me."

"I bet it is."

Her eyes drifted shut again as she pressed her lips against my nose. And for a moment, I forgot that that was it. That the moment—right there—was as good as it would get for us.

It was the greatest thing we'd never have.

The thought created a knot in the pit of my stomach, and I couldn't shake it. "You want to shower?"

"Okay."

I kissed her once and tried to smile. "I'll go after you, and then maybe we can get something to eat?"

"Sounds great."

*   *   *

Last night, when she'd been in my arms, I'd asked her to stay—not in those exact words—but she'd known what I'd meant. She hadn't responded, and that had been enough of an answer for me.

I'd wanted to tell her that I loved her—or at least I thought I did. But then she'd told me how she felt about me, and the word *love* hadn't felt like enough.

I had three and a half days to find words that were enough. Even if she didn't stay, at least she'd know how I felt about her.

She'd told me she'd wait outside while I showered. When I stepped out of the house, she was leaning against my car, and my mother was with her.

"I invited your mom. I hope you don't mind."

What was I supposed to say? That I did mind? That I wanted her all to myself and that I wanted her to be *mine*? "That's cool."

"I also rang Mary, and everyone else is going to meet us there."

"Okay."

"And Josh, too."

My smile was tight, but I nodded anyway.

We got in my car and drove to Clayton's restaurant, her hand on my leg the entire drive.

My mom linked arms with me as I watched Chloe walking ahead and into the restaurant. "It might be the last time she gets to be with everyone, Blake. Don't be selfish. Let her have this moment."

I looked down at her. "When did you get so smart?"

"Honey, I write romance novels. You don't think I know what goes on in the minds of two people in love?"

Chloe

I frowned when Mary, Dean, and the kids walked in.

"What's wrong?" Blake asked. He must've been watching me.

"Harry's not here," I said into his shoulder.

He put his arm behind me and brought my temple to his lips. "I'm sorry."

They all joined us in the corner booth.

"Harry's coming," Dean said. "He wanted to meet us here. Said he had something he had to do."

I felt a weight lift off my shoulders.

"Dean, Mary, this is my mom, Celia." Blake made the introductions. They talked among themselves for a while as I watched the seconds tick by. My eyes moved from the clock to the front door, waiting for Harry. When I saw him walk in with a skateboard under his arm, my heart leapt. I couldn't contain my smile. Blake squeezed my shoulder once before standing up to bump fists with him. He took a seat on the other side, suggesting that Harry sit next to me. It was a small gesture, but one that didn't go unnoticed. I was thankful that he'd thought of it. I was thankful for *him*.

"Hey," Harry greeted.

"Hi," I squeaked. I was nervous. I wasn't sure what Harry would say to me.

"Can I sit?"

"Of course."

He sat down and placed a bag on the table. "I got you something," he said quietly.

"You didn't have to get me anything." I was still looking down at the table. Too ashamed to face him after what had happened between us.

"It's not really for you. It's more for me." He tipped the bag and emptied the contents.

A phone.

"It's an upgrade from your old flip phone. This one has Internet and stuff."

I finally managed to look up at him. He was smiling, but the moment was awkward.

"I bought enough credit for a year. They charged it while I was buying it. I loaded Facebook on it and made you an account."

"What do you mean?"

"I mean you have a Facebook account now. I'm your only friend. You can chat, send me pictures. Whatever." He slid the phone over to me. "And it's a gift. Mary always says never to look a gift horse in the mouth. I don't really know what that means, but I think it means that if you get a gift, then you have to use it. This is my gift to you—you *have* to use it. You have to stay in touch. Send me messages. Pictures of where you are and what you're doing. You have to let me know that you're okay, and that you're *healthy*."

Mary sniffed, pulling me out of my thoughts. She buried her face in Dean's arm.

"I didn't mean to make you cry, Chloe," Harry said.

"Thank you. I love it," I said, wiping my cheeks.

"Promise me you'll use it."

I laughed. "You're going to have to show me how."

He grinned and picked up the phone.

I tried to listen to his instructions, but instead I noticed Blake watching us the entire time, his eyebrows drawn and a frown on his face.

He stayed that way until the bell above the door chimed, and Josh ran in, carrying Tommy. "Hey, everyone," Josh's words rushed out, and then he set Tommy on the floor. Tommy stood on wobbly feet. "Okay, Tommy. Do it!" Josh ordered.

Tommy dropped himself on his diaper-covered butt.

Josh rolled his eyes, picked him up, and set him on his feet again.

We all watched.

"He did it this morning, took his first step," Josh informed us, his eyes trained on Tommy. "Go on, buddy, do it again."

Tommy stood still. His little eyes moving from one person to the other.

"Come on," Josh encouraged. "You're making a liar out of your daddy."

Tommy moved.

We held our breaths.

But then he fell on his butt again.

Josh sighed and set him on his feet.

Tommy pulled out his pacifier and pointed to Blake. "Hunt."

Blake's eyes went huge. "He can say my name!"

"You want Uncle Hunter?" Josh said excitedly. He pulled Blake out of the booth and stood him two feet in front of Tommy. "Go to Uncle Hunter," he cooed.

"Hunt," Tommy said again.

And then he took a step. Followed by another. And then another. He fell on the fourth, but it didn't matter. We were out of our seats and cheering by the time Blake picked him up off the floor and sat him on his lap. "I'm your Uncle Hunt," he said through a smile.

CHAPTER TWENTY-FIVE

Blake

Graduation day.

The last day of Chloe.

It sucked.

Almost as much as the fact that when I woke up that morning and opened my eyes, Dad was hovering above me with what looked like a gift basket containing a basketball and Duke Blue Devils jersey. "What the fuck is this?"

For a second, I got scared. I let his intimidation work. And then I remembered Chloe and, all of a sudden, dealing with Dad didn't seem so hard. Not compared to saying good-bye to her.

"What does it look like?" I threw the covers off me and stood toe to toe with him.

His eyes widened in surprise, but for only a second, before he recovered and glared at me. His lips turned into a snarl when he growled, "Did you tell them you were enlisting? Basketball is not a future, Hunter. What the fuck kind of lessons and achievements are you going to get from throwing a damn ball around?" His voice got louder with every word.

The thing was, if he would have actually sat down with me, tried to talk it out, maybe made suggestions as to why I should have chosen to enlist rather than play college ball, I would've listened to him. I would have heard him out, really considered his point of view. But all he'd done was make me want to tell him to fuck off and that he had no fucking clue about my life or me. So I bit my tongue and contained the rage that had been building for so long. Then I brushed past him, got in the shower, and dressed in the stupid graduation gown.

One day left.

I was going to miss the shit out of her.

Chloe

Arms around my waist gripped me tight. I panicked for a second, but then a familiarity set in. *Blake.* I was airborne. My legs kicked out in front of me as I mumbled some form of apology to the family whose ice cream I had just started to scoop. Blake and Josh's laughter filled my ears. I stopped kicking and gave in to the inevitable.

The sunlight hit my eyes when they opened the storeroom door that led to an alleyway behind the building.

Blake set me carefully back on the ground. "I didn't see you at the ceremony," he said.

"I told you I wasn't going. I was only working a half shift here, and I wanted some extra time with Dean and Mary."

"Fair enough. But what about *my* extra time?" He pouted.

I leaned back against the wall and hid my hands behind me. "I'm sorry."

Truth was I was avoiding him. I didn't know how I would've reacted had I been at the graduation ceremony. I hated good-byes. So much so that I did everything I could just to avoid farewells. Luckily for me, I'd had years to get used to the idea of leaving everyone. When the kids had been heading off for school, I had told them I'd see them soon. Dean and Mary had taken me out to lunch, and then I'd gone to work. Mary had cried when she'd gotten in their car. I knew because I'd watched her. Letting them go actually wasn't as bad as I'd thought it would be, especially since I'd promised Harry I'd keep it touch, and I had every intention of keeping that promise. I hadn't said how often I'd contact them, but it would be often enough that they would know I was *healthy.*

Now came the hardest part of all: saying good-bye to Blake.

"We gotta be quick," Josh interrupted my thoughts.

"We got you something. A good-bye gift, I guess."

My heart sank. "You didn't have to get me anything."

"Yeah, well . . ." He shrugged. "Something to remember us by."

Josh held out something long and flat, wrapped in newspaper. I already knew what it was, without having to look. Stepping forward, I took it from his hands.

He shoved my shoulder. "Open it."

Blake's low chuckle caused the ache in my chest to tighten. He shoved my other shoulder. "Yeah, open it."

Josh laughed, shoving me again. "Yeah, open it."

I smiled and shook my head. "What is wrong with you guys?"

"Just do it," Blake said, his voice low, serious.

I made a show of ripping the newspaper off and being surprised by the skateboard hidden underneath. "This is amazing!"

The storeroom door opened, and Trent, who had been hired to take my place stepped out. "It's getting busy. I don't know what the fuck I'm doing."

"Alright, fucktard. Calm your tits," Josh yelled.

Trent went back inside without another word.

I laughed. "A little harsh?"

Josh shook his head. "I've hated that asshole ever since I went to school with him."

My eyebrows pinched, and I looked up at Blake. "He goes to our school?"

He rolled his eyes and shook his head. "Chloe, you've met him! How do you not know these things?"

I shrugged.

Then I was engulfed in Josh's arms. "I know you didn't want good-byes," he whispered in my ear. "So I'm not going to say it. I'm just going to say that I'm forever thankful I met you. And I'll remember you always, Chloe." He released his hold and took a step back.

I wiped my eyes with the back of my hand, containing the sob that was bursting to escape. I had held it back the entire day. I hadn't cried with the kids, or with Mary and Dean. But I was on the edge now, and I didn't want Blake to be the one to see it.

Josh nodded once, and then he was gone.

"It's got your name on it," Blake mumbled.

"What?"

"The board. Underneath. It has your name."

I looked down at the board in my hands as I processed what he'd said. Then I flipped it over. Not Abby, in bright-red letters.

I laughed. "Always with the red," I thought out loud and looked up at him. "You always write in red. What's with that?"

He smiled sadly. "It's you."

"Me?"

"Yes." He stepped forward and placed his hand on my waist, pushing me back against the wall.

I set the board down next to me. "What does it mean?"

"Red-letter days. It's when something unexpectedly phenomenal happens."

I choked on my sob.

"You're my unexpectedly phenomenal, Chloe. *You're* my red-letter day."

My head dropped onto his chest, but his fingers laced in my hair, tilting my face up to look him in the eyes, like he'd done so many times before. His gaze roamed my face, searching for something I knew wasn't there. "It's still not enough, is it?"

My silence was his answer.

"No good-byes?" he asked.

I shook my head. "No good-byes."

"Okay," he whispered, his lips grazing mine. "Then I guess I'm just going to have to kiss you."

With one hand in my hair and the other gripping my waist, he kissed me.

It could've been seconds, minutes, hours—it wasn't long enough.

When Josh opened the door with a look of regret on his face—and an apology for interrupting us—we knew it was time.

That last kiss was our perfect good-bye.

Blake

I'd been searching for days for the words—something bigger and greater than *I love you*—and I'd stood there, during our last hours together, with nothing to say. But then she'd asked about the red ink, the red letters, so I'd told her *she* was my unexpectedly phenomenal.

But it hadn't been enough.

There'd been no words exchanged after the kiss, just a silent agreement that it had been our good-bye.

I watched the seconds of the clock tick by, waiting for her shift to be over. I was so consumed by the clock on the wall that the ticking of the seconds matched the thumping in my chest. Then Josh nudged me with his elbow. "She's leaving."

My eyes snapped to the exit, where she was walking out the doors, skateboard under her arm.

My heart stopped, but the ticking got louder.

Or so I thought.

But I had it wrong.

The ticking stopped. But my heart thumped harder.

And suddenly, everything that had happened in the past three months flashed before my eyes. Like a predeath slideshow. Only it wasn't death. It was Chloe. *All Chloe.*

I bounced on my feet.

And looked from the clock.

To the door.

To the clock.

Back to the door.

My hands fisted.

My body went rigid.

I turned to Josh.

He was smirking.

"Josh . . ."

That was all I had to say for his smirk to widen. "Hurry up, dude! She's leaving!"

And then I ran.

Out the exit.

Through the parking lot.

And to her car.

She was pulling out of the spot.

I jumped into the passenger's seat.

Literally, jumped.

She hit the brakes, her eyes wide. "What the hell are you doing?"

"The Road."

"What!"

"Just drive!"

She stared a moment before a huge smile took over. "Are you sure?"

Adrenaline pumped through my veins. "Just drive, Chloe." And for a split second, I panicked. Maybe she didn't want me there. "Please?"

Her eyes lit up. "Oh my God," she mumbled, before hitting the accelerator and peeling out of the parking lot.

We drove twenty minutes out of town before she pulled over. Her smile never faltered and she didn't say a word. But when the car finally came to a stop and the squeal of her hand brake filled my ears, I got nervous.

She pushed open her door and stepped out.

I followed.

She started hastily walking down a hidden path, and it was only then that I realized where we were. Her mom's lake. I had been too preoccupied, watching her drive, waiting for her to stop and kick me out, to notice where we'd been going.

She paused for a moment after the trees cleared and the lake was in view. I saw her shoulders lift, and I could picture what she was doing. She would have her eyes closed, be filling her lungs with the clean air that surrounded us.

I cleared my throat and stood next to her. "Chloe?"

She turned to me, confused, then a hint of a smile played on her lips. She took my hand, linking our fingers together, and led me to our rock. Or at least that was what I called it. A flat piece, hanging over the water's edge. We had sat there, together, more times over the past nine weeks than I thought anyone had in an entire lifetime. She sat down, legs crossed like usual, and pulled me down with her. I sat behind her, with my legs on either side of her and my arms wrapped around her waist.

It was perfect.

And then it wasn't.

"What are you doing, Blake?" She sounded so sad, I almost regretted getting into the car with her. *Almost.*

"I'm not ready to lose you."

She tilted her head to look up at me. I kissed her. Just once. I couldn't help it. She smiled against my lips, but when she pulled away, her smile was gone, replaced by a sadness that had the power to destroy me. "That's not an answer," she said.

I tensed. She was right. I tried to think of something that would satisfy her. "I have a proposition," I said on a whim.

"I like the sound of that," she joked.

"Are you being a pig?"

"Yes."

We both laughed.

"Duke's fall semester starts August 19. After—"

"I'll take it," she cut in. "I'll take anything you give me."

Chloe

I didn't get it. I didn't understand why he'd chased after me, or why he was still there. He knew me. He knew my story. He knew *everything*.

"Stop it," he murmured into my ear.

"What are you talking about?" I squeezed his hands and wrapped his arms tighter around me.

"I see the gears in your head spinning and, whatever you're thinking about, stop it."

"Okay," I said quietly. "What do we do from here? Where do we go?"

He laughed. "Chloe, this is your journey. I'm just here for the ride. We do whatever you want."

"I didn't really have a plan," I told him. "I was just gonna drive."

He nuzzled his face into the crook of my neck. "That sounds like an amazing plan to me."

And it was.

Until about two hours into the drive on the highway when he'd started to fidget in his seat. He'd changed the station on the radio numerous times, searched on his phone about hardwiring his iPod into said stereo, quizzed me about my lack of sports knowledge, and tried to fix the been-broken-forever console with a stick and a piece of gum.

Then he was bouncing in his seat, chewing his nails. He barely ever chewed his nails. *"Did you know that the human head weighs eight pounds?"*

I glanced at him quickly. "I did actually. The kid from Jerry Maguire taught me that."

"I love that kid!"

"Me too!"

"I wanted to be a sports agent because of that film. You know, if basketball didn't work out."

"Oh yeah?"

He nodded enthusiastically. "Yup! Before that I wanted to be a fireman. And a racecar driver. Oh! And lion tamer. How good would that be? A lion tamer. I'd call my lion LeBron, and we'd go everywhere together. He would be my best friend and we'd go to the park and laugh at all the people with their petty dogs and I'd have a kick-ass lion. I'm going to do it. Do you think there are laws? Or an adoption program? All lions need love too. Maybe I can find a blind lion. It would be harder to train but it would be worth it because—"

"Oh my God," I laughed and placed my hand firmly on his knee to stop the bouncing. "What is with you?"

He froze but eyed me sideways. Then he sucked in a huge breath. "Chloe, I'm fucking bored."

I looked at the clock on the dashboard. "We've only been driving a couple hours."

"I know, but I'm not used to just sitting around. I'm always doing stuff."

"Okay." I tried to settle him. "What do you normally do? What can *we* do to stop this boredom?"

He rolled his eyes. "Quit talking to me like I'm a kid, for one."

I giggled. "Well, tell me what you normally do."

He shrugged. "I don't know. Shoot hoops, skate, run, fuck."

I choked on air.

His eyes shut tight. "Ignore that last one."

I did. "Pass me my bag?"

He reached into the backseat and then handed me my bag. I pulled out a lollipop, ripped the wrapper off with my teeth, and held it in front of his mouth.

"A lollipop?" he groaned. "Really?"

"It's to shut you up."

"I'm not Sammy!" But he opened his mouth and took it anyway.

Two seconds later, he waved the stick in my face, sans lolly. "That didn't last long. What else you got?"

"It's a lollipop. You're supposed to suck it, not bite it."

"That's what he said."

"Pig." I reached into the bag and pulled out another one. "Suck it this time. Make it last."

He took the lollipop from my hand. "That's what he—"

"Shut it."

He laughed but put the lollipop in his mouth and crossed his arms over his chest. Even when he acted like a kid, he was still stupidly hot.

Blake

We found a hotel to stay at in Myrtle Beach. Even though it was only an hour-and-a-half drive from home, it took us four hours to get there. Most likely because she didn't believe in maps.

"Did you want to just stay the one night, Blake?"

I shrugged. "Whatever you want."

"Can we book for two and then go from there?"

The lady behind the desk nodded and took Chloe's card. I offered to pay. She wouldn't let me. But something was off, the lady kept eyeing me weird, and I had to bite my tongue to stop myself from asking her what the hell her problem was.

Okay, I was on edge.

I'd been in a car for four hours, and my mind was starting to run a little wild. I was happy I was with Chloe—don't get me wrong. But I had left a lot of things unfinished at home. And I had left a lot of things *at* home. Like clothes. Running shoes. Josh. Tommy. Mom.

"I mean no disrespect, but are y'all runaways?" the lady asked.

Chloe laughed. "No, ma'am. We're actually here on our honeymoon."

My eyes widened, but I tried to hide it when the lady smiled at us, and Chloe wrapped her arms around me. "Well, why didn't you say so?" the lady asked. Myrtle, her name was. *No shit.* "I'll upgrade you. No charge." She held her hand to her heart. "Young love," she sang. "Bless your hearts."

*   *   *

I dropped Chloe's bag in the middle of the room.

She sat on the edge of the bed and kicked her legs out in front of her. "What's bugging you?"

"Nothing," I lied.

"I can get another room," she said quietly. "And I'll take you home in the morning."

"What?" My head whipped to hers, but her face was down, watching her feet moving back and forth. "Why would you say that?"

"I don't know. You just seem like you regret being here."

My eyes drifted shut, and my shoulders sagged. I felt like an asshole. "I don't regret it, Chloe. Not for a second." I pulled the sheets down on one side of the bed and stripped to my boxers. After climbing in, I waited for her to do the same, but she didn't. She just sat there, frozen. "Chloe?"

She turned to me now, her mouth pulled down into a frown. My insides twisted, and I hated myself, because I knew I was the reason she looked like that. I sat up on my knees and lifted her off the bed, placing her under the covers and into my arms. "I'm an asshole."

"A little." She turned so we were face-to-face. "Talk to me."

"I don't regret being here with you. Not at all. There's absolutely nowhere else I'd rather be right now. Believe me. I just didn't think things through, I guess."

"Like what?"

"Like clothes, I have no clothes. Right now I want to go for a run to kill the ache from sitting in the car for so long, but I only have my work clothes. And work, I just left. It was my only source of money and now it's gone. Fuck. I have no money. You can't pay for everything! I just need—"

"Blake," she cut in. "There are stores. Stores sell clothes. We can buy clothes. Work will find someone else, easily. And money—I have money. Lots of it."

"Where . . . I mean how do you have all this money?"

She shrugged. "My mom and aunt left it to me. Their parents left it to them. They both died so young they never really got a chance to spend it."

I frowned, wondering for a moment if *she'd* ever get a chance to spend it. I pushed down the ache that thought had caused and moved on. "You can't pay my way."

"It doesn't cost me any extra to have you here. Hotels, gas—it's all the same. But like I said, I can take you home tomorrow—"

"No. Fuck, Chloe. I don't want to be without you. That's why I'm here." The desperation in my voice was evident, because it was the truth. And because I was so scared of the day I'd wake up and she wouldn't be there.

"Okay," she said.

But the air was still thick, and the mood was still sad. "Chloe?"

"Mmm?" she said into my chest.

I pulled back and lifted her chin with my finger. I made sure she was looking at me before I spoke. "I don't ever want you to question this—the reason why I'm here—or whether I want to be here or not. Ever. I'm here because I want you. Because I've always wanted you."

Her breath became shaky. "Will you kiss me already?"

I smiled. "You don't ever have to question that, either."

CHAPTER TWENTY-SIX

Blake

"Chloe," I whispered in her ear. "Chloe. Chloe. Chloe."

I was bored. Edgy. Anxious.

"Chloe." I poked her cheek.

Nothing.

"Chloe." I poked harder. "You sleep like the fucking dead."

That made her smile.

"Oh cute, pretending to be asleep while I go out of my mind with boredom."

She sat up. "What the hell time is it?"

I threw my hands up. "I don't know. Time to get up. Let's go."

*　　　*　　　*

We couldn't find a Footlocker, so we ended up at a small sporting-goods store. I didn't care, just as long as I got a decent pair of running shoes and some extra clothes. She walked around the store while I tried on different sneakers.

"Babe!" she yelled out, and I couldn't help but smile. "Did you want a basketball?"

"Yeah, good thinking."

"There's like eighty here. Which one?"

"A Spalding twenty-nine and a half."

She laughed. "I have no idea what you just said."

Shaking my head, I made my way over to her.

"What's the difference?" she whispered.

I picked up the Spalding. "This one's a pro ball. Different material, sizes, grip."

"Oh." She nodded but then shrugged. "I won't remember that." She turned her head, looking around the store. "You should get a skateboard, too," she said. "We can skate together. How exciting." She clapped her hands together. Then it dawned on me—that I'd never seen her like this. This happy. This free.

"You mean I'll skate, and you'll roll?"

"Hey." She poked a single finger into my chest. "I've been getting better. You even said so. And now I can practice more since I have my own board." Her eyes widened as she caught sight of something over my shoulder. "Go get the board and meet me at the counter. I need to get something."

I did as she asked and waited for her at the counter. After a couple of minutes, she was back, wearing a Duke cap too big for her head and holding a few jerseys. She took the cap off and set it on the counter, along with the three basketball jerseys. One blue, one black, and one white. All Duke. "What's the difference?" she asked the sales clerk.

I stayed silent, waiting for the moment. *You know . . . that moment when something significant happens, but you don't realize it until it's over.*

"White's home. Blue's away. Black's alternative," the clerk answered.

Her eyes moved from the clerk to me. But I couldn't speak. I couldn't form words. I could barely breathe.

She shrugged. "I'll take them all."

"Okay," the clerk laughed.

"Shit. And this." She pulled out another cap from under her arm and reached up to put it over my head. Then she eyed me up and down, her head tilted to the side. "Oh!" she squealed, turning back to the clerk. "Do you have those little letters that go on the back?"

"Yup," he said, but his eyebrows were drawn in as he looked between us. "What name do you want?"

"Hunter."

And there it was.

That moment of significance.

I put my arm around her shoulders, drew her into me, and kissed her forehead.

"Number?" the clerk asked.

"Twenty-three," she said quickly, then looked up at me. "Wait. Do you change when . . . I mean *if* . . ."

I nodded and opened my mouth to speak. Nothing came out. I cleared my throat. "Eight." My voice broke. It felt like forever since I'd used it.

"We can heat press the names and numbers here. You want it on all of them?"

"Yes please," she answered, but her eyes never left me. She pressed the front of her body against mine. "Are you okay?"

I nodded once.

Then the clerk cleared his throat. "You're not Blake Hunter, are you?"

My smiled was tight. "Yes, sir."

"So, Duke? I didn't know. Was it announced?"

"No, sir."

"You got a few offers, right?"

Chloe pulled away. All the way away, until she was no longer touching me.

I nodded. "A few."

Her eyes narrowed at me before she looked away.

We paid and left the store, neither of us uttering a word. When we got in the car, I reached for her hand, but she pulled it away. I didn't know what had happened between the store and now, but the mood had grown noticeably colder.

"Chloe?" I said cautiously.

"Blake."

"Chloe?"

"Blake."

"Chloe?"

"Just give me a minute," she said. "I'm trying to think!"

I sank into my seat. And I waited.

"Blake?" she finally said.

"Yes, Chloe?"

She faced me. Then moved her eyes from side to side, as if she was about to share a huge secret. I sat up straighter and turned to her.

"How big a deal are you?" she whispered.

My lips curved into a smile.

"This isn't funny, Blake. I mean, I looked you up. I knew you were *good*, but that guy in that store—that you've probably never been to before—he *knew* you. That means you must be a somebody, right?"

I shrugged.

"Oh my God," she mumbled under her breath. "And offers? It wasn't just Duke?"

I tried to contain my smile. She was so damn cute.

"How many offers?"

I shrugged again.

"You're not talking to me?"

215

I shook my head. It wasn't like earlier, when my emotions had gripped me, and the words hadn't been there. I just liked messing with her and watching her get more nervous with each question.

She squinted as she took me in. I didn't know what she was looking for, but whatever it was, she must've found it, because her eyes went huge. "You're like . . . a celebrity!"

The notion was so crazy it made me laugh. "I'm not a celebrity!"

"You are so!" She nodded frantically. "A sports celebrity!" Her hands covered the squeal that escaped her. "Oh my God." She pushed open her door and stepped out of the car. "I've kidnapped a sports celebrity! I'm going to hell. Or worse. *Jail.*" She was pacing and rambling. "I'm going to sports jail. Where all the sports fans are going to throw rocks at the girl who stole their sports-celebrity-hero-god."

I dissolved in a fit of laughter.

"This isn't funny!" she yelled, but I couldn't stop.

When we got back to the hotel, I changed and went for a run. I asked her to come with me. She laughed in my face and told me that she'd rather poke herself in the eye with a pen than be seen running with a sports god.

*   *   *

It was another quick run. I thought I'd be gone for ages, but the second after I'd left the hotel, I just wanted to get back to Chloe.

"Your mom's been calling. I think you need to . . ." Her words died in the air as she took me in. I had taken my shirt off midrun, because I was so sweaty. She'd seen me shirtless before but probably not like this. She blushed and looked away, pretending to be engrossed with whatever was on TV.

I took a seat next to her and started to take off my shoes. "Did you answer?"

She pursed her lips and shook her head.

"How many times did she call?"

She shrugged, refusing to meet my eyes.

I ran the back of my finger along her bare thigh, trying to get her attention. "What did you do while I was gone?"

She stood up quickly. "Nothing. I'm making coffee. You want some?"

I laughed under my breath. "Yeah. I'm just gonna shower real quick."

"I might um . . . go . . . I'll be back . . . You shower." Then she picked up her keys and left the room.

And I couldn't wipe the damn smile off my face.

*   *   *

She must not have been gone for long, because by the time I'd finished my shower, she was back. Admittedly, I'd had a long shower. A nice, long, *cold* shower.

I sat out on the balcony and dialed Mom's number. "Blake?" she answered. She sounded pissed.

Chloe came out with two coffees. She set them both on the table and started to walk away. I curled my arm around her waist and brought her down on my lap. She didn't resist. "Hey, Ma."

"You didn't come home last night. Your car is still at the bowling alley, and Josh won't tell me what happened! Where the hell are you?"

I frowned. "Don't be mad."

"Never start a sentence with that, especially with your mother!"

I switched the phone to speaker and placed it on the table. Chloe turned to me, biting her lip. She looked scared. I *was* scared. "I've kind of . . . left."

"Left!" she shrieked. "What do you mean, you've left?"

"I'm with Chloe," I said, as if it was a valid reason for my actions. "She was leaving, and I left with her. I had to. I'm sorry."

"HUNTER!" she screamed.

We both flinched.

But then she started to laugh. It started low, then built up to something she couldn't control. I started to get worried. Maybe she was crazy. It wouldn't surprise me—being cooped up in that guesthouse all day, making up stories could do that to a person, right?

"Ma?"

She laughed harder.

Chloe tried to get up, but I held on to her tighter.

Mom finally stopped laughing long enough to sigh. "Oh, Blake," she said. "I've never been so damn proud of you in my life."

"What?" Chloe and I said at the same time.

"Is that Chloe? Is she there?"

"Yes, Mrs. Hunter, I'm here."

"Good," she said. "I want to speak to both of you."

Chloe's eyes went wide.

"Okay?" I said.

"Okay," she repeated. I imagined her rolling her shoulders back, trying to calm herself down. "I need to wire some money to you. It might take a few days—"

"No," we both cut in.

Then Chloe spoke over me. "We don't need the money. I have enough."

"That's rubbish." Mom's words were final. "I'm sitting on piles of it, and I have no use for it. I live in a guesthouse, for Christ's sake. Blake, are you there? Blake!"

"Yeah, Ma, I'm here."

"I'll transfer you some money. Don't let Chloe pay for everything. Be a gentleman, for God's sake—" She paused, the kind of pause I knew meant she wasn't done speaking. Her voice lowered when she asked, "Is she still driving that . . . *antique* convertible?"

I couldn't control my guffaw. "Yes."

"Right," Mom said. You could hear her frantically typing away. "You'd better buy a new car."

"No!" Chloe yelled. "You can't—"

"Chloe," Mom said. "If your car breaks down and you guys get stuck in the middle of nowhere and get attacked by serial-killer joggers"—I laughed—"I'll always blame myself. Make an old lady happy."

"You can't buy a car," Chloe whined.

"Why not? Consider it a graduation present for Blake." More typing of keys from her end. "Where are you?"

"Myrtle Beach," I answered.

"Great. I'll call with details soon." She paused again. "Blake?"

"Yeah?"

Her tone turned serious. "I'm proud of you for following your heart, doing something that makes you happy. You deserve it."

Chloe turned to face me, a perfect pout on her perfect face. She kissed my nose—the freckles, I guess.

"And you take care of Chloe," Mom said. "She deserves that, too."

"I will," I answered. "She's my red-letter day."

"She's your unexpectedly phenomenal?" Mom giggled. "Holy shit. I need to put that in my next book." Frantic typing. "Okay, kids. Keep in touch. Love you both." Then she hung up.

"What the hell just happened?" Chloe laughed.

I shook my head. "I have no idea."

She picked up her coffee and handed me mine, but before I could take a sip, my phone chimed.

Myrtle Beach Chrysler-Jeep dealership. Grand Cherokee. Chloe gets to pick the color. Happy Graduation. I love you. Mom.

*   *   *

Mom wasn't the only one who called. Dad did, too, over twenty times. We stopped by a store and picked up a new SIM card for my phone. I texted Josh and Mom my new number. I also told Mom to give Josh my old car; his was unreliable at best.

Chloe found a homeless shelter nearby and gave them her car.

Mom had handled all the financing by phone, so by the time we got to the dealership, all I had to do was sign for ownership, and Chloe had to pick a color.

She chose red.

CHAPTER TWENTY-SEVEN

Chloe

I woke the next morning to an empty bed. When I sat up to look around the room, all his stuff was still there. Relief washed through me. Then I saw it. Red ink on torn white paper, sitting on his pillow.

Back soon. Gone for a run.
P.S. You're beautiful when you're sleeping. Just thought you should know that—in case nobody else ever gets a chance to tell you.

I swallowed the lump that had formed in my throat and read the note over and over. *In case nobody else ever gets a chance to tell you.* I wondered for a moment what he meant—but it was only a moment before reality kicked in. The best kind of reality. Blake was there—with me. And we had until August 19 to make it count.

I got up, used the bathroom, and brushed my teeth, then climbed back into bed and waited for him to return. I had to wait only a few minutes before I heard him walk over to the side of the bed and stand over me.

"Like the dead," he whispered and laughed to himself.

I shot up and wrapped my arms around his neck, bringing him down with me.

"Jesus Christ, Chloe, you scared the shit—"

I pressed my lips to his. Rushed and frantic at first, but then the kiss slowed enough so that he could position himself on top of me and between my legs. He tasted salty from the sheen of sweat that covered his face and his entire body. He was shirtless again. And the picture of him in my mind made my hips jerk up and into him.

He moaned but pulled back quickly. "Shit," he spat out, letting his head fall onto my shoulder. "I need to shower." He kissed me once. "A cold one."

And then he was gone. I waited for him to get in the bathroom before kicking my legs wildly, like a teenager who had just made out with a boy she'd been crushing on forever. Because that was what I was. A teenager, crushing on a boy for the very first time in her life.

I got out of bed, made us coffee, and waited out on the balcony for him. When he came out, he just stood in front of me. "You're in my seat," he said. My eyebrows bunched, but I got up anyway. He sat down, but before I could move to another seat, his arm curled around me and brought me down onto his lap. "I think every room we get should have a balcony."

"Okay." I picked up my coffee and used it to hide my smile.

He kissed my neck a few times, and his lips remained there when he spoke. "Chloe?"

"Yeah?"

He pulled back and swiveled my legs so I was sideways on his lap. "I think that—I mean, I want to—" He cursed under his breath before continuing, "I want to take things slow with you. With *us*. We only have a couple months, and I want to remember all of it.

I don't just want to have sex with you and become another forget-table guy."

I opened my mouth to interrupt, but he cut me off.

"I know," he said. "I know that's not what I am, but I don't want to risk it. And I'm scared that if we have sex, then that's the only thing we'll remember from this time we have together, that's all this adventure will become—sex. Because I'm positive that once I have you in that way, then I'll need to have you always. And that's just not good enough for me. It's not good enough for *us*."

"Okay," I said, because a part of me agreed with him, and another part of me wondered what the hell I'd done that made me deserve him.

*   *   *

Sometimes the wrong path can lead us to the right road. And toward the greatest thing that will ever happen to us.

We stood in front of the fridge and stared at my handwritten quote on the magnet I'd just placed there. I hoped he understood what I meant by it. I hoped he knew that I was talking about him. That *he* was the best thing that had ever happened to me.

"Why are you leaving it here?" he asked.

I shrugged. "Maybe one day someone will book this room, see that message, and those words might be exactly what they need to see. Maybe they'll smile after reading it. Maybe a smile is all they'll need to keep them going."

"You got another one?"

I reached into my bag and pulled out a blank magnet and a red pen. He smiled when he took it from my hands. Then he leaned on the counter, wrote on the magnet, and stuck it right next to mine.

When life gives you melons, you might be dyslexic.

*   *   *

"It's a giant peach," he said.

I leaned back against the car and looked at the roadside water-tower attraction. "I know, how cool is it?"

"I don't think *cool* is the right word." He tilted his head to the side. "I don't know that there is a word to describe it."

"*I* think it's cool."

"*I* think it's odd that I can't stop staring at it."

I laughed. "I think you secretly think it's cool."

"I think the word *cool* is outdated."

I turned my back on the giant peach and stood in front of him. "I think *you're* outdated."

He peered down at me from under the brim of his Duke cap. "I'll outdate you." He pulled my shirt until I was flush against him. Then he lowered his head toward mine.

My eyes shut.

I waited for his lips to touch mine.

But they never did.

I opened my eyes.

He was gazing over my head. "I can't stop staring at the giant peach."

*   *   *

When we had left the hotel that morning, he'd asked if he could negotiate some terms with me. I'd told him that it was *our* trip, not just mine, and negotiations weren't needed. He had three requests: (1) an endless supply of lollipops, (2) we drive for only two hours at a time before stopping, and (3) we drive no more than six hours a day.

We found somewhere to stay a few hours away. I didn't exactly know where we were, and it didn't really matter. Where he was— that was where I wanted to be.

The first thing he did when we walked into the room was look for the balcony doors. He slid them open and stepped outside. I made us coffee and followed after him. His legs were already kicked out, and he was waiting for me take my spot on his lap. He smiled sadly when I did.

"Are you okay, Blake?"

"Yeah, why?"

"You always get sad at the end of the day."

"I'm that obvious, huh?"

I turned to face him. "Is something wrong? Are you homesick?"

He laughed. "No. I'm not homesick. It's just another day over. That's all. I hate it—counting them down and knowing our days are limited."

"I know." I forced a smile. "So what do we do?"

"Nothing," he sighed. "I'm just being grumpy." He positioned me so I sat sideways on him. "And this is gonna sound really stupid, but I miss you."

I chuckled. "You miss me? How? I'm with you all the time."

"I know! I told you it would sound dumb, but I do miss you. We're always in the car or eating somewhere. And I feel like I'm sharing you with The Road, and I just want you all to myself, and it makes me feel selfish because this was your thing." His words were rushed. "But I miss you. I just want to talk to you, and only you, like we did all the times at your mom's lake. Or on your swing seat." He sucked in a breath. "I'm sorry. It's stupid that I feel like this."

"It's not stupid." And it wasn't. I felt the same way, but I didn't know how to voice it. Blake—he always had the words. "We can stay here for a few days. It's nice and quiet. We don't have to do anything. Just lock ourselves away from the rest of the world."

His eyebrows furrowed in confusion. Maybe that wasn't what he'd meant.

"I mean—if you want to," I added. "I'd like that, just you and me. But it's cool if you—"

"That sounds perfect, Chloe." He smiled. "More than perfect."

＊　　＊　　＊

The entire night he'd been sitting there shirtless, watching whatever the hell movie had been playing. I'd tried not to look at him. To ogle him. To devour him.

I kept tossing and turning, trying to get comfortable with the throbbing ache between my legs. I wanted him. And I knew he wanted me. The endless kissing, touching, feeling—it wasn't enough anymore. Not for me.

He pulled back from our kiss, his lips red and raw. "We need to slow down, I don't want to sleep with you yet. But if we keep going, I'm going to lose control. You need to stop me before it gets too far." His eyes were dark. Darker than I'd ever seen them. "Please, Chloe."

It took a moment before I worked out what he was asking. I nodded once and wrapped my legs tighter around his waist.

"Okay."

And if he did lose control—it didn't show. Every move, every touch, every taste felt calculated. His hands moved up my sides, taking my shirt with it. We broke away from the kiss only long enough for him to lift the top over my head. But when we continued, something in him had switched. No longer slow and gentle, his kisses became desperate. Passionate. Perfect. *He* was perfect.

His hand slid up my back and settled on my bra, where it stilled—asking for approval, I guessed. I moaned into his mouth and pulled myself closer with my hands on his shoulders. Effortlessly, he unclasped the bra, slowly sliding it down my arms. I pulled back to let it fall, but his grip on my waist kept me there.

He bit his lip, his eyes moving from one breast to another. "Beautiful," he whispered before kissing me again.

It took only seconds before we were there once more, teetering on the edge of whatever control we had left. His thumb brushed against my nipple; the other one laced and fisted in my hair. He yanked hard but not hard enough that it hurt.

My head tilted back so his mouth could move to my neck. I was grinding my hips, rubbing my heat where I wanted him the most. His hips rose, meeting me there. I was so wet, so close.

His mouth moved lower and lower, onto my collarbone, where his lips paused to suck. Hard. *And I loved it.* And then he moved. Lower again. I pushed my chest out. Ready. Waiting. I *needed* him where he *wanted* to be. The warmth of his mouth on my nipple set me off. I ground harder into him. Faster. We groaned simultaneously. And I didn't even know when or how they got there, but his fingers brushed against my sex, over my panties, rubbing lightly.

"Shit," I repeated the word over and over between pants.

Then he pushed the material aside and pushed two fingers inside me. His mouth moved from one breast to the other, and whatever control I had was gone. I was *done.* I thrust into his hand as his fingers worked me over the edge. I didn't even notice when he pulled back. Not until every last shudder went through me, and I finally managed to open my eyes.

He was watching me, eyes hooded, mouth partially open. I moved in to kiss him. Just once, before I made my way down his body. His neck first, sucking the way he'd done to me. Marking him. Making him mine. He slid his fingers out of me. I kissed lower, over his chest, as I slid down his body. My tongue slid to his stomach—his perfect stomach—paying special attention to the dips of his muscles. Then my hands moved and curled around the band of his boxers.

"Chloe." He covered my hands with his. "You don't have to—"

I didn't listen. He didn't continue protesting. Once my mouth was around him, he was silent. Apart from the moans toward the end and a single word—my name.

* * *

We spent three more days in the hotel room, and we did exactly what we both wanted. We didn't have sex, but we shared, we talked, we laughed. And at some point, we fell even more in love. We didn't voice it. We didn't have to. We both knew. But someday, real soon, I'd tell him.

And for the first time in my life, I made a plan for the future.

Blake Hunter—he was my *future*.

* * *

Think a little less, live a little more.

"Ha!" he said. "I like that one."

"Me, too." I smiled.

He picked up his blank magnet and scribbled on it. *Today will live forever in the memory of tomorrow.*

"I love that. Where's it from?" I looked up at him.

He shrugged and kissed my forehead.

"One of my mom's books."

"You read her books?" I asked.

"Every single one."

CHAPTER TWENTY-EIGHT

Chloe

He leaned against the car and pulled me into him, my back to his chest. "What's it supposed to be?"

"An egg, I think."

"What's its purpose?"

"A water tower? I'm not sure."

"Why do you always make me stop at these random things?" He pulled the lollipop out of his mouth and pointed it to the egg-shaped tower. "Do you think they built it with this in mind? That people would pull over and want to spend longer looking at it?"

I laughed. "You can't stop looking at it, can you?"

"No," he said, astonishment clear in his voice. "And I have no idea why."

*   *   *

I stared at my breasts in the bathroom mirror.

They *looked* the same.

Only they weren't.

I had imagined this moment so many times. I even thought that I'd prepared myself for it. But things had changed so much over the past few weeks that I had almost let myself believe that it would never happen.

But now, *now* it was happening.

I wiped the tears off my cheeks and attempted to inhale a few calming breaths. Then I shut my eyes and waited as every single possible emotion passed through me. And then I settled on one. I didn't want to feel anymore. "I think we should go out tonight," I shouted to Blake on the other side of the door.

"Yeah? You wanna go to dinner or something?"

"No. I'm thinking I might want to lose myself for a little bit."

His footsteps got louder as he walked to the bathroom door. The handle moved but it didn't push open. I'd made sure to lock it. "Open the door, Chloe."

I rushed to get dressed and opened the door. His eyebrows bunched as he looked down at me. "You want to go out and have a few beers?"

"Yeah." I feigned casualness in my tone. "Just for something different, you know?"

"Okay," he agreed. "We might get carded, so dress whore-ish."

I would have been offended by his suggestion if not for the fact that I'd already planned to.

Blake

We hadn't been carded; they'd let us right in. Luckily, the bar was only a block away from the hotel, so we didn't have to worry about getting back. We hadn't had to worry much about anything since we'd hit the road.

But at that moment—I was worried. After her fifth shot of tequila, I asked if she was okay.

"Quit looking at me like that. I'm fine."

I hadn't realized I was looking at her like anything.

She brushed past me and headed toward the pool tables. "I'm taking a piss," I told her. I went to kiss her quickly, but she pulled back and walked away. I tried to ignore it—the hurt from her actions and the concern over the way she'd been acting all night.

When I walked out of the restroom, she was leaning against one of the pool tables, her shorter-than-short skirt barely covering her ass. She had a cue in one hand and a beer in the other, but that wasn't what set off the rage in my head. It was the guy standing in front of her. Too close in front of her. I made my way over and stood next to her, hoping my stance and physical appearance would make him fuck off. His eyes moved from Chloe's breasts to me, and a disgusted snarl appeared on his face. "This your boyfriend?" he asked her but kept his eyes on me.

I sized him up and smirked. I could take him. Easy.

I leaned back and waited for her words of rejection so this asshole would get out of her face, but her dismissal never came.

"He's whatever," she said.

My heart stopped. Or picked up pace. I couldn't tell.

When I turned to her, she was looking down at the floor, her head bent and eyelids heavy from the alcohol.

"Chloe!" I snapped. "What the hell's gotten into you?"

"Fuck off, *Hunter*. You met me a few months ago, and you think you know me? Seriously, fuck off. You don't know shit. I'm not some fucking damsel that needs saving. You think you can stick around and that'll save me, you're wrong."

I got that she was drunk. Beyond drunk. But even when she had been loaded at Will's party, she hadn't talked to me like this. A ball formed in the pit of my stomach, and I stood straighter, staring at her, trying to work out what the fuck I should do.

Then the asshole stepped forward. "You wanna get out of here?" he asked her.

And I lost it.

I'd never been this pissed before.

Without even thinking, I grabbed her arm—rougher than I should have—and dragged her out of the bar.

I didn't want to say something I'd regret, so I tried to compose myself before asking, "What's wrong, Chloe?"

"Nothing!" she yelled. "Nothing is fucking wrong with me. And you—you have no right to control me like that. From where I stand, you and me—we're nothing. I haven't promised anything and neither have you." She started walking hastily away from me.

I grabbed her arm and made her turn to me. "What the fuck are you talking about?"

"You!" She pushed against my chest. "August 19. That's all you've promised me. Maybe that's not enough anymore!"

My heart dropped. It felt as if all the air had been knocked out of me. "What do you want me to say, Chloe? What the hell do you want me to do? Tell me, and I'll do it!"

Her shoulders sagged, and a sob took over. "Nothing, okay? I want you to do nothing."

She started walking back to the hotel. I followed, a few feet behind her, completely lost in my own thoughts.

What the fuck just happened?

Once we got to the hotel, I changed into my running gear, craving the numbness I knew the run would provide. "I'll be back soon."

She got into bed without bothering to change and nodded, refusing to look at me.

Chloe

"Chloe." I could hear his voice, but he sounded far away. Then something nudged my leg. "Chloe," he said again.

I waited for the room to stop spinning before opening my eyes.

Blake was hovering above me, chewing his thumb. "Hey."

"Hey," I replied, sitting up to try to clear my head.

He sat on the edge of the bed, his head down. Then his gaze lifted and locked with mine. "I'm gonna take off. I just wanted you to know . . . so you don't wake up in the morning and wonder what happened."

He was leaving?

I sat up straighter and tried to stop myself from throwing up. Not because of the alcohol but because of what was happening. And even though I'd expected it to happen, even *needed* it to happen, I'd never *wanted* it to happen. Not for a second. "Okay."

All it took was that single word—that one response of approval—and I could see his heart shatter right in from of me. He sniffed and looked away. I followed his gaze, and my heart tightened like a vise. His bags were already packed. "Now?" I squeaked.

He stood up slowly. "I got another room for the night. I'm leaving in the morning. You can have the car until you get something else, then just contact my mom. She'll take care of it."

The ache in my chest became so painful I wanted to reach in and rip my heart out, throw it against the wall, and watch it as it slowly stopped beating and died. Maybe that was what was happening to me; maybe I was slowly dying.

I nodded.

He reached for his bag, picked it up, and took one step toward the door.

And that was when it happened.

My heart kicked back in, and I panicked. I lost all restraint from earlier. I jumped to my feet on the bed and wrapped my arms around his neck. "Blake, please," I cried.

He dropped his bag and turned to me, but his hands didn't touch me. "What, Chloe? What do you want?"

"Don't," I begged.

He shook his head. "Don't what? I don't know what the hell you want."

All I could do was cry. The words were there. *Don't leave me.* But I just couldn't bring myself to say them out loud—to break the promise I'd made myself to never let anyone in.

He removed my arms from around him and took a step back, the sadness and regret clear on his face. "You can't even say it, can you? You don't even know what you want." He took another step closer to the door.

The thought of him leaving, walking away, and never seeing him again sent my mind into overdrive. "I do!" I reached for him again. "I want *you,* Blake." I jumped off the bed and wrapped my legs around him. And then I kissed him. With everything I had. But he didn't kiss me back. Instead, he tried to pull me off him. "Chloe. Stop."

I held on to him more tightly. "Please."

I physically felt it. The moment when his body won out, and he gave in to me. His hands moved down my back, onto my ass, gripping it hard, and hauling me closer to him. Then he finally started kissing back. But it wasn't Blake, not the usual him. Not the one that liked things slow, liked to savor me so he could get to know me. It was another part of him kissing me. It was pure need. Pure lust. He dropped me on the bed and looked down at me. I never released my hold.

He shook his head. "Chloe."

I didn't know if it was a question or a warning, but either way, it didn't matter. Not when I started kissing him again. Not when I pushed his sweats past his hips, just enough to free his erection. Not when he cursed under his breath and said my name again. Not even when I held it in my hands and brought it to my entrance. I didn't bother removing my panties, and neither did he. He just pushed the material aside and thrust his fingers into me.

"Fuck, Chloe, I can't do this," he said as he dropped his head next to mine.

I gripped his hair tightly and kissed his neck. "Please, Blake. I *need* you."

He groaned before pulling his fingers out and replacing them with his erection.

I winced from the shock of him filling me.

It was rushed, rough, and over quickly.

I cried the entire time.

He stilled on top of me. "Mother fucker!" He punched the pillow next to my head, and jerked himself out of me. He sniffed as he hastily sat up on his heels.

I wiped the tears of embarrassment from my cheeks and jumped in the shower. I cried as I tried to wash the filth off me, but it didn't work, because the filth wasn't on me. It was *in* me. I was ashamed.

I'd used sex as a way to keep him there, and it'd worked.

For now.

*　　*　　*

When I stepped out of the bathroom, he was sitting on the edge of the bed, his head in his hands. "I didn't use a condom," he muttered.

"Oh," I said, surprised. It hadn't even occurred to me while we were having sex. I always used a condom, even in my cross-faded states, I'd made sure of it. But with Blake, I hadn't even thought about it. "I have an IUD. I'm protected."

"That's not—" he sighed. "That's not the point." But he wasn't talking to me. "I don't even know what the hell the point is." He tied the laces on his running shoes and stood up. "I'm going for a run."

And even though a part of me had thought he would, it still surprised me that he was. He'd told me why he ran; he'd said he did it to feel numb—that when things got to be too much sometimes, he wanted to feel nothing. That moment was his moment of *nothing*. He walked to the door with his head down, refusing to make eye contact. I was sure he was disgusted by me, ashamed of what I'd just done.

I wiped frantically at my tears. "Are you coming back?"

He froze midstride, then lifted his gaze and nodded once. "Yeah, Chloe. I'll be back," he said quietly, but with so much pity that I hated myself.

Once he had left, I ran to the bathroom and threw up.

Blake

Josh answered first ring.

"I'm sorry for calling again," I said as I sat on the curb in front of the hotel.

"Dude. You never have to apologize for that. What's going on? You want us to come and get you now?"

The word *yes* caught in my throat. I wasn't sure how long I'd been silent, not knowing how to respond, when he sighed loudly. "What the hell happened, man? Did you go back and tell her you were leaving?"

"Yeah."

"And?"

It took everything I had to answer him. "I fucked up, Josh."

"What does that mean?"

"We had sex."

He sighed again. "And I take it that's a bad thing?"

"I don't know what the fuck happened." I dropped my head between my knees, my hand gripping the phone tighter. "One minute I had my bags packed, ready to leave, and the next thing I know, she's . . ." I couldn't even finish the sentence. "She was wasted and she asked me to stay. She threw herself at me, and I didn't fucking say no. I took advantage of her, Josh. I'm exactly like every other forgettable asshole she's ever fucked." I wiped my eyes, grateful that Josh couldn't see me crying.

He was quiet a long moment before he asked, "Do you honestly believe that?"

I shook my head, my tears falling freely. "I don't want to, Josh, but maybe I had it wrong. Maybe I thought this was something more than it really is. Maybe I'm nothing to her . . . or I'm just a fling, someone to have a good time with until she decides she wants to be invisible again." I let out a bitter laugh. "How did I not see this coming?"

Josh cleared his throat. I heard movement on the other end, as if he was sitting up and pushing the covers off him. "You wanna know what I think?"

"I think you're gonna tell me anyway."

"I think you're wrong."

"About which part exactly?"

"All of it." He paused a beat before continuing. "I think that it's human nature that when people get scared, they do stupid things. All you have to do is look at Natalie for proof. As far as Chloe goes—you and I may not agree with the way she lives her life, but we can't really disagree with her reasoning behind it. Chloe kept everyone at arm's length, even the people she calls family. But you, Hunter, you're there with her. She let *you* in. And you—you haven't *cared* about anything the past couple years. You existed, but you didn't live . . . yet somehow, there you are, with a girl that you may be in love with, and you finally *care*. Whatever happens, if you stay or if you leave, you need to decide whether it's worth giving all of that up."

Chloe

For two hours I lay in bed, wide-awake, waiting for him to come back. I wondered if he'd come in silently, get his bags, and leave.

I waited. And waited. And finally, at around five in the morning, against my will, I succumbed to exhaustion.

*　　　*　　　*

I wasn't sure how long I'd been asleep before the sound of the door opening startled me awake. I didn't dare move. If he was going to leave, he had every right, and the perfect opportunity to do it. I heard his footsteps and then the shower running. It was only a few minutes, but it felt like an eternity. When the pipes clanked and the water switched off, I pulled the covers over my head—hiding out—surrounded by my own self-pity and self-loathing. He sighed—the sound deafening in the dead silence of the room. Then the bed dipped and he lay down behind me, gently placing his arm over my waist and pulling me to him, the other arm under my pillow and around my chest.

And then he held me. Tight.

All while I silently cried in his arms.

I cried for me.

I cried for him.

I cried for the future we'd never have.

And I cried because he had absolutely no idea about any of it.

*　　　*　　　*

He wasn't in bed when I woke up. What was there, though, was a throbbing in my head, no doubt from my crying. My endless, fucking crying. As I sat up, I noticed his bags but no note on the pillow. He always left a note.

Then I heard his voice. "Yeah, Ma."

I turned to see him sitting out on the balcony, holding his phone to his ear.

"I know," he said. "I love you, too."

He pulled back, looked at the screen, tapped it once, and placed it on the table. And then he just sat there.

I got out of bed and made us coffee, like I did every morning. I refused to look at him when I brought it out to him. I just set it on the table and turned to leave him alone, but I didn't get far before his arm curled around my waist and he pulled me down onto his lap.

We stayed like that, with me on his lap and his arm around me, neither of us speaking.

He rested his chin on my shoulder and kissed my cheek softly. I must have been so tense, so stiff in his arms that he felt the need to say, "You can breathe, Chloe. It's okay."

I finally did.

"What happened last night . . ."

I didn't know if it was a question or not, so I began to answer. "I'm not—"

His hand gripped my shirt, causing me to stop. "It wasn't a question. I just . . . I need a minute to find the words." He inhaled a heavy breath.

I waited.

"What happened last night shouldn't have happened. I shouldn't have taken advantage of you the way I did." I went to interrupt him, but he cut me off. "Just let me finish, please?"

I nodded.

"I know you well enough to know that when you said you wanted to lose yourself that something deeper was going on. I wish that you would have shared it with me, but you didn't, and that was your choice. I can't force you to talk to me, no matter how upset it makes me that you didn't. I chased after you when you left because I wanted to be with you, Chloe. I wasn't ready to say good-bye, and you knew that. We both knew that. And we both knew that our time was limited. We talked about that. If you wanted more than that . . . if you wanted me to promise you something more . . . you should've asked. But I didn't know, and you never told me."

He positioned me so I was sideways, and he could look at me. "But if last night is what it's going to be like . . . if things get hard for you, and you choose to keep pushing me away, then I'll leave."

He sniffed and wiped his face on my shoulder. The wetness from his tears seeped through my shirt. "Because I don't deserve that, Chloe. If you push me away, I'll leave, and I'll never come back. I won't ever call you; I won't ever breathe your name again. I know that's how you've lived your life—wanting to be invisible, so I'll give that to you. But you should know that that's not what I want. And I don't think that's what you want, either. I think you're afraid. I think you realize how close we've gotten and how deep our feelings are getting, and you got scared. And you pushed me away because that's what you're used to."

I swallowed down the words I wished I could say. The ones that would tell him that I was afraid that I might have cancer. The ones I couldn't voice, no matter how much I wanted to. Because I wasn't ready. And because they would change *everything*.

I blinked.

Tears fell.

"Chloe." He placed his finger on my chin and made me face him. And when I did—the walls around me crumbled. And so did I. I wailed into his chest, gripping his shirt tight, holding on to him. When I'd calmed down, he held the side of my face and tilted my head up. "So you have to tell me. What do you want? Do you want me? Do you want *us*? Do you want *more*?"

I nodded.

But he still looked unsure.

I squared my shoulders and held his head in my hands. "Yes, Blake. I want you. I want us. I want a future. I want a forever with you."

And even through his own tear-filled eyes, he managed to smile. A smile that took all the hurt, all the pain, all the anguish, and buried it deep in my past.

A smile that turned my world *red*.

It had never really made sense when he'd explained it in the past, but I finally got it.

Blake Hunter—he was my red-letter day.

"Can I kiss you now?" he said.

I let out a relieved laugh. "Please."

And just like his smile—his kiss took all the pain away.

"Blake?" I pulled back slightly.

He kept his eyes closed. "Yeah?"

"Last night—"

"Never happened."

"But I was—"

"Shut up and kiss me."

*   *   *

Love me when I least deserve it, because that is when I need it the most.

He tensed when he read my magnet aloud. Then he placed his magnet right next to mine. "Ready?" he asked.

"Yeah, babe. I'm ready." I took one more look at his magnet before picking up my bag and walking out of the room.

You can run, you can hide, you can choose not to see, but where the road takes you will always lead to me.

CHAPTER TWENTY-NINE

Blake

She was wearing the blue Duke jersey, my name and potential number on the back, and I'd never wanted to play for Duke as much as I did right now.

"Should we just skate down? It's only half a mile to the pier."

"Whatever you want, babe." But I was already pulling our boards out of the trunk.

I skated to the pier. She held on to my shirt and rolled along behind me. There was a street art show going on, and she wanted to check it out. I'd do whatever she wanted.

"I wish I was good at art," she said from next to me.

"Have you tried it?"

She shrugged. "Not really. I just can't do anything creative."

And it struck me then, that even though we'd spent all this time together, I really didn't know much about her at all. "What do you do?" I asked.

She laughed. "What do you mean?"

"I mean, when you're not with me, skating, or practicing shots from the three-point line. What's your deal?"

She shrugged. "Not much, really. I don't really have any hobbies, if that's what you mean."

"Yeah." I followed her to the next artist—a chalk drawer. "But there must be something you like to do . . . or are good at. Something?"

"Not really." She dropped some change into the dude's hat.

"I call bullshit. I bet you sing or play guitar or something phenomenal."

She laughed. "No, Blake. I really do nothing." She started walking toward an ice-cream truck, but stopped a few feet away and turned to me. "Maybe it was because I was fostered or something. Like, I didn't want to do anything permanent, because I didn't know if *I* would be permanent." Her eyebrows bunched, and she pursed her lips. Then sadness washed over her features. "Maybe it was because I didn't think I'd be around long enough to enjoy it." She shook her head. "That sounds so stupid."

"Baby, it's not stupid." I hugged her with one arm, the other busy carrying both our boards. "I get it, though—why you would be like that. Maybe it's time we find something for you."

She pulled back and looked up at me. "What do you mean?"

"Well, we're always fucking around with the skating and the basketball. Maybe we find something you like and do it together. We can learn together. You like music? We can buy guitars. You want to learn magic? We'll buy a—"

"I like *you*," she cut in. She smirked and placed her hands under my shirt, fingers splayed flat against my stomach. "Can I learn *you*?"

"You're changing the subject and avoiding talking about this."

She pouted and dropped her hands. "Why does it matter?"

"Because," I said. "It matters because you deserve to have something of your own. To want something for yourself. Even if it's not forever."

"Okay, Blake." She nodded. "I'll think about it. I'll do it for you."

I sighed. "Babe, I want you to do it for you. Not for me or anyone else."

"Okay," she agreed. Then her gaze moved toward the ice-cream truck. I watched as her eyes narrowed and a glare appeared.

"Chloe?"

She jerked her head toward the truck. "That girl won't take her eyes off you."

"And?"

"And it's pissing me off."

I chuckled.

"Wrong time to laugh, asshole."

I laughed harder.

She gripped my arm. "Oh my God," she gasped.

I followed her gaze just as the girl walked into a wall.

"Oh my God," she said again. Then, through a laugh, "That girl was so busy checking you out, she didn't even see a wall right in front of her!"

I took her hand, and we walked to the ice-cream truck.

"I bet you're used to it, huh? Girls looking at you. God, I feel so average right now."

I dropped her hand and the boards. "Chloe." I stood in front of her and made sure she was looking at me. "Don't ever talk like that about yourself. Ever." I was beyond serious, and my tone let her know.

She frowned. "I'm sorry."

"Don't be sorry." I released a breath and tried to calm down. "I just hate when you look down on yourself."

She tried to smile. "You need to give me a break. I'm an eighteen-year-old girl, and you're my first boyfriend . . . and you just happen to be stupidly hot. So what if I get petty and jealous?"

She shrugged. "I'm allowed. I bet if a guy looked at me like that, you'd probably feel the same."

I let her words sink in before speaking. "A, if a guy looked at you in *any way*, I'd probably beat his ass. B, I didn't know I was your boyfriend."

Her eyes went wide. "I just assumed—"

"Good," I interrupted. "Assume away, girlfriend."

*   *   *

I felt her release her grip on my shirt as I skated us back to the hotel. I quickly turned around, hoping she hadn't stacked somehow. With Chloe's coordination, I never knew. She had one foot on the ground, the other on the board, her gaze fixed through a window and into a store. I flicked the board up and held it as I walked over to her. "Chloe?"

She didn't respond.

I followed her gaze into the store; it was a clothes store full of formal wear. Her brow furrowed as she watched a group of girls talking and laughing, dressed in what looked like prom attire. "It's a little late for prom," I said.

"I don't know," she said quietly. She frowned and looked down at the ground. "I've never been to a prom."

"Yeah? That's not surprising."

She looked up at me. "What do you mean?"

I shrugged. "You're not exactly the prom type. I just don't see you getting your hair done and getting all dressed up to spend a night out with your friends, you know? You didn't even really have friends."

She nodded, but her frown deepened and tears started to fill her eyes.

"What's wrong, babe?"

She shrugged. "I guess regrets are useless in times like these."

"You want to go to prom?"

"No," she said quickly, shaking her head. "I'm just being stupid. Let's go."

She pushed off the ground and attempted to skate away, but I grabbed on to her arm to stop her. "Wait here, okay?"

She started to speak but I was already stepping into the store.

I made my way over to the girls, who smiled warmly when they saw me coming. "Are you girls going to prom?" I asked them.

They nodded in unison. "Kind of," one of them said, stepping forward. "It's not a school one. We kind of just organized it because we all go to small schools and didn't really have a decent prom. Plus, all our boyfriends are in college and couldn't make it, so we're just having a big ol' fake one in my barn." She paused for a beat and eyed me curiously. "Why?"

I smiled. "My girlfriend, Chloe," I pointed to her watching us from the other side of the store window. Their smiles widened. "She's never been to a prom. You think you might be able to make room for two more?"

"That's so sweet," one of the other girls said.

"I'm Jasmine," the girl hosting the prom said. "Send your girlfriend in. We'll take good care of her. I promise."

I couldn't help but grin. "What time does it start?"

"Eight."

"Perfect."

I headed back out and dragged Chloe into the store. The girls introduced themselves, all while Chloe stood by awkwardly, almost shyly.

"You've never been to prom?" Jasmine asked her.

Chloe just shook her head. Jasmine clapped her hands. "This is going to be so much fun."

Chloe looked up at me, chewing her lip, her eyes unsure.

"I'll pick you up at your room at seven thirty." I kissed her cheek and walked out before she could protest.

A half hour later she texted me: *All these girls jog. You know what that means, right? It was nice knowing you, Blake Hunter.*

Chloe

The girls weren't serial killers, like I'd first suspected. They were actually really nice. I was afraid they'd be a bunch of Hannahs, but I was so wrong. It didn't take me long to find a dress, and once I had, the girls helped with the shoes and accessories. I was the first to admit that I was way out of my element. Jasmine's mom owned a salon two doors down from the clothes store and was able to fit me in last minute to get my hair, nails, and makeup done. It had been awkward at first, but then I decided to let myself have this one moment, before it was all over.

*   *   *

Later, I kicked my legs back and forth as I sat on the edge of the bed, waiting for Blake to knock on the door. My light-purple dress shifted with each kick. I looked at the alarm clock on the night-stand. He would be there any second. My palms sweat from the nerves that were wreaking havoc in my mind. It felt like a first date, or what I assumed a first date would feel like.

I exhaled loudly, stood up, and started pacing the floor, then I went to the bathroom and checked my hair, now formed into loose curls, which cascaded down my shoulders. I checked my makeup, and then I started pacing again. I did this four more times before there was a knock on the door.

"Shit." I brushed my hands down my dress and checked in the mirror again, then I swallowed my nerves, placed a hand on the door handle, inhaled and exhaled a few calming breaths, and finally opened the door.

He was wearing a tux, perfectly fitted to his broad shoulders. He held a white corsage in one hand, the other hand in his pocket. His head was bent, looking down at the ground. Then, slowly, his gaze started to move up. My entire body heated up as his eyes kept trailing higher until they finally landed on mine.

He blew out a forceful breath and shook his head slowly. "I didn't think it was possible for you to become more beautiful, but I was so wrong, Chloe."

I smiled at his words, trying so hard to avoid tears of happiness.

A slight smile graced his face as he lifted the corsage. "I got you this."

I raised my hand for him. "It's beautiful," I told him.

He shook his head. "No, Chloe. I don't think the word beautiful should ever exist unless it's used to describe you," he mumbled, his eyes narrowed, concentrating on securing the corsage on my wrist. I waited for him to straighten up before stepping forward and kissing him. I felt him smile against my lips, and then he pulled back, the smile still in place. He held his arm out, bent at the elbow, waiting for me. "You ready, girlfriend?"

My smile matched his. "Yes, boyfriend."

I stopped us in front of his car, but he just laughed. "We're not taking the car," he stated, before pulling me with him around the corner and to the front of the hotel where a stretch limo was waiting.

I gasped, long and loud. "Blake!"

He linked his fingers with mine and continued over to the limo. "It's not prom without a limo."

Blake

I laughed as I watched her fiddling with all the buttons in the limo. She squealed when she found the one that operated the sunroof.

248

She spent a good few minutes standing there, with half her body sticking out.

She slumped down on the seat next to me and sighed. "This is so exciting for me."

"Really? I couldn't tell," I laughed.

She threw an arm over my waist and moved closer to me. "What do normal teenagers do in a limo, then?"

I raised an eyebrow. "You really wanna know?"

She nodded.

I leaned in and kissed her neck, then placed my hand on her thigh, slowly shifting her dress higher until my fingertips skimmed her skin. "Fool around," I murmured against her skin.

She laughed and pushed me away, her nose scrunched in disgust. "I don't like pre-me Blake Hunter," she said.

I chuckled. "I don't think I do, either."

*   *   *

When Jasmine said she was hosting the prom in her barn, I had imagined a run-down shack. What this was was the Hollywood mansion of barns. At least a hundred kids filled the barn, more than half of whom were dancing to a song I'd never heard before. Chloe froze next to me, her grip on my arm tightening. I watched as her eyes widened and she looked at me. "Wow," she said. "It's just like in the movies."

"You made it!" We both turned to see Jasmine approaching us, dragging a guy behind her. She stopped when she got to us and looked me up and down. "You clean up nice."

I chuckled as her boyfriend threw his hand out. "I'm Chase."

I shook his hand. "Blake." I jerked my head toward Chloe. "This is my girlfriend, Chloe."

They barely had time to shake hands before Jasmine had a hold of Chloe. "You boys have fun," she shouted over her shoulder. "I'm showing off Chloe."

Chloe looked back at me with a grimace.

"Have fun," I mouthed.

"So this is really her first prom?" Chase asked, now standing next to me, watching our girls walk away.

"Yup."

"Kind of hard to believe, considering she looks like that." He paused for a moment, then added, "That came out wrong. I apologize. I was just trying to pay your girl a compliment."

My shoulders relaxed. "It's fine. She wasn't really all that social in high school."

Awkward silence filled the space between us. "So you wanna dance?" he asked. "I do a mean Hammer dance."

I laughed.

"Come on, I'll take you to meet the others."

He led me to a table far enough away from the speakers that I could actually hear conversation. He introduced me to three other guys with beers in their hands. Chase pointed at a chair and positioned it so it faced the dance floor, then pointed to Chloe, who was standing with the girls from earlier that day. I sat on the chair and watched as they huddled in a circle as they spoke to each other. Chloe threw her head back and laughed at something someone must have said, then Jasmine started to Hammer dance.

"Dammit!" Chase said. "She always mocks my dancing."

I laughed and turned away from the girls. Leaning my elbows on the table, I said, "So you're in college now?"

He nodded. "Yeah, I'm at The Citadel—"

"That military school?"

"Yeah," he said slowly, as if he was surprised I knew what it was. "How did you—?"

"Do you like it there?"

He nodded again. "It's perfect for me, but it's not for everyone." He paused for a beat. "You just graduated, right? What are your plans?"

I looked over at Chloe, who was watching me with a hint of a smile on her face. "Have fun," she mouthed.

I turned my attention back to Chase. "Right now? My plans are Chloe."

He just smiled and leaned back in his chair.

After an hour of talking ball with the boys, I heard the music stop for a moment, and the atmosphere changed. The lights lowered, and the music started again. The song was slower, and half the people left the dance floor. The boys moaned, knowing too well what their fate was. Me—I'd been waiting for this moment all night.

I stood and made my way over to Chloe, whose back was to me. I straightened up before tapping her on the shoulder. She turned around and smiled when she saw me. "Girlfriend," I greeted her, and her smile widened. "Dance with me?"

She nodded and gave me her hand. I led her to the middle of the floor and held her close to me. "I don't know how to dance," I whispered in her ear.

She giggled into my chest. "I don't, either." She threw her arms over my shoulders. "So it's kind of perfect."

I don't know how many songs we danced to while I held her. She didn't speak, and neither did I. But she was right; it was kind of perfect. We spent the next couple of hours sitting and talking with Jasmine and Chase and their friends. They were good people. The type of people I wish I'd had around me in high school. I told them about school, about Josh and Tommy, and about Duke and the army. Chloe listened to everyone intently and spoke only when asked questions. Jasmine asked her how we'd met, and she smiled and laughed as she retold the events of that night. When Chase asked her what the hell she was doing in a park in the middle of the night, she just shrugged and looked at me. "Maybe fate knew that I needed saving," she said.

It was close to two in the morning when the party died down and people started to leave.

Chase stood up and dramatically pointed at Jasmine. "Hungry. Feed me, woman," he bellowed.

Everyone laughed.

"Diner?" she asked him.

Everyone got up and started to pack their stuff.

"You guys coming?" Chase asked us.

Chloe turned to me. "Can we?" she asked shyly.

"Of course, babe."

*　　*　　*

Time flew as we all ate and talked shit. By the time conversation had slowed down, Chloe was in my jacket, snoring lightly under my arm. "She's out," Chase said, motioning to her.

Jasmine giggled. "She looks so peaceful when she's asleep."

"I know," I said, rubbing my eyes. "It's one of my favorite things about her—when she's sleeping."

Chase chuckled. "Because she's not talking?"

I laughed but then turned serious when I glanced down at her sleeping form. "No, because it's the only time she doesn't carry the weight of the world."

Silence descended on the table, but they didn't ask questions. Jasmine sighed. "The sun will be up soon," she mumbled.

I looked at the time. "Shit. We gotta go."

*　　*　　*

Chase pulled me aside as Chloe was saying her good-byes. He gave me his number and told me to call him if I ever needed advice about my Duke vs. army dilemma. I thanked him and told him that I'd like to keep in touch either way.

*   *   *

I told her that we'd be a while and that she could sleep in the limo. She was too tired to question me. She just lay across the seat with her head on my lap and slept the entire forty-five-minute drive to the field.

I woke her when we got there, and told her to look out the window.

"We're not at the hotel?"

I shook my head, my eyes never leaving her. Then she gasped so loud, it made me laugh. "Blake!"

Our driver opened the door, and I stepped out, hand out to help her do the same. We walked hand in hand over to the hot air balloon. Well, I walked. She skipped.

"You did this?" she asked, her eyes wide with excitement. "Why?"

"Because prom should be a night you'll never forget, and I wanted to make sure this was memorable for you."

*   *   *

She stood in front of me with her head against my chest as we watched the sun rise from almost two thousand feet in the air. "This is so beautiful, Blake," she said, and I could hear her holding back her sob. She inhaled deeply and tilted her face up, soaking in the morning light, her eyes closed.

"It reminds me of the day we met."

She smiled, but kept her eyes closed.

"I remember you doing the same thing. Do you remember what you said?"

She nodded. "I said it was perfect, and you agreed."

"Yeah. But I wasn't looking at the sun rise, Chloe, I was looking at you."

Her eyes snapped open. "Liar," she whispered.

I shook my head. "It's the truth."

Tears instantly welled in her eyes.

She blinked.

They fell.

I wiped them away and inhaled a shaky breath. Then I let out the words I'd been holding on to for weeks. "I've fallen so hard in love with you, Chloe."

She gasped, her eyes wide.

I continued, "And I don't know how to express it. I don't know what to do to show you how much I've come to love you."

"You're already doing it."

She didn't tell me she loved me back. But she kissed me in a way that reminded me that she didn't need to say in words how she felt. I already knew.

After a while, she pulled back from the kiss, her tears still flowing.

"You okay?" I asked.

She laughed once, but it was sad. "It's just moments like this—you make me not want to miss out on anything. You make me want to live forever, Blake."

*　　　*　　　*

I'd walked her to her hotel room door and told her that I'd booked the room next door for the night. When she'd pouted and asked why, I'd told her that I hadn't wanted to be presumptuous in believing that we'd spend the night together, considering it was kind of our first date. She'd laughed but she hadn't argued.

That was a half hour ago.

I opened the bathroom door after showering and heard a knock on the door. It was only eight in the morning, too early for housekeeping.

I smiled when I opened up and she was on the other side, her hair wet from her own shower. She wore the white Duke jersey, which reached midthigh. "I don't like sleeping without you." She exaggerated a pout.

I laughed and opened the door wider for her.

She waited until I was settled in bed before scooting in next to me and resting her head in the crook of my arm. "Thank you, Blake."

"What for?"

"For giving me this night. For giving me this memory."

Chloe

I leaned up on my elbow so I could look down on him.

He sighed and looked me right in the eyes. "Thank you for giving me *you*, Chloe."

I moved in and kissed him, softly, gently, the way he always did with me. He moaned and positioned me until I was on top of him, straddling his waist. His hand flattened on my back as he sat us up, and drew me closer to him. Then his hands skimmed up my thighs, shifting my shirt up, and rested on my waist a moment before moving higher and higher. His kisses travelled lower and lower, down my collarbone and to my chest. The heat of his mouth warmed my skin. My hips pushed forward; my body arched, ready, waiting.

His hands drifted under my shirt and up my sides. He turned me onto my back and lifted my top over my head, all in one swift move. Leaning on his elbows and hovering above me, his eyes roamed my face and down to my chest. Then he descended, his mouth open against my nipple. My hands reached up, gripping his hair, holding him tighter against me. His palms flattened on my thighs, spreading my legs for him. We let out simultaneous moans when his hardness pressed into my center. His lips moved up again, tasting my mouth. His hand gripped my thigh, bringing it up and around him so he could get closer.

He started moving down my body again, his mouth now on my stomach as his fingers curled around the material of my sleep shorts and panties. His mouth moved lower, as did his hands, pulling both items of clothing down my legs and off my feet.

He stood at the end of the bed, his eyes burning with lust as he took in my bare-naked form. "Fuck, you're beautiful."

He crawled back onto the bed, removing his shirt. He positioned himself between my legs, taking my mouth with his. We started moving, thrusting into each other. I wanted to feel him. All of him. Everywhere. On me. Inside me. My fingers trailed down his back. My hands raised and pushed against his chest. I rolled us over so he was underneath me.

And then it was my turn to taste him.

His neck. His chest. Every single dip of his abs. That perfect vee. I pulled on his boxers, freeing him. "Chloe," he breathed. It was a question. An answer. I hovered on all fours above him.

"Chloe." It was almost a warning. A plea.

I moved down and kissed him with everything I had, like my life depended on it. I laid my chest flat against his. "Make love to me, Blake."

"Are you sure?" he asked, his eyes closed and his jaw tense.

"Yes," I whispered.

He rolled us until I was under him and kissed my neck up to my ear. "I love you so much, Chloe."

And then he moved.

And so did I.

And we were there.

Loving each other.

In this room.
In the middle of a road trip.
On an experience of our lifetimes.
And a journey toward my death.
If he felt my tears, he never mentioned it.

CHAPTER THIRTY

Chloe

"This is by far the greatest thing you've ever dragged me to look at."

I laughed. "I know, right?"

"I'm not even kidding right now, Chloe. I mean, it's a manmade UFO . . . to welcome aliens when they land on earth so they're comfortable when they meet humans. How the fuck is that not the greatest thing in the world?"

"Wow!" I pulled out of his arms and sat on the hood of the car. "You're really into this one."

He followed and stood between my legs, shoving the lollipop back in his mouth. "Don't you think it's strange—" he mumbled around the stick. I took it from his mouth and put it in mine so he could talk properly. "Don't you think it's strange that we've been on the road for this long and we've only crossed one state border?"

He smiled when I laughed, squinting to block out the sun. I pulled his Duke cap farther down his forehead. "We should take another picture of us and send it to Harry."

He nodded in agreement and took the phone out of my back pocket. "Have you figured out how to use it yet?"

"Yes. I haven't been living under a rock. I just had no need for things like Facebook."

He snapped the photo, tapped the phone a few times, and shoved it back in my pocket. "You're the only eighteen-year-old I know that doesn't know how to use technology." He scrunched his nose in disgust. "You make me sick," he joked.

But I was too busy looking at him, watching as the sun beat down on his face, making his eyes extrablue and the freckles across his nose darker than I'd ever seen them.

"What?" he asked.

I tapped my finger on his nose. "You. These freckles. You're just so damn cute. How did I land you?"

He laughed and brushed my hand away. "Pretty sure I landed *on* you."

I ran my fingertips across his nose again. "I'm in love with these freckles. I kind of just want to make out with them."

He swatted my hand away, feigning annoyance.

Blake

"Okay, thank you, I'll see you later." She hung up the phone just as I took a seat in the booth at the diner we stopped at for lunch.

"Who was that?"

She shook her head and looked down at the table. "Um, just the bank, about releasing some of my money." Then she raised her head. "We should go . . . before the bank closes." She stood up. "You go pay the bill. I'll wait in the car." Then she was off, rushing out the door.

She was seated in the driver's seat when I came out, which was odd, because ever since we'd picked up the Jeep, I'd been the one to drive.

I climbed into the passenger's seat. "You're driving?"

"Yup." Then she sped off, tires spinning as she did.

"Where are we going?"

"Duke."

"What?"

She shrugged. "It's where the bank's head office is."

"Okay, you're going a little fast. We'll make it before the bank closes."

Her eyes darted from the clock to the speedometer. "I know," she said, bouncing in her seat. "I just don't want to risk it."

*   *   *

When she'd said we were going to Duke, I'd thought she meant Durham. Not Duke University. And definitely not Cameron Indoor Stadium, where she was pulling into. I eyed her sideways. "What are you doing?"

"Come on. We're late!"

"Late for what?"

She unclipped her seat belt and then mine. "Hurry!" she squealed.

She took my hand after we stepped out of the car and rushed toward the stadium, looking at her watch every few seconds.

"Chloe, what the hell is happening?" She was practically running now, which was strange, because Chloe never ran.

"Oh thank God, he's still here." She stopped suddenly and flattened her hands on my back, pushing me closer to the building. My head was turned, trying to look at her, so I didn't see the man who began chuckling in front of me.

"You must be Chloe," he said, and my head whipped forward.

"Hey, Coach," she said from behind me, as if the man standing in front of me wasn't a legend whose very presence made me nervous. "I'm Chloe." She pointed her thumb at me. "You already know Blake."

He held his hand out.

I wiped my palms on my shorts and shook his hand. "C-C-Coach," I stuttered.

Chloe giggled but stopped when I turned to glare at her. "Sorry." She frowned and then turned to the head coach of the Duke Blue Devils. "So, I'll come back in an hour?"

Coach nodded.

She smacked my ass. "See you in an hour, babe."

We both watched as she walked away.

"Your girlfriend's something else," Coach said.

"Yeah." I turned to him. "She's kind of amazing."

He smiled. "Let me show you around, son."

*　　*　　*

For the next hour, I got something not many people get to experience. I got one-on-one time with the head coach of a Division I college team. He showed me around the center, the gym, the locker rooms, and the facilities. We ended up sitting in the stands, right behind the Duke Blue Devils' bench.

"My coaching staff told me about your situation, Hunter."

"Yeah." I wiped my palms against my shorts again. He was intimidating as a coach, but this felt so much more nerve-racking. "I need to thank you for allowing me . . . I mean . . . for keeping the spot open for me. I know that it's not common, especially given—"

"Hunter," he cut in. "I know what it's like to be in your position. You know my history, right?"

"Yes, sir."

"So you know I'm ex-army?"

"Yes, sir."

Then the familiar sound of a basketball bouncing on the hardwood floors echoed through the stadium. Followed by more bounces. Feet shuffling. Shoes scraping. I sat up in my chair and leaned forward, waiting for the moment the players walked out.

"You look like a kid that's seeing his heroes up close for the first time."

I laughed. "I am."

"You could be someone's hero." He stood up and patted me on the back. "In fact, according to your girlfriend and the skateball league, you already are."

I shook my head and let out a disbelieving sigh. "Chloe," I mumbled.

"Chloe," he repeated, throwing his hand out for me to take, "is probably waiting for you outside."

I gripped his hand, and he helped me to stand.

"I'll walk you out."

She was sitting under a tree, earphones in, bopping her head. It reminded me of her in high school. *High school.* It sounded so long ago.

"I'd keep her," Coach joked.

"I plan to, sir."

*　　　*　　　*

She smiled and pulled out her earphones when I came into view. "How was it?"

I sat down next to her. "I don't think I have the words right now."

She reared back in mock horror, holding her hand to her heart. "Blake Hunter, speechless? I never thought I'd see the day."

I nudged her side with my elbow. "We missed the bank."

"Oh yeah, about that . . . There was no bank." She batted her eyelashes.

I sat there, and I watched her, because I couldn't take my eyes off her if I'd tried. I shook my head to clear my thoughts. But then I asked her something that'd been bugging me ever since I'd realized she'd chosen to take me there. "Why did you do this? Come here . . . organize all this?"

"I just wanted to give you the opportunity to make your own choices. That's what you wanted, right? To be able to choose your own future?"

I couldn't answer.

Her eyes narrowed in confusion, but she added, "I think your dad's probably been drilling army into your head since you were a kid. It's only been what . . . two years since you started taking basketball seriously? Or the other way around, really. Basketball started taking you seriously. I don't know, Blake. I just thought if you were here, if you got to meet Coach, got to see the campus, got to see the facilities, maybe Duke would be on an even playing field?"

I just shook my head, unable to form any words. Unable to believe what she was saying, and what she had done for me. So I changed the subject. "What did you do while I was gone?"

She sat up straighter and scooted her crossed legs closer to me. "Actually, I went into town and looked around."

"Yeah? Is there something you want to check out tomorrow?"

She sighed. "No, Blake. I mean I checked out houses and stuff, to live in, for me to rent. Or us. For us to rent."

"What?" I wasn't sure if I'd heard her right or if I'd just wanted to hear what she'd said so badly that I'd dreamed her words.

"If you want to . . . I was thinking, if you go to Duke, we could rent somewhere close. I don't know if you want to live on campus, but it's not really my thing . . . so if you want to, you can live here, and I'll live there . . ."

"And if I choose the army?"

"Well . . . I checked out the area. I like it. If you do decide army . . . I'll wait for you."

"You'll wait for me?" I asked. I had to make sure that I understood exactly what she was saying.

"Yes," she said quietly, looking down at the space between us.

"Chloe. Are we doing this? Making plans? *You're* making plans?"

She nodded.

"With me? You're making plans with me?"

She nodded again. And she must have seen the elation on my face, because she smiled.

"Are you sure?"

"Yes, Blake, I'm sure."

"Best red-letter day in the history of the world."

CHAPTER THIRTY-ONE

Chloe

If I could dream the same dream, a million times over, it would be of you—sleeping peacefully in my arms, every morning, for the rest of my life. Gone for a run, beautiful girl.

That was what the note on his pillow said when I woke up. Red ink. How could you not love him when he said things like that?

*　　*　　*

"You wanna just stay here for a couple of days? We can have a proper look around, see if we really wanna live here?"

He pushed off his arms. "Forty-eight," he said, before moving in to kiss me.

It was one of the best parts of my day. When he came back from his morning run and did his sit-ups and push-ups in front of me. Shirtless. Sweaty. Showing off muscles I'd never known existed. I watched, my head on the edge of the bed, and after each one, he'd kiss me. He said it was his motivation to keep going. To keep pushing himself. He said *I* was his reward. "That sounds great."

"How many more?"

"Fifty-one." He kissed me again.

"I wonder if I could do a hundred push-ups." I got out of bed and got on all fours next to him.

Arms outstretched, he watched as I got into position. And then he laughed so hard that his arms buckled beneath him and he fell on the floor. "I dare you!"

"It can't be that hard."

"Babe, I make it look easy, but I do five hundred of these a day."

I stretched my legs out behind me and tried to copy his form. "So one hundred should be easy, right?"

"Sure," he laughed. "Go ahead."

Two.

I got to two before collapsing.

"You're so weak!" His cackle was so loud I was sure you could hear it in every room of the hotel.

"Shut up!" I lunged for him, but hitting him was like smacking a brick wall.

He stood and made his way toward the bathroom. Shaking his head and chuckling to himself, he mused, "I can't believe you thought you could do a hundred."

I leapt up and brushed past him, ripping off my clothes as I did. I froze just inside the bathroom door. His eyes lit up as they roamed my naked body. A smirk appeared instantly. He stepped forward, his hand already out, ready to touch me.

I slammed the door in his face, making sure to lock it. "I can't believe you thought I'd let you touch me!"

He banged his fists on the door. "Chloe, this shit isn't funny!" he yelled. "My dick's about to snap off!"

Blake

"Blake!" she yelled from the shower.

I opened the bathroom door in time to see her cover herself.

"You can't just walk in! I'm in the shower!"

She moved to the corner of the tub to hide herself more.

"Babe, I've seen you naked."

"Get out!"

"You were the one calling me!"

"Turn around! Don't look!"

I took a step forward. Just enough that I could see her eyes narrow and the snarl on her lips. And a nipple. There was definitely a nipple.

"Quit looking and turn around!"

I chuckled but finally did what she asked. "What do you need?"

"My lotion. It's in my bag. Can you bring it to me?"

I left the room, went to her bag, and rifled through it, looking for the lotion. I found the lotion, but I also found something else.

I couldn't hide the smirk from my face when I went back into the bathroom, hands hidden behind my back. She was already out, one towel wrapped around her hair and another around her body. "Did you find it?" she asked, hand held out expectantly.

I nodded, trying desperately not to laugh.

Her eyebrows bunched, her head tilted slightly as she took me in. Then it all played out in slow motion. Her eyes went huge, and a gasp escaped. She knew. "What else did you find?" she whispered.

"Nothing."

"What's behind your back, Blake?"

I squared my shoulders. "Don't know what you're talking about."

Her face flushed instantly. "Oh my God," she breathed before quickly looking away.

"It's kind of huge." I stood behind her, so we were both facing the mirror. "I mean, is that what your expectations were? I think I'm close, Chloe, but I can't be sure." I wrapped one arm around her stomach to hold her in place. I moved my other hand to the space between her and the mirror, revealing her bright-purple vibrator. "Should we compare?"

And just like I'd suspected, her feet kicked off the ground, and she tried to bolt for the door. My grasp tightened, keeping here there. "Why are you trying to run? Are you embarrassed?"

"Blake!" she squealed, trying to wriggle out of my hold.

I let her go, just long enough to shut the door so I could stand in front of it, keeping her in the tiny space of the bathroom.

"Oh my God." She covered her face, but the blush had taken over, from her chest up to the tips of her ears. "This is so bad."

My body shook with laughter as I examined her toy. "I have so many questions right now, I don't know which one to ask first."

She grunted.

It made me laugh harder.

"Fuck it," she said. She uncovered her face and raised her chin. "So what? I have needs. Big deal."

"*You have needs?*" I repeated. I held the vibrator up between us. "That's some pretty *big* needs."

"Shut it!" she yelled. But she was smiling, too.

"Does it have a name? I mean . . . did you name it?"

She threw back her head in laughter, the blush almost completely gone. "Yes."

"Yes?" I stepped toward her. "What's its name?"

"Pussy Hunter!" she yelled through a chuckle.

I froze, remembering Josh's little rant the first night we'd all hung out. "Pussy Hunter? That's cute." Then my face fell. "Wait. Have you used it? I mean . . . since I've been here with you? Have you got off using this?" I waved it in front of her face.

Her lips thinned to a line.

"You have! When?"

She looked away.

"When?" I repeated.

She shrugged. "I dunno. One night you were walking around shirtless, and then you went out for a run, and I . . ."

My eyes narrowed. "You used it when I went for a run?"

She laughed. "Babe, I was thinking of you the entire time."

"Cute," I said, before examining it further. "How does this thing even work?"

"No!" she squealed, lunging for it.

I pulled back and held it above my head and out of her reach.

"Blake, I'm serious. Stop!"

Then I found the dial at the bottom . . . and I turned it. The power of it scared the shit out of me. It shot out of my hands and into the air. We both watched as it landed in the bathroom sink. The buzzing and rattling against the porcelain was loud enough to echo off the walls in the small room.

"Holy shit!" I said, shocked by its intensity. We both walked to the sink and looked down at it.

"Aww . . . poor Pussy Hunter," she joked, before breaking out in a fit of laughter.

*   *   *

"How many more do you have to do?" She hung her head upside down off the edge of the bed, watching me.

I pushed off the floor and straightened my arms. "Twenty-three," I said as I completed the push-up.

"Hurry up."

"Why?" Another push-up.

"Because I'm getting tired, and I want to cuddle for a bit before I fall asleep."

Another push-up. "I'm a man. I don't cuddle."

She laughed at that and ran her fingers through her hair. It hung loose and still a little wet from her shower.

And then I noticed something I'd never noticed before. Her hair was darker at the roots. My eyes squinted, trying to get a better look, but she moved quickly and sat up on the bed, legs crossed. "Drop and give me twenty more, Hunter!" she commanded, her finger pointed at me. Her fake glare was too fucking cute. I gave her twenty more, never once taking my eyes off her. I watched as the amusement left her eyes and was replaced with something else. Want. Need.

She mumbled something under her breath before getting between the sheets. I got up, switched the light off, and joined her. "I always thought you were a natural blonde?"

She tensed in my arms. "Is it bad? Is it really noticeable?"

"No," I said quickly. "I just noticed when you were running your fingers through it before. It's not bad or obvious. I just thought I would've noticed earlier."

"Oh," she said, but she seemed uncomfortable.

"There's nothing wrong with you dying your hair, Chloe. Heaps of girls do it."

"I know," she sighed. But something was wrong—maybe I'd offended her.

Reaching over her, I turned on the lamp on the nightstand. "Did I say something?"

She shook her head but refused to look at me.

I laid my head on her pillow so we were close enough that she had no choice. "I'm sorry if I said something wrong. It's not like I care that you dye it."

"I know. But I don't want you to think I'm vain and care about—"

"Chloe, you're the least vain person I've ever met. Personally, I think you'd look just as beautiful with darker hair or blonde hair or no damn hair at all."

She smiled. "I was born blonde. I've been blonde most of my life, but the last few years my hair started getting darker." She pressed her lips softly against mine, kissing me once. "My mom was blonde," she croaked. "I felt like I was losing a part of her when it started to get darker. I liked having that connection—something we both shared, even after she was gone."

Blake

"I miss my mama," I told her.

She pouted. "You wanna go home and see your mama?"

"No." It was my turn to pout. "I don't want to go home. There's nothing there. But I wouldn't mind seeing her. I honestly do miss her."

"You want to call her? Ask her to meet us here? I'm sure she'd come in a heartbeat. It's only a couple hours' drive."

"No. I feel like I'm hijacking this."

Her eyebrows quirked. "This?"

"The Road."

She laughed. "Don't be stupid. I'm calling her now." She reached over and took the phone off the nightstand. Then she just stared at it before lifting her gaze to me. "I don't know how to use it," she whispered.

Chuckling, I took it from her, dialed Mom's number, and gave it back.

"Mrs. Hunter?" Whatever Mom said made her grin. "He's good. I'm taking good care of him." She giggled. "We were both wondering if you'd like to meet us in Durham tomorrow? Or the next day . . . when you can. I'm sure you have deadlines and such—" Mom must've cut her off. "Okay! We'll see you tomorrow at noon." She hung up and handed the phone back.

"She didn't want to talk to me?" I said, feigning disappointment.

"Sorry, baby."

I sighed dramatically. "Nobody loves The Hunter."

She laughed—my favorite of all her laughs. The uncontrollable kind that consumed her entire body. "Oh jeez," she cooed when she could finally take a breath. Then she turned serious. "*I* love The Hunter." My breath caught, but her finger covered my lips.

"I wanted to tell you after you told me," she continued. "I wanted to say that I loved you, too, but I didn't want you to think that I was saying it for the sake of saying it. Or because you did first. I wanted you to know that I was saying it because it was the realest thing I've ever let myself feel."

I moved the hair away from her face so I could see her clearer, so I could remember the moment my life had a greater meaning than just me.

"Blake," she said through a shaky breath. "I'm so in love with you. And that love—it might not be forever. But while we're both here—that love is *always*."

*   *   *

You must make a choice, to take a chance, or your life will never change.

She reached up on her toes and kissed my nose. "You're my change, Blake Hunter," she said quietly.

I smiled and stuck my magnet on the fridge. Then I kissed her temple and tugged on a strand of hair.

You were born phenomenal.

CHAPTER THIRTY-TWO

Blake

Mom's eyes narrowed as she looked between Chloe and me. "So, you've been gone all this time, and you've crossed *one* state border . . . twice?" She took a sip of her drink and placed it carefully back down on the diner table.

"Yeah, but there was this peach and this egg and this man-made, welcome-to-earth UFO," I said seriously. "What else is there to see?"

"You should have seen him at the UFO." Chloe giggled. "It was like the greatest thing he'd ever seen."

"It was!" I was too excited. Turning to Chloe sitting next to me, I added, "Apart from you, of course. You're definitely the greatest thing I've ever seen."

She scrunched her nose.

"That was pretty lame, Blake." That came from my own mother. "Remind me to teach you some better lines if you're attempting to woo her."

I shrugged and stuck my nose in the air. "No woo attempt needed. She's already bat-shit crazy in love with me."

I got a backhand to my stomach. That one came from my own girlfriend.

*   *   *

Chloe went back to our new hotel; the balcony on the other one was too small. She wanted to give Mom and me some time, which was perfect because we both had something we needed to say.

Mom settled her arm in the crook of my elbow as we walked through the park near the hotel. "I kicked your dad out. He's living with his mistress. We're getting a divorce, Blake. I'm sorry."

I wanted to care, but I just couldn't find it in myself to do so. "I don't know what to say . . . that it's about time?"

She laughed.

"I mean I get that he's my dad and all, but he's kind of an asshole. If you knew that he was cheating, why did you stay married? It's not like you guys lived together—not really. And I was old enough to know what was happening . . . so it's not like you did it for me."

We stopped walking and sat on a bench. She turned before speaking so her entire body was facing me. "I don't know, a lot of reasons. It's hard. We got married under the wrong circumstances, I guess. We weren't really dating when I got pregnant with you, and he wanted to do the right thing. So he proposed, and we got married. I don't know that we ever loved each other, not in the true-love sense." She sighed. "I used to believe so much in the idea of love that I thought we'd get there someday."

"And now? You don't believe in love anymore?"

"Oh no," she said quickly. "I still believe in *love*. Just not between your father and me."

"Is that why you started drinking?"

She nodded. "I didn't mean for it to get so far out of hand—for it to turn into an addiction the way it did."

"I'm not judging you, Ma." I settled my arm on the back of the bench. "You fought it right? You knew it was a problem and that it had affected your life, and you fought it. You beat it, and you came out on top. I can't really ask for much more."

She laughed quietly. "Who raised you?"

"You did," I assured her. "When it was important, you were there."

"I don't know, Blake." She brushed something off my shoulder. "I think you raised yourself, and you did a pretty good job of it."

Silence fell upon us as I watched a sadness take over her. Her eyes misted, and she visibly swallowed. I knew she was on the verge of tears. I'd seen it before but not like this. When I'd been in middle school, I'd gotten most improved and MVP in this tiny junior league. Back then, basketball had been just a sport, not a future, but she'd still been so proud of me. Before I'd gotten my license, she'd been the one driving me to practices—early mornings, after school—and all my games. She'd always been my endless support and probably the reason I am where I am, and I'd never even thanked her for any of her encouragement. I'd never even told her about how it helped to get me to where I was.

She sniffed and wiped her cheek.

"Ma?"

"Yeah, honey?"

"Thank you."

She let out a nervous laugh. "For what, sweetheart?"

"For being my mom. For supporting me, even when you had no idea how much it would pay off."

"I don't really understand what you're talking about, Blake."

I released all the air in my lungs. "I got into Duke, Ma. I got a full athletic scholarship. Basketball."

She raised her hands to her mouth. Then she cried into them. She wrapped her arms around me so tight I could barely breathe. But I didn't care.

"Why didn't you tell me?" she laughed.

I shrugged and looked away. "I still don't know if I'm going to take it."

"What?" she screeched, then understanding dawned. "Because you want to enlist?"

I faced her again, and nodded slowly. "I want to do both. That's the problem. I don't know which one I want to do more."

"Wow," she said slowly. "I wish I could make that choice for you. Either way, I'll support you. You know that."

"Yeah, Mom. I know." I tried to smile, but I could still see the sadness in her. So I changed the subject. "So, I was wondering if you could do me a favor?"

"Anything."

*   *   *

Chloe met us outside the hotel to say our good-byes.

Mom hugged Chloe longer than necessary, but Chloe didn't seem to mind. "Thank you for coming to see us, Mrs. Hunter. Oh, and the car, thank you so much for the car."

Mom patted the side of Chloe's face and smiled. "Anything for you two," she said, then to me, "Get a haircut, Blake. You look like a gigolo."

I closed Mom's car door and watched as she drove away.

"Yeah," Chloe said from behind me. "My own private gigolo." She smacked my ass.

"Should you have been paying me this entire time?"

She winked. "Maybe you're not worth it!" Then she bolted, running away from me and back to the hotel room.

She got about ten feet before I caught her. "What the hell makes you think you can outrun me?" I picked her up and threw her over my shoulder. "You can't even do two push-ups!" I smacked her ass and carried her back to the room. She laughed the entire time.

Chloe

I was sitting up in bed, with his head on my lap, playing with his hair. We were supposed to be watching a movie, but I didn't think either of us was paying attention.

His eyes caught mine when he turned to look up at me. "What are you thinking?"

My eyebrows bunched.

"You always play with my hair when you're lost in thought. What's up?" He moved to get into bed and under the covers, tugging me down so we were lying face-to-face. "Talk."

What could I say? I love you, but I'm scared that I'm dying? I faked a smile. "What did you and your mom talk about today?"

His eyebrows rose, as if he knew I was talking bullshit. He sighed before answering. "Her and Dad are getting a divorce—"

"I'm sorry, Blake."

"Nothing to be sorry about. Mom and I are fine with it. She thought I'd be upset about it, but I'm not. I'm happy for her."

His eyes drifted shut when I reached for his hair again, moving it away from his eyes. "What else?"

He leaned in closer, kissing me softly. I opened my mouth, inviting him. But he pulled back before he could get there. "I told her about Duke."

My face lit up. "You did? And?"

"She said she would support me, whatever I choose."

"Was she proud of you?"

"Yeah," he said, nodding. "I also told her about how much I love you," he whispered against my lips. His own moved to my neck. "I love you so much, Chloe." His deep voice vibrated against my skin. "So much," he repeated.

CHAPTER THIRTY-THREE

Chloe

My eyes fluttered open when I felt his lips on my back, moving lower and lower. I turned quickly. "What are you doing, boyfriend?"

He made his way back up, kissing each of my breasts on the way. We'd fallen asleep naked after making love for the third time. No. Fourth.

He smiled into my neck, bringing my body flush against his. I reached up to stroke his back. "No run this morning?"

He pulled back so I could see his face. His beautiful face and the beautiful smile that graced it. "No. Just wanted to lie here and hold the girl I love. I couldn't leave you, even if I tried." He shook his head, trying to move the hair away from his eyes. "Mom was right, I need a haircut."

Laughing, I moved in to kiss his chest, skimming my lips along his collarbone. He let out a frustrated groan and pushed gently on my shoulders, making me look up at him. "We need to get out of this bed," he said and then looked around the room. "Actually, we need to get out of this room." He pulled away, and got up. "I'm gonna get rid of this gigolo hair before you get any ideas," he stated, before covering his hard-on with his hands and making his way to the shower. "You're gonna be the end of me."

*   *   *

Heads turned when we walked into the salon. One hairdresser even froze mid-blow-dry. Her client yelped before she realized what she'd done. As always, Blake didn't even notice.

"Can I help you?" the girl behind the desk said. She didn't actually say it—more like *purred* it. And the eighteen-year-old insecure girl in me wanted to wipe the flirtatious smile off her Barbie-blonde head. He must've known, sensed it somehow, because he threw his arm over my shoulders, pulled me into him, and kissed my temple before answering her, "My girlfriend likes to tug on my hair when we . . . you know? I'm thinking it needs to be cut back a lot. She's startin' to hurt me."

A few giggles were heard.

I blushed and covered my face in his chest. And then I stomped on his foot. Hard.

He released a pained cry before laughing. "See? She likes it rough."

An older woman came over and shooed blonde Barbie away. She winked at me before looking up, up, up to Blake. "Your girlfriend's beautiful. You shouldn't embarrass her like that." Then to me, "You want anything done today, sweetheart?"

I started to shake my head, but then an idea came to mind. "Would you have time to dye my hair?"

She eyed my hair quickly. "Just a touch-up on the roots?"

"Um. No, ma'am. I was thinking maybe go back to my natural color. I feel like being phenomenal today."

Blake chuckled and placed an open-mouth kiss on my cheek, sucking hard.

"Gross." I pushed him away and wiped my face. He laughed harder.

The woman behind the desk giggled. "I'll wait until we have two free stations next to each other. I have a feeling he won't like being far away from you for too long."

He raised his chin. "Your feelings are correct, ma'am."

*   *   *

He sat next to me, bouncing in his seat, his new haircut revealing more of his perfect face. "How much longer?"

I rolled my eyes and reached down into my bag and pulled out a lollipop for him. He took it, no questions asked. "Seriously, though," he mumbled around the candy, "how much longer?"

"I don't know, but look." I showed him a flyer displaying a drive-in theatre nearby. They were showing *Hoosiers*, his favorite film. "Perfect," he whispered. "You think you'll be done in an hour?"

I nodded.

He jumped up. "Good. I'll come back." He started to leave but turned halfway, took the steps to cover the distance between us, and kissed me. "Don't go anywhere. I love you." And then he was gone, out the doors and into the sunlight. I'm sure I wasn't the only one who watched him leave.

"He a baller?" a man sitting in the waiting area yelled out.

My hair covered in plastic wrap, I looked around the salon, making sure he was talking to me.

"Yes, you!" he said.

I reared back, a little afraid of his tone.

"That's Dennis," the woman from earlier whispered. "He's a little crazy but means well. He's the town's basketball historian. You best answer him before he loses his mind."

"Yes, sir. He's a basketball player."

"Duke?" he bellowed, arms crossed over his fat gut.

"Not sure, sir."

"Whaddaya mean you're not sure, girl? He is or he ain't!"

"Dennis!" the woman reprimanded. "Be nice to my clients or I'll kick your fat ass out of my salon."

His eyes went wide. "Sorry, Missy," he drawled.

"He signed with Duke, sir," I answered. "But he's still deciding whether to enlist in the army or to play ball."

He stood and strolled over to me, taking the seat Blake had just vacated. "Hmm," he mused, "that's a tough choice." He kept nodding, as if he was the one to make the decision. "He a good man?" he asked.

"Yes, sir. Blake's the best man I know."

"Blake?" He eyed the ceiling, deep in thought. "Hunter?"

I smiled. "Yes, that's him."

"And you love him?"

"Yes, sir. I love him," I assured him.

"Well, then, you decide for him. A man is only as good as the woman behind him. Or under him! Or on top of him!" He winked while his body shook with laughter.

I paled, eyes wide.

"I'm just messin', girl. But not really. What do *you* want for him?"

Forever, I thought. I want him forever. "It's not my choice. It's his. It's important for him to make his own decision."

"He told you that?"

"Yes."

"Before or after he fell stupidly in love with you?"

I laughed softly. "Before."

"Well, things change, girl. Maybe now he wants you to tell him what to do. Maybe he's given you the cards, and now you have to deal them."

*　　*　　*

Blake's eyes widened when he stepped into the salon and saw my hair. It was the most natural it'd been since I'd started dying it. We paid and left, but he wouldn't look at me. I didn't think it was that bad. His strides were long and quick. I had a hard time keeping up with him.

"Blake!" I dug my heels into the ground. "What's wrong? You haven't mentioned anything about my hair. Do you not like it?" And there was that insecure teenage girl again. He grunted but didn't say anything else. He took my hand and started walking to the car again. I stayed frozen, refusing to move, and refusing to let him move me. Dropping his hand and crossing my arms over my chest, I narrowed my eyes at him. "Talk!"

He let out a frustrated groan and then looked around, searching for something. His eyes lit up. He must've found what he was looking for. *Probably a ditch to throw his ugly girlfriend in.* He grabbed my arm, pulling me toward an alcove between two stores.

"You think I don't like your hair?"

I nodded, pouting as I gazed up at him.

He looked around again before he cleared his throat. Gently, he tugged on my hand and led it down to his crotch, where I could feel how hard he was. I bit my lip, containing my moan at the feel of him in my hand.

He raised his arms, flattening his palms on the wall on either side of my head. "Does that feel like I don't like it?" he whispered in my ear. "I need to get you back to our room, Chloe. Now."

*　　*　　*

"Oh my God!" I quickly snapped on my bra and pulled on my shorts. "We're gonna miss *Hoosiers*."

He laughed, lazily shrugging his shirt back on. "I've seen it a million times. I can tell you exactly what happens."

"That's not the point. I want to see it. I want to see it with *you*. I want to fall in love with basketball the way you have. I want to feel what it feels like for you."

*   *   *

"When did you do all of this?" I asked as I took in the trunk of the Jeep. He'd set up a blanket, food, drinks, and a jar full of lollipops.

"While you were at the salon somehow getting *more* beautiful."

"This is amazing."

He grinned and took up his position, knees up, legs spread, waiting for me. I sat cross-legged between them, like we'd done so many times out at my mom's lake.

His arms wrapped tightly around me as he softly kissed my neck. "I love you," he said. And it didn't matter that it was the seventh time he'd said it that day. Each time it was said held a greater significance.

I tilted my head up to kiss him. "I love you, too."

Blake

We watched the movie in silence. She got so caught up in it that she didn't even realize that I was so caught up in her. I could watch the movie whenever I wanted, but this moment, with her, it was once in a lifetime. She sniffed, wiping at her tears as the final scenes played.

I knew what was happening without looking. It was the state championship game; they were tied at forty, twenty-four seconds on the clock. Hickory, the underdog heroes, had just called a time-out. Coach Norman Dale had given them the play, using Jimmy as a decoy. The players hadn't wanted it, and Jimmy had spoken up, "I'll make it," he said. And the story went back to game play.

She leaned forward, her eyes glued to the screen as the seconds ticked by. I knew the moment the shot was about to be made. The sound of a ball hitting the hardwood floors. Once. Twice. Crossover. Third time. The music blasted. Chloe held a hand to her heart. Then that swoosh—that unique sound a ball makes when it passes through the hoop, nothing but net. And then the cheers. Not just on the screen but from the people around us. She let out a sob, so relieved that the shot had made it, and that Hickory had won. On the screen, the crowd swarmed the court, people hugged, people cried. In my head, it was silent, all but for the thumping of my heart.

"Chloe."

She turned to look up at me, her eyes welling with tears.

She blinked.

They fell.

I wiped them away.

And then she smiled.

And that was all I needed to say the words.

"Marry me?"

Chloe

My breath caught.

My heart stopped.

My eyes closed.

Nothing but *red*.

"Chloe." His voice sounded far away. "Did you hear me?"

I opened my eyes to see his beautiful face watching me, waiting. "What did you say?"

His hand went in his pocket, and he pulled out a little black box. "I'm asking you to marry me," he said. And then he flipped the lid.

I looked away, too afraid that I might be dreaming.

"Marry me," he said again, his voice softening and his confidence waning. "I know it's not much," he continued, "and I get that we don't really know what's going to happen or what our future might be. But we're eighteen, so it's okay that we don't have that stuff worked out yet. And I know that I have nothing to offer you, just this car and a bunch of maybes. And I know it's selfish, to want you like this, to need you the way I do—"

"Yes," I cut in. Because I knew it, too. I knew that I was being selfish—to want the same things as he did. But a part of me wanted that selfishness to be okay, because he knew about my chances. He knew what might be coming. He just didn't know how soon.

"Did you say yes?" He lifted my chin so I would look him in the eyes. "Is that what you said? Did you say yes?"

I nodded, and then he lunged at me. Kissing me. Hugging me. Holding me. Then he took my hand in his, pulled the ring from its box, and slipped it on my finger. And then it was my turn. I jumped on him. Hugging. Kissing. It was a messy kiss, but we didn't let that stop us. Through laughter, through tears, we never stopped kissing. "I love you," I cried.

And then we did it all over again.

"I need to call Mary," I managed to get out.

He handed me his phone.

It rang twice before she answered. "Hello?"

"Mom!" I squealed.

And then I froze. My heart dropped to my stomach.

Blake took my hand and squeezed it once. He smiled and nodded, encouraging me to continue.

I closed my eyes and I saw her, my mother, in my vision, in my memory. And that was exactly what she was. A memory. An *irreplaceable* memory.

A calmness washed over me and I smiled.

Mary stayed quiet on the other end.

I wiped my tears, and inhaled deeply. "Mom," I whispered, afraid of how it would make me feel. But all it did was make me feel lighter, as if a weight had been lifted. It felt right. "Mom, it's Chloe."

Silence.

And then I heard her shaky exhale. The line clicked, and Dean's deep voice filled the space of the car. "Who the hell is this making my wife cry?"

I laughed. I couldn't help it. I missed them. And I *loved* them. "*Dad*, it's Chloe. Put Mom back on the phone."

"I'm here," she choked out. "Sweetheart, I'm here."

"Mom! Blake just asked me to marry him!"

CHAPTER THIRTY-FOUR

Chloe

The diamond sparkled in the moonlight. The wind blew into the alcove of the balcony, causing my freshly washed and dyed hair to whip around my neck. I shivered and wrapped the dressing gown tighter around me, and then I closed my eyes and took a deep breath.

Everything felt normal.

The same.

Only it wasn't.

I could be dying, and Blake—he had no idea. *I have cancer.* The words played in my head, but they sounded wrong. *I think I might have cancer.* That sounded better but not great. Not reassuring. Not the way it should be. He had the right to know, especially now. But I could barely breathe at the thought of how it would hurt him. A bitter laugh escaped, and I tried to reason with myself. *He knew it could happen. It was not my fault.*

Before I had a chance to find the right words, his voice pulled me out of my thoughts. "What are you doing out here?" He slid the balcony door closed behind him and took a seat opposite me. "So?" he asked, reaching out for my arm to pull me to him.

I pulled away, wanting to be face-to-face so I could see his reaction when I told him the truth.

He sensed my mood and leaned in closer, his elbows resting on his knees. His eyes locked with mine. "What's going on, babe?"

"Are you sure you want to do this, Blake?"

He let out a bitter laugh and leaned back in his chair. "Wow. One night, and you've already changed your mind."

"I haven't changed my mind, but I'm giving you a chance to change yours."

"I don't want to change my mind, Chloe. What's this about?"

"I just want to make sure that *you're* sure. That you know about—"

"The cancer? Yes, I know about it. And I still wanna marry you, so what's your next excuse?" He skimmed over the subject as if it didn't mean anything.

"It's not an excuse. It's a reality."

"One that I already knew before I fell in love with you, before I asked you to marry me. Chloe . . ." He sighed and leaned forward again. "What's really going on here?"

I sucked in a breath and let the words leave me. "I could have cancer, Blake."

"Like I said, I already knew that. It doesn't—"

"No, Blake. I mean *now*. I could have cancer *now*."

Blake

Her words hit me like a ton of bricks. And even though they were clear, formed, premeditated, I still found myself asking, "What?"

She nodded slowly. "If you want to take it back, now's your chance."

I got up and started pacing, too edgy to stay in my seat. A million questions passed through my mind. She stood behind me and placed her hand on my back. "Blake?"

I flinched.

I fucking flinched.

I didn't mean to—because I knew she'd take it as a rejection.

Her sob was enough to make me turn around. She was halfway to the door before I caught her arm. "I'm sorry." I pulled her into me, holding her close. "I'm just trying to process everything, okay? I'm not . . . I'm not taking anything back, Chloe. I promise that's not what this is about. I just need time. You need to talk me through this." I pulled back and tilted her head up to look at me. "I'm just scared. And I don't want to be. I'm supposed to be the strong one—the one to hold you up. And I'm crumbling because I'm so fucking scared of what you're saying right now."

"I'm scared, too," she whispered.

*   *   *

My eyes snapped shut as her shaky hand guided mine to her left breast. "Do you feel it?"

She hadn't stopped crying since we came in from the balcony. I didn't console her, I couldn't. On the inside, I was crying, too.

She told me that she had discovered it the day of the "night that never happened." That was why she'd acted the way she had. Josh had been right; she'd gotten *scared.*

I nodded as I felt the lump, like thick skin, close to her underarm.

Her voice came out a shudder when she spoke. "I always knew there might be a chance—that this might happen—but I never prepared myself emotionally." She let out another sob and pulled away from my hand, closing her robe as she did. "I never got tested,

Blake. I'm sorry." She sat on the bed and let her head fall into her hands.

I kneeled in front of her, stroking her hair.

"I never thought that I'd have someone like you to explain that decision to. And now it's too late. Now you have to deal with it, too," she sobbed. She gazed up, and shook her head, her eyes wild as they bore into mine. "Blake, you can't deal with this. You're *eighteen*. You shouldn't have to deal with a dying fiancée." She clasped the ring and began to slide it off her finger.

I covered her hands. "Stop! I'm sorry, Chloe. I am. But you can't do this. You can't take away your answer. You said yes, and you meant yes. I told you the other night, if you push me away—if you do that again—I'm leaving, and I meant it." It was an empty threat. One I had absolutely no intention of keeping. I would never walk away from her. Not now, and not even then.

"Blake, you can't possibly still want to marry me. Not now."

"No," I answered truthfully. "Not now. But afterwards. *After* you fight this . . . after you've beaten this . . . after you come out on the other side, then we'll do it. Promise me you'll still want me then?"

She laughed and cried, all at the same time.

I pulled on her hands so she was straddling me and placed her hand over my heart, my other hand skimming the lump on her breast. "What I feel in here," I covered her hand on my chest and, with the other, stroked my fingers across the thick skin, "completely outweighs what I feel here. The love I have for you . . . Chloe." I sighed. "What's happening now, it doesn't change a thing. Do you understand me? Not a damn thing is going to take this away from us. *Ever.*"

She held my face in her hands and kissed me with her tear-stained lips. "You, Blake Hunter, are my unexpectedly phenomenal."

Chloe

My mother hadn't left me many material items when she'd died. She'd been too young to possess a lot, but she had left a letter. One I was told to open if the disease ever got me. I used to wonder what magical words she might have in case I needed them. Now I needed them.

Like I had when I'd been a kid, I sat on the chair in the corner of the room and stared at the letter in my hand, tracing my name on the envelope with the tips of my fingers. I watched as Blake slowly moved onto his back, his arm out on my side of the bed, waiting for me to crawl in beside him, throw my arm and leg over him like I did every night. And in that moment, there were no insecurities, no petty teenage jealousy. There was just me—and Blake—and our maybe forever.

And that was all the courage I needed.

I lifted the envelope, taking one more look at its unopened form before quietly peeling back the flap and pulling the letter out.

I unfolded it.

Once.

Twice.

Three times.

A gasp escaped before I covered my mouth with both hands, dropping the letter onto my lap.

To my beautiful girl, Chloe, it said.

White paper.

Red ink.

CHAPTER THIRTY-FIVE

Chloe

He wasn't in bed the next morning, and neither was a note on his pillow. For a second, my heart dropped, believing that he'd left in the middle of the night. And then I remembered everything he'd said, everything he'd declared, and I knew it wasn't possible.

Sitting up, I searched the hotel room, smiling when I saw his figure out on the balcony.

Two coffees in hand, I made my way out there. He was sitting on the chair—phone in one hand, pen in the other—frantically writing something on a notepad. "Morning, babe." I set his coffee on the table. "What's all this?"

I didn't wait for an invitation before taking my regular seat on his lap. "I'm just trying to wrap my head around things . . . what we need to do from here . . . but my phone keeps fucking up, and I can't get to certain sites, the signal keeps cutting out . . ." He was rambling, lost in his own thoughts.

I looked at the notepad; his now-familiar handwriting graced the page. Words like *symptoms, malignant, chemo, mammogram* all stood out.

"I'm sorry," he said quietly.

My gaze shifted to him.

"I'm sorry if I don't do things right or if my emotions get the better of me, but all of this . . ." He motioned to the notes on the table. "This is all new to me . . . so if I get off track or go a little crazy with the research, I apologize now. I just need to know that I'm doing everything I can to take care of you." He paused. "I think I'm going to enlist, Chloe."

I did everything I could to contain my reaction. It was his decision and one that he'd made on his own, but deep down, it wasn't the choice I wanted him to make, though I'd never tell him that. "Okay." I nodded and smiled, but the smile was tight. "That's good, Blake. I'm glad you made a decision."

He let out a heavy breath. "If we get married and I enlist, we get free housing, more pay, and you could be covered under my healthcare, so at least that's one less thing to worry about. I called my recruiter, Hayden, and told him everything. He said that he'd help me out—do everything he can so that I could serve out my time here and take care of you while you're going through treatments. I'd have to go to basic for ten weeks and then AIT, but still, I might not have to travel like I would with ball. Maybe Mom can be there when I can't be. I wouldn't do it if I knew that I had to leave your side . . . I couldn't do that . . . but so far it's the best option and—"

"Wait. Do you want to enlist because of the free housing and healthcare or because you *want* to?"

His face fell.

"Blake?"

I waited for a response, but it never came.

"Before you knew about my cancer, yesterday—when you proposed—what did you want?"

He swallowed before lacing his fingers with mine. His gaze lowered, fixed on the engagement ring. "Duke."

A relieved laugh bubbled out of me.

He eyed me sideways. "What?"

"So you're going to Duke."

"But—"

"But nothing, Blake. We'll make it work. I promise. Did you look up the best treatment centers in the state?"

He shook his head. "No, I was just—"

"It's here, Blake. Duke Cancer Institute is one of the best hospitals for cancer treatment. You choosing Duke doesn't have to change anything. You can get what you want. I can get what I *need*. And we can do it together."

"Okay," he agreed. "But you have to promise me something."

"Anything."

"Promise me you'll let me carry some of the burden. Don't pull back and don't push me away. This is *our* life now, *our* future."

I sucked in a breath and held back the tears. "Okay, I promise."

Minutes felt like hours while we silently sipped our coffees.

"I wish Mary were here."

He nodded slowly, a grimness washing over him. "I wish my mom was here, too. She'd be good in this situation. She'd take charge, make appointments, whatever we needed, you know? I mean . . . do we even know what we do from here?" He laughed, low and slow at first, and then he let it out, unconfined. It was a beautiful sound. A beautiful sight. *He* was beautiful.

"What?"

"We're eighteen, and we need our mommies!"

"Yeah," I agreed. "But at the same time we're only eighteen. We're not supposed to have all this figured out yet."

He ended his laughing fit with a sigh.

"I think it's time to go home, Blake."

*　　　*　　　*

And in the end, it's not the years in your life that count, it's the life in your years.

"I love you, babe," he said as he stood in front of the fridge and read my magnet. He picked up our bags off the floor and kissed my cheek. "I'll meet you in the car."

"Wait. You're not doing a magnet today?"

He winked. "It's there."

I turned back to the fridge, my eyes already searching for it. And there it was. Top left corner. Red ink, as always.

Be strong when you are weak, brave when you are scared, and humble when you are victorious.

CHAPTER THIRTY-SIX

Chloe

Mary cried when we told her the news, just like we knew she would. Dean—he left the room, went out to the backyard, and sat in the playhouse. Mary said to leave him be—that he just needed time. He was there for an hour, then Blake went out there to talk with him. They were there for another two hours. When they came back into the house, Dean wrapped me in his arms, told me he loved me, and went back to his normal self.

Blake never told me what they'd spoken about.

Harry, the only one old enough to understand, announced that he was a man and he wouldn't cry about it, but when I went to his room to talk to him, I heard him sobbing. I left him alone so he could get it out. Maybe it was important to him to keep up that front, but it pained me to know how much he was hurting because of me.

We told them we'd be back the next day, hopefully after we knew what the next step would be. For the time being, we had no idea what the lump was. And it was important to us that we all remained positive.

Blake's mom gushed when she saw the ring on my finger, but when she saw Blake's face, hers fell instantly.

"We need your help," he croaked.

She sat on the couch opposite us while we told her everything. His hand held mine the entire time, gently squeezing when he knew I needed the encouragement to keep going. She sat frozen, crying silently and listening to everything we had to say. When she knew we were done, she smacked her hands on her knees and stood.

"Well, then," she said, quickly wiping the tears from her face, "looks like we have some stuff to organize."

Blake nudged me with his elbow, a hint of a smile on his face. He raised his eyebrows and nodded toward his mom. A kind of "I told you so."

Before I finished making us all coffee, she was on her laptop, on her phone, taking names and numbers. She was in full control. Something we both admitted to needing.

She made an appointment for a mammogram the next day with Dr. Ramirez, and told us we could stay in the main house until things were sorted out; it had been empty since his dad had left.

She worked fast, almost too fast, but it was for the best. The earlier we knew, the sooner I would be able to get treatment if I needed it.

I asked Blake to get our bags and meet me up in his room. Once he had left, I turned to Mrs. Hunter. "Thank you."

She smiled sadly, took a seat next to me, and held my hand.

"Go on," she said. "I know there's more."

"Blake told me that you helped him with the ring when you came to see us. But it was before either of you knew about . . . you know . . ." Even though I'd had my entire life to deal with and understand cancer, I had a hard time actually saying the word.

"What are you saying, sweetheart?"

I wiped the wetness off my cheeks. "I'm saying that if you don't want us to go ahead with this . . . if you don't want Blake to marry me, or even be with me, I understand." I looked down at her hands, covering mine. "I'm sure it's hard as a mother, to know that your only son is in love with a girl that could be dying. I'm sure that it's not the type of life you wanted for him—to be with someone like me—to have to deal with so much, so young. And as much as I love him, I'll walk away. I'll tell him that it was my choice; he'll never have to know this conversation existed. You just say the word."

"Oh, Chloe," she sighed. "You couldn't be more wrong. Blake told me about your chances . . . that it might happen. But he doesn't care, and neither do I. I'm not going to lie; it scares me that he has to deal with all of this, especially so young. But you know what's also great?"

I shook my head.

"It's great that you've found a love so deep while you're both so young. It means that you can deal with this together, and the love that you have—it'll help you through it all. So when you do beat this—you'll have the rest of your lives to keep on *living*." She squeezed my hands as her eyes held mine. "When Blake asked me to help him with that ring, I didn't even think twice, Chloe. Blake—he's always been smarter than he gives himself credit for. If you think for a second that him asking you to marry him was a split-second decision, you're wrong. He contemplated it for weeks, not just the days leading up to it. He would've thought about the cancer, he would've thought about you, and he even would've thought about me. I want what's best for him, and the best for him is you, Chloe, however healthy you are." She smiled before adding, "Regardless of all the black-letter days you might have to endure, there's always a red one waiting for you."

I cried. Harder than I'd ever cried before.

We hugged each other good night at her door. "Keep your head up, Chloe. You never know. It might not be cancer at all. It might be benign."

*　　*　　*

It wasn't benign; it was cancer, just like we'd all expected.

Blake wasn't joking when he'd said that his mom would take charge. Within two weeks, she'd purchased a block of townhouses in Durham, a block away from Duke. One for us, one for her, and one for Dean and Mary, for when they visited. She'd called the Duke Athletic Department and committed Blake to playing and attending there. He'd wanted to defer, but we'd both pushed him to start that coming fall. Nothing should have to change, and his mom had guaranteed that she would be with me when he couldn't. He'd made a joke about starting up a two-player team and calling it Team Uncoordinated Losers, but he'd been smiling as he'd said it. And that smile had been enough to let me know that things would be okay.

For a while.

His mom had made all the appointments for us. Blake had said that she actually looked as though she was enjoying herself, not because I was sick, but because she felt as if she had a reason to be a mom again.

Then one night, I told him that she'd make a great grandmother. We spent the rest of the evening naming our future kids.

I said Clayton.

He said Jordan, LeBron, Kobe, Shaquille, Barkley, and about ten other names.

I laughed and asked him if he planned on making enough babies to create his own basketball team.

His eyes lit up. "Can we do that? Oh man, that would be so good!" was his actual response.

God, I love him.

CHAPTER THIRTY-SEVEN

Six Months Later

Blake

I crawled into bed and under the covers. It was already warm from her body heat. She was in bed a lot lately, always tired from her treatments. Carefully, I curled my arm around her stomach. "Baby," I whispered in her ear.

Her cheeks rose as a smile formed. She turned in my arms, her eyes still closed. She leaned in, her mouth already puckered. I pressed my nose against her waiting lips—our standard morning ritual. And then I waited. I knew what was coming next. Her hand trailed up my arm, over my shoulder, up my neck, and into . . .

Her eyes snapped open. "Where is your hair?"

I shrugged.

Tears instantly pooled in her eyes, and she pouted. "You shaved it all off?"

I nodded.

"Because of me?" She wept.

"You're just so damn beautiful with no hair, I wanted to be the same. I kinda look like Gollum, though."

"You do not." She giggled. "You look . . ." She trailed off.

"I look like what?"

"I don't know." She sulked. "I don't have the words. I just love you."

"I love you, too, baby. Happy birthday."

Her pout turned into a smile. "Did you come in here to give me a present?"

"You told me not to get anything."

Her smile widened. "You don't have to."

Then her hand was on my dick, and my eyes went huge. She started softly stroking me through my shorts, but I had to pull back. "Babe—"

"I'm feeling good today, baby," she said quickly, moving so she was lying on top of me, her legs on either side, and her ass on my junk. My palm flattened against her back, pulling her down toward my waiting mouth. Then I kissed her. Softly, slowly. She started moving on me, getting me harder and harder.

And then I remembered.

I pulled back. "Shit."

"What's wrong?" Her hand went straight to the chemo tube in her chest, checking to see if it was still in place.

"You have visitors."

"What?" She quickly got off me. "Who?"

I leaned up on my elbows, smirking, as I watched her rush to the walk-in closet. "Just some people who wanted to wish you happy birthday."

She stuck her head out of the closet and glared. "Who, Blake?" she yelled.

Laughing, I rolled out of bed and joined her in the closet, taking a seat on a chair in the corner. "Just some people." I shrugged again. I knew she'd get annoyed and call me an asshole, but she was kind of adorable when she got pissed.

She turned to me, wearing nothing but panties, an old shirt, and a frown on her beautiful face. "I have nothing to wear, and I'm ugly."

I got up and was next to her in no time. She was looking in the full-length mirror. To me, she hadn't changed much. She was a little thinner, her skin a little gaunter, and her hair was gone, but she was still beautiful. "You wanna know what I think?"

Her shoulders slumped. "No, I already know what you're going to say." She rolled her eyes. "You're going to say that you think I'm beautiful, and that I haven't changed, and if anything, I've just gotten better with time."

I chuckled. "So if you know that's how I feel, then what . . . ? Wait . . ." My eyes narrowed. "Are you trying to impress some other asshole? Who is he, Chloe? I'm gonna find him and beat his ass. Right now."

She threw her head back and laughed. A sound that was rare— but that just made it ten times more rewarding.

I picked a dress off the rack and handed it to her. "Here, I've always liked you in this one."

She placed her hand over her tube. "But it doesn't cover this."

"So?" I raised my eyebrows, waiting for her answer. She took it from my hand, but she looked uncomfortable. I added, "Baby, do you think it matters to whoever is waiting downstairs?"

"It's Dennis," she deadpanned.

"What?"

"Dennis. He's the other asshole I'm trying to look good for."

I laughed. "Dennis, that fat old bald man that calls you 'girl'? The one that memorizes ball stats from 1863?"

She nodded.

"Shit, I got my work cut out for me."

She slowly peeled her shirt off, put on a bra, and shrugged on the dress I'd handed to her. When she reached for her wig, I stopped her. "Leave it, babe. I told you I thought you'd be beautiful with dark hair, blonde hair, or no hair at all. And I was right. You're beautiful without it."

*   *   *

She gasped, loud and slow. "You guys!" she yelled.

My teammates laughed.

"When did you—? How did you—?" And then she cried—the good kind of cry. She tried to bolt, like I knew she would, so I held on to her waist to make sure she stayed put.

"What's wrong?" I teased.

She buried her head in my chest.

"Chloe," Grant, our team captain, sang. "You don't want to show us some love?"

She raised her head, looked up at me, and whispered loudly, "Blake. The entire Duke basketball team is in our living room."

"I know."

"It's not funny!" she said a little louder.

I laughed.

Then she stomped on my foot. Hard.

That got laughs.

She finally looked at the team. "Where did all your hair go?"

They cheered just as Mom came out with a birthday cake. We sang *Happy Birthday*, and Chloe blew out the candles, crying the entire time.

Josh and Tommy showed up a little later, and so did Mary and Dean and the kids. It didn't take long for her exhaustion to settle in.

"I need to take a nap," she said. "But you stay down here. I'll only be an hour."

I led her upstairs, helped her change, and got her into bed.

"Why did the team do that?" she asked once she was settled. "Why did they shave off their hair? For me?"

"And for me, too. They wanted to do something. It was Grant's idea. They all raised money and made a charity event out of it. The money went to Duke Cancer Institute."

"I like them. They're good people." Her eyes started to drift shut as she slowly lost the will to stay awake.

"Sleep, baby. I'll come up and check on you in a bit."

"I love you, Blake," she whispered. "Thank you for giving me this life."

A second later, she was asleep. I stayed up there for another half hour, watching her chest peacefully rise and fall.

Though I'd never admit it to her, it was hard. Keeping up with college classes, basketball, taking care of her . . . sometimes, it got the best of me. The pressure and the uncertainties of our life made every day a struggle. Mom being around helped, but when Chloe was in for a session or a doctor's appointment, and I had practice or games and couldn't be with her—I hated it.

At first, I'd been a mess on the court. I'd been distracted, and the coaches and the players, they'd understood. But I hadn't thought it was fair to them for me to take up a spot when my head and my heart weren't always in the game. I'd tried to quit once. Chloe—she didn't know this. Coach had said to give it a year, and if I still felt the same—if the pressure was still too much—he'd let me walk. He'd be disappointed, but he'd let me go.

Sometimes I still thought of quitting. But then there'd be days like today. Where the support of everyone around us was overwhelming, and I knew that it'd be worth it. Grant—he was nothing to me. Not really. But he knew enough to understand what it would mean to Chloe if they did what they had done.

He'd told me the idea one day after practice, once everyone had left the locker room. He'd said that he'd run the idea by the team, and they'd all been eager to do it. Not just for her, but for me. I was glad that he'd waited for everyone to leave, because I'd cried like a bitch. He'd sat next to me and let me get it out. He'd said that we were more than just teammates; we were brothers, and I didn't need to feel the pressure of it all—not when I had fifteen of my brothers to carry some of the weight.

So I'd done it—I'd asked for help. They'd worked out my schedule and what classes I had to go to and what classes they could cover for me. For those, they took notes or had friends take notes, and I was able to spend more time with Chloe. Which was all I'd wanted in the first place.

I wiped my eyes as I watched her flip to her side, relaxed and sleeping. And I knew it then—even without the support of everyone around us, it would be worth it. Chloe—she was worth it.

She was worth everything.

*   *   *

I checked on her a few more times while people were there, but it didn't seem as though she was going to wake up anytime soon. Mom helped clean up and took Tommy to her house, asking Josh if he could stay with her until Josh was ready to leave. I told Josh that he could stay the night, and Mom was more than happy to have Tommy with her.

Josh and I settled on the back patio.

He took a swig of his beer. "How are you, fucktard?"

I laughed. It seemed like so long ago since we'd talked shit and worked in that bowling alley. "It goes alright, shitstain."

He leaned forward, resting his elbows on his knees. "Are you sure?"

"Yeah. Some days are rougher than others. She's having a good day today, more upbeat than yesterday."

He laughed. "I asked how *you* are."

"We're one and the same, Josh. I'm whatever she is."

"So no regrets?"

I shook my head. "None."

"Even with the cancer?"

"I didn't choose to fall in love with her; I just did. Just like she didn't choose to have cancer; she just does."

The back door slid open, and she stepped out. "I missed my own birthday party." She laughed. "What kind of person does that?"

She walked over and curled up on my lap, running her hand over my head. "Thank you." She kissed my cheek. "I had a good birthday."

"You're welcome."

"Hey, C-Lo," Josh interrupted.

Chloe turned to him.

"He kinda looks like Gollum, no?"

She laughed. "He does not. He looks hot."

Josh shook his head. "You always get the girl, bald head and all."

Chloe chuckled. "Free-Pussy Hunter," she mocked.

I shook my head at her. "Cute, babe. Throw me under the bus."

She laughed harder, moving closer and kissing my neck.

"Fuck, that was a good night," Josh said. "Hey C-Lo, when you get better we should go back there, for old time's sake."

Her face lit up. "Fire truck yeah, we will!"

CHAPTER THIRTY-EIGHT

One Year Later

Chloe

Tommy sat on Blake's shoulders as we watched Josh take the first-place podium. He'd started competing on the pro skateboarding circuit around a year ago and made a huge splash when he had. People had thought he had died when he'd just disappeared off the face of the earth right before Tommy was born. It'd taken one competition for him to be noticed and for sponsors to start knocking on his door. He'd declined sponsorship, wanting to make sure that his time with Tommy wouldn't be determined or limited by their requests. He was still living in the garage apartment because he wanted to make sure that there was enough money to give him and Tommy a good start.

"You guys didn't have to come out today. We could've met you at the hospital," Josh said, coming up to us after the ceremony had ended.

I backhanded Blake in the stomach. He faked hurt. That made Tommy laugh. "This guy can't sit still. I had to get him out of the house or he was going to lose his mind."

"I ate an entire bag of lollipops on the way here," Blake bragged.

*   *   *

Dr. James sighed and dropped a stack of folders on her desk. Her lips clamped shut as she forced a smile.

That wasn't a good sign.

Blake's knees started bouncing higher, faster. I settled them with my hands. "Sorry, baby, I'm just scared."

Before I could respond, Dr. James spoke up. "You brought your army with you." She motioned to her office door. Behind it, everyone was waiting. *Everyone.* Our parents, the kids, Josh, Tommy, and the entire Duke basketball team.

"I'm sorry about that," I said quietly. "They all wanted to be here . . . either way."

She nodded and took a seat.

"I've got your results." Her tone was stern, and for a moment I panicked. Dr. James was an amazing doctor, but more than that, she'd become a friend to both of us. She knew all about our relationship, our lives, and us. And she knew how to swiftly switch from friend to doctor—and right now she was *all* doctor.

"And?" Blake asked. His face had paled; the nerves and the anticipation had gotten the best of him.

She handed us a thick letter-size envelope. "I think you should read them for yourselves."

Blake and I eyed each other for a long moment before he reached for it. He pulled out the document and laid it on the table between us. We leaned in, slow and simultaneous. My eyes scanned back and forth, reading each line, but they weren't the results I'd expected.

"This is just a list of her treatment history," he said, his eyes never leaving the page.

I looked up. Dr. James was sitting back in her chair, her fingers steepled against her chin. "Keep reading. Keep flipping the pages."

We scanned each page for something different, something that would pop out. My fingers itched to turn the papers faster, searching for the final results of my treatment—whether or not I was cured.

Blake inhaled deeply before blowing out a shaky breath. His gaze moved to me. I tried to smile, but I was getting less and less positive about the outcome.

"I love you," he whispered.

"I love you, too."

We both turned back to the document.

Continued to flip the pages.

And then we stopped.

We didn't need to read the words to know what they meant.

"Blake," I sobbed. I couldn't peel my eyes away from the page in front of me.

White paper.

Red ink.

I cried into his chest.

"You did it, baby." He kissed my hair. My short-but-still-there hair. "You beat it." I didn't know how long we spent, sitting there, crying with each other. The weight of the world had finally lifted. "I'm so proud of you." He held my head in his hands and searched my face.

Dr. James sniffed.

We both turned to her. "Happy red-letter day," she said, wiping at her eyes. "You're all clear, Chloe. Go plan your wedding."

I let out a cry so loud Mary must've heard it, because she screamed, "What? What is it?"

We all laughed.

309

Blake pulled out his phone and tapped a few times.

A second later, cheers were so loud they vibrated the walls of the office. And then . . . a trumpet . . . the Duke Blue Devils fight song.

My eyes went wide as I turned to Blake. "A marching band!"

His hands went up in surrender. "I didn't do that." He laughed through his tears.

Dr. James just shook her head. "You've got a lot of supporters." After a pause, she said, "I got you guys an early wedding present."

She pointed to a shoebox on the corner of her desk. "Go ahead." She smiled. "Open it."

Blake laughed. "You open it, babe, you deserve it."

A lifetime supply of red pens.

I laughed.

I cried.

And then I did it all over again.

Dr. James stood up and made her way to the door. The cheers outside were still going strong.

"It looks like it's time to celebrate. Go plan that wedding. Go have enough babies to make that basketball team."

*   *   *

So that was what we did. Minus the basketball team of babies.

We were married two months later. In the spot where it all had started. On a running track, in the park where Blake had first saved me. My wedding gift from him—a plaque in front of the bush where I had randomly appeared. *To My Wife: My Unexpectedly Phenomenal.*

We had the reception at the abandoned half-court, which was no longer abandoned. Josh and Dean had teamed up and created a league of skateballers.

310

Of course, no wedding could be planned to take place in two months, unless it was planned by Celia Hunter. That woman could make anything happen. Blake had invited his dad, but he hadn't shown, which was probably a good thing, because Celia's boyfriend was a six-foot-eight ex-pro-baller. They'd met at one of Blake's awards nights. I had been too sick to attend, so I'd asked her to go in my place. I guess it had been fate. His name was Jimmy. Blake always laughed about it—it was the name of his favorite character in *Hoosiers*. The one that made the shot right before he'd said "Marry me?". Jimmy had asked Celia on a number of occasions to marry him. She'd said she had a man. His name was Blake, and she didn't have room for much else.

Dean and Mary had adopted Amy and Sammy and now had all three kids permanently. They'd stopped fostering once they'd been approved for Sammy. Three kids are enough, Mary had said. Dean—he wanted enough to make his own skateball team.

As for me—I hadn't told anyone, but I'd enrolled in some community-college classes for next semester. I didn't know what I wanted to do yet. And since The Road had been my life plan, I'd never thought about it. So I was going to take a little bit of everything until I worked it out. But like they say, *it's not the years in your life that count, it's the life in your years.* And I sure as hell was going to make my life count.

Oh yeah, my wedding dress—it was red.

EPILOGUE

Blake

Nine years later

Flowers and gifts surrounded her headstone. It didn't surprise me; she made an impact on a lot of people in her lifetime. I stood tall in front of the shrine. It had been three years since she had passed, and each year got easier without her. My eyes trailed over the letters, her name printed in bright-red ink: C. A. Hunter, just above the large pink ribbon.

Small hands gripped my fingers. "Dad?"

I smiled down at our son. His little five-year-old face was scrunched as he tried to block the sun from his eyes. I jerked my head toward the headstone. "Say hello, Clayton."

His gazed moved to the shrine, his head dropping as the words left his mouth. "Hi, Grandma."

Then Chloe was next to me. Her hand on the crook of my elbow, the other arm carrying our youngest son, Jordan. "Wow," she said, her brown hair whipping all over her face. "Look at all the stuff people have left."

I took Jordan from her and set him down on his wobbly feet. "This is your Grandma, buddy. It's a shame you didn't get to meet her. She was kind of amazing."

We stayed for a few minutes as a family before Chloe took our boys for a walk. She thought I needed some alone time, and she was right.

Mom had passed quickly and unexpectedly. Unlike Chloe, she'd had absolutely no idea that death was coming. *Seven months.* Seven months was all it had taken. She'd fought, every day, until her last. And when it had been time, she'd left in peace.

The last book she'd written became her most successful. Chloe had helped her write it. It was about a boy who went for a run in the middle of the night and the girl who was there to save him . . .

*   *   *

To my beautiful girl, Chloe,

I hope there never comes a time when you have to read this, but if you are, then that must mean you're scared. And I'm here to tell you that that's okay. Not that it's okay in the sense that things will be okay, but it's okay to be scared. It's okay to be afraid of the things ahead you. I am. I'm scared. But I have the support of the people around me, who will help me get through this, who will help me when I need them the most, because they love me, even when I don't deserve it.

You're too young to remember, but I used to tell you this story. A story about red-letter days. A girl in my sorority, Celia, used to tell it to us. She used to come up with these fascinating stories of love and life. We all told her she should be a writer, but she said it was a pipe dream.

She told us about black- and red-letter days. Black were for those days that were doomed, or when bad news would be handed to you. Like the day I found out I had cancer—that was a black-letter day. You—you're my red-letter day. When I gave birth and held you for the first time, that was the start of many, many red-letter days. Celia—she explained it in words that left such an impact that, to this day, I still remember them. Red-letter days are a positive experience or when something unexpectedly phenomenal happens—you, my beautiful Chloe, are my unexpectedly phenomenal.

So, if you get to this, and you have some time left, I want you to do something for me. I want you to fight. I want you to hold on to the people around you, and I want you to fight it. And if things don't go your way, and you find yourself losing the battle, then I want you to look back on your life and think about all the living you did. Do not let cancer be the story of your life. And don't ever write 'The End.' Not until all your days are red-letter days.

I love you.
Mom

ABOUT THE AUTHOR

 Jay McLean is an avid reader, writer, and, most of all, procrastinator. She writes what she loves to read—books that can make her laugh, make her smile, make her hurt, and make her feel. She currently lives in Australia with her fiancé, two sons, and two dogs. Follow Jay on Instagram and Twitter @jaymcleanauthor. For more information, visit her blog at www.jaymcleanauthor.com.

51046064R00200

Made in the USA
San Bernardino, CA
11 July 2017